KINGS OF GROVE ACADEMY

PANDEMONIUM

USA TODAY AND
INTERNATIONAL BESTSELLING AUTHOR

KATIE MAY

FOREWORD

This is a dark contemporary reverse harem romance with strong language, sexual situations, and scenes of graphic violence. This particular book deals with issues readers might find triggering, such as self-harm, suicidal ideation, and sexual assault. I want you to read my book, but more than that, I want you to take care of yourself. Don't hesitate to reach out to me with any questions or concerns!

INTRODUCTION

Pandemonium is the third book of a slow-burn, contemporary, academy romance. Despite the characters being in high school, I definitely do not consider this young adult. It contains strong language and sexual situations, as well as murder and violence. It's a reverse harem romance, meaning that our main character, Ellie, won't have to choose just one man to be with at the end of the series. If such material offends you, I recommend putting this book down.

Our female lead, Ellie, also starts off as innocent and naive, though she does become stronger with each new book in the series. I love writing about character growth, and this series has it more than any other. Badasses aren't born as badasses, and Ellie is no exception. I can promise that by the end of the series, you'll grow to love her as a character.

The men, on the other hand, are all hardened alphas

and serial killers. However, there is no bullying whatsoever from the guys. They worship the ground Ellie walks on and will do anything for her.

I hope you enjoy!

Our female lead, Ellie, finally convinces her older brother, Fischer, to allow her to live in the dorms on campus. After their parents died a few years prior, he became extremely protective of her, but since he has become a state senator, he can't be around as often as he would like.

Ellie is close friends to the five kings of the school, but she always feels as if there's a divide between them. She doesn't know quite how to define their relationship, despite their closeness.

The guys, however, are keeping secrets, all under the pretense of protecting Ellie. They're serial killers who target members of the elite organization known as POP—The Paragons of Prosperity. POP is ruled by a masked man only known as The Divine One.

Ellie's guy friends are terrified of telling her the truth because they fear she'll hate them once she discovers everything they have done and all of the people they have killed in her name. Their decision to keep POP a secret from her has caused a lot of tension and division within the group.

Ellie gets chosen to compete in the Culling, a series of trials that will prove whether or not she's fit to become a member of POP. She keeps her involvement in the Culling a secret from her guy friends because she's not sure if she can trust them. More than that, she doesn't want to put them in harm's way.

The first trial finds her abandoned in a corn field and forced to find her way home. During this task, she stumbles upon Zane's bloody barn, where the guys dispose of their victims' bodies through the meat grinders. The second trial has her trapped in a room with only an hour to escape. The third takes place during the Halloween carnival, where she's kidnapped and comes face to face with one of her friends, Blair. The two girls are told to kill each other. Ellie refuses, but Blair attempts to kill Ellie. However, the gun they were given wasn't loaded, and The Divine One kills Blair for being impure.

At the end of the book, Landon confesses that the Culling isn't designed to create new members of POP. It's to find a worthy human sacrifice.

Throughout book two, Ellie finds herself spiraling down a black hole of depression after she witnesses some members of POP sacrificing an innocent girl to their so-called goddess, Cassia. They believe Cassia will grant them wealth and power if they offer up pure sacrifices on a continual basis.

After discovering her guy friends knew about POP this entire time, Ellie cuts them out of her life, though they do everything in their power to win back her trust and respect.

The Divine One tells Ellie that as a test to prove herself

to POP, she needs to give them a senator named Reece Whipers for reasons unknown.

Slowly and surely, Ellie begins to forgive her guy friends under the condition that they don't keep anymore secrets from her.

Over Thanksgiving break, POP members and The Divine One are able to sneak onto Ellie's property. Mania believes that some members of Fischer's security team may be involved with the cult...and maybe even Fischer himself. Landon, Dominic, and Zane decide to investigate the security team.

At the end of book two, Ellie and Beckett are kidnapped by mysterious foes and Ryker, who was tracking them, is hit by a car.

Characters:

Ellie — the protagonist of the story, who lost her mother and father years earlier. Since then, she's been looked after by her older brother, Fischer. She's quiet and studious but has somehow managed to gain the attention of the guys of Mania and the members of POP. She's an unwilling member of POP and seems to be favored by The Divine One.

Landon — the leader of Mania, a gang of men who aim to destroy POP. He's been in love with Ellie for many years and is fiercely protective of his friend group.

Dominic — the second-in-command of Mania. He's Landon's best friend and can come across as an asshole. He has a strange obsession with getting Ellie in his clothes, though she firmly believes he hates her. He was adopted when he was a baby, though his birth-father still makes him attend weekly family dinners. He suspects his birth-father is a member of POP.

Zane — the most eccentric member of Mania. His

parents leave him alone for months at a time, so Mania uses his house and barn to cover up their murders. He's clinically insane and obsessed with Ellie.

Ryker — a member of Mania. He's silent, preferring to watch from the shadows, and is the only member of Mania not swimming in money. His mother is a junky who abuses him. Near the end of book two, he confesses his feelings to Ellie, but when he calls her his girlfriend, she rejects him.

Beckett — the final and newest member of Mania. He's a foreign exchange student from England who is obsessed with clothing designs. He met Ellie when he was sixteen after saving her from getting assaulted by douchebags.

Victoria — Ellie's posh, elegant, French roommate.

Piper — Ellie's outgoing, hyper roommate and the girlfriend of Blair.

Jane — Ellie's soft-spoken, studious roommate.

Blair — Piper's girlfriend and a member of the Culling. She is killed by The Divine One at the end of book one after she tries, and fails, to kill Ellie at his orders.

Fischer — Ellie's older brother. He's a state senator and is often away for long periods at a time.

Roy — a boy Ellie went on a date with. He still seems to have feelings for her, despite her repeated rejections.

Dane — a charming, flirtatious boy who expresses an interest in Ellie. He is murdered by Mania in book two.

Paulina — a typical mean girl and Dane's stepsister. She transfers schools after the death of her stepbrother in book two.

Mr. Moreau — a new teacher who seems to have a lot of interest in Ellie. Ryker beats him up after he finds Mr. Moreau touching Ellie inappropriately. He quits his job in book two.

The Divine One — the leader of POP who always

conceals his or her face with a mask and his or her body with a cloak. Ellie believes him to be a man, but she isn't entirely certain.

Melody Ladouceur — a woman who was born over one hundred years ago and the daughter of the town's founders. When she was accidentally kill, her parents found themselves coming into great riches and power, thus starting the Paragons of Prosperity.

Harvey — Dominic's biological father and a suspected member of POP.

Dana — Harvey's wife who constantly tries to win Dominic's affection through whatever means necessary.

Senator Reece Whipers — A mysterious senator that The Divine One instructed Ellie to bring to him for reasons unknown.

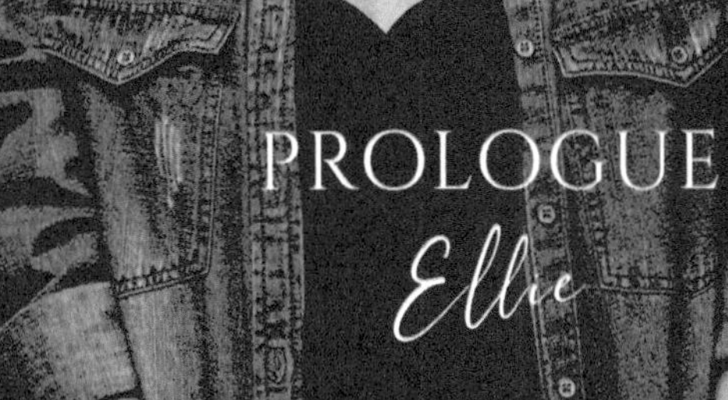

PROLOGUE
Ellie

The smell of burnt flesh is nearly overpowering. *Definitely* overwhelming.

I have to bite down on the urge to gag every time the pungent stench of charred skin and melted bones assaults my senses. I try to breathe through my mouth, but I swear the taste of ash on my tongue is somehow worse than flayed flesh in my nostrils.

The snakes in my stomach weave themselves into a dozen tight knots as I exchange a glance with first Landon on the right of me and then Dominic on the left. Their grim faces mirror my own.

Behind us, flames lick at the sides of the house, eating it alive, burying it beneath mounds of rubble and debris. All I can hear is the hissing and crackling of the fire, growing in height until it seems to spear the velvety-black sky above.

Not even the moon is visible anymore; the congested, gray smoke has completely obscured it, trailing across the sky like dark fingers. The trees in the distance are nothing but torches of fire. I can feel the heat from their flames on my skin.

Zane moves to stand beside me, covered in soot and blood—though I have no idea if the blood belongs to him or someone else. With Zane, it could go either way.

A strand of pitch-black hair falls forward into his eyes, but he doesn't lift a hand to push it away. For the first time I can remember, he's silent. Somber, even. His gaze is firmly fixed on the body at our feet.

"I can't believe we did this." Beckett moves to join our group, a frown carved onto his painfully handsome face. His accent sounds even more pronounced than usual, an indicator of his distress. "Bloody hell, I can't believe we did this."

He repeatedly forks his fingers through his chocolate-brown hair as those mismatched eyes I've come to love sweep over the group.

"It's done." Landon's lips compress into a tight line as guilt momentarily darkens his expression.

I imagine it's the same guilt I'm feeling—the sensation of plunging off the tallest building and knowing only a flimsy rope is keeping you from splattering across the pavement. One wrong move will cause your rope to sever and send you spiraling hundreds and hundreds of feet towards the unforgiving ground below.

Dominic folds his arms over his chest and scowls. "Zane, Beckett, the three of us need to make sure they're gone. If they're not...kill them. Don't hesitate."

At one point, I would've flinched at the blatant display of violence. Of murder. But now, I don't even bat an eye. This is my new life, my new reality, and though it's twisted and tainted by shadows, it's what has kept me alive all these months.

Zane and Beckett nod seriously before separating to do as instructed, Dominic only a step behind them. Once it's just Landon and me, I turn to face him completely. The flickering flames at his back give him an ethereal glow, lines of red and orange and yellow and blue eating at his skin.

I can't help but notice how disheveled he looks. How haggard. The violet crescent moons beneath both his eyes only emphasize that, as do the streaks of dark soot on both of his cheeks.

Meeting my stare evenly, he says, "Ryker's dead."

His jaw clenches as that familiar pang of guilt once again carves me open.

My eyes automatically flick towards the body at our feet.

Ryker's body.

Landon blanks his expression before continuing. "We need to get rid of the body. Then, hopefully, this will all be over."

CHAPTER 1
Ryker

Blood trickles down my chin as I struggle to orient myself, struggle to see past the darkness coating my vision as if drawn in charcoal. I blink repeatedly, but my lashes seem to be plastered in concrete. They're unnaturally heavy as they flutter against my cheeks, and I half wonder if they're leaving behind dark smudges.

A groan tears its way out of my throat as I blink some more until finally, slowly, agonizingly, the world comes back into focus.

At first, I believe myself to be peering through a warped funhouse mirror. My own face is reflected back at me from every angle—this horrid display of mottled, bruised skin, scars lacerating my neck and the top of my chest where my shirt doesn't cover, glass in my hair.

But then I realize it's not a mirror after all but the windshield. Or, more specifically, the shattered remains of it. There seem to be hundreds and hundreds of glass shards.

Some of them hang suspended to the top of the car, holding on for dear life as they twinkle with the setting sun, painting the car in shades of rose-gold and palest green. Others cover the dashboard and passenger seat.

And a few...

A few remain embedded in my skin, causing blood to leak steadily.

Fuck.

I try to recall what happened, try to remember the last few minutes, but my memory seems foggy and indistinct. The more I try to grasp onto it, the more it moves farther and farther away until it's nothing but a hazy mirage in the distance.

I try to lift a hand to my face but frown when my arm doesn't cooperate with me. Searing pain ripples through me as I twist myself to stare at the disfigured lump of meat that was once my arm. It's still there—I didn't fucking lose a limb—but the bone stands out at an odd angle, and I can see pieces of glass decorating my skin like a fairy farted glitter on me.

I cough around the blood in my mouth and then use my free hand—the one not broken—to wipe it away. Red stains my palm, and I glance down at it in growing alarm.

Blood.

So much blood.

A fleeting memory returns to me then—a car rushing at me, its headlights brilliant and bright and all I can see. That car must've hit me, though now that I'm more cognizant, I note that there doesn't appear to be anybody else around.

Something squeezes my heart in an impenetrable iron vise.

There's something I need to remember...

Someone...

Her face appears to me—bright, luminescent eyes on a face just a little too pretty to be real, brown curls that I ache to run my hands through, perfect pink lips stretched into a tentative smile.

Ellie.

Oh my god.

Ellie.

Panic beats through me as I struggle to open the mangled car door. The pain from my broken arm has me biting my lower lip to keep from screaming, but that doesn't matter right now. Nothing matters except finding my girl.

She had been with Beckett at her new self-defense class. I watched her leave and then followed her, using a tracker I implanted in her right shoe. And then the tracker had stopped in the middle of the road, and my jealousy over seeing the two of them together turned into alarm. When I'd arrived at the blinking dot my iPad indicated, it was to see Beckett's Jeep on the side of the road with the passenger door wide open.

There wasn't a sign of Ellie or Beckett to be seen.

POP—The Divine One—must've taken them.

Panic, true panic, has remained foreign to me for many, many years. I used to wonder if I was broken, if there was something fundamentally wrong with me that made it so I didn't feel the same emotions others did. My entire world seemed to be characterized by ice—there was, and still is, a coldness around my heart that refuses to thaw.

But then I learned that there's one person who makes my body burn, makes my skin go up into flames, makes my heart warm. One tiny slip of a girl with eyes that see straight into my soul.

Ellie.

For her, I would willingly walk into the fires of hell with a wide smile on my face.

For her, I would burn.

The thought of someone having her, touching her, hurting her...

Bile sears my throat as I struggle futilely with the driver's side door, but the damn thing doesn't budge. Ignoring the pain reverberating through my broken, beaten body, I crawl across the center console and try my luck with the passenger door. That, fortunately, slides open with only the slightest creak of protest.

The cold winter air slaps both of my cheeks as I fall to the ground, and my knees sink into the frosty snow.

Fuck.

Slowly, I push myself to my feet and stare at my surroundings, though the wind whipping at my face carries with it a white mist that makes seeing difficult.

I appear to be on a back road far away from the academy and town. I don't recognize any of the landmarks —though I'm not sure if you can call pine trees landmarks. Snow decorates their branches, white and fluffy, and falls in clumps on the ground as the breeze rushes through it.

Cursing, I turn back towards the car and reach first for my phone, even knowing it's dead. I shove it into my jacket pocket regardless before grabbing the iPad that would show me Ellie's location. While before, there was a single crack running down the center of the screen, it's now covered in lines branching outwards like a demented spider web. I try to turn it on, but the screen remains black.

Fuck.

Blood trails behind me as I stumble through the snow, coloring the white surface with streaks of red. I imagine the police will have lots of questions when they inevitably stumble upon Landon's car, but those questions won't be answered today. I have no plans to remain here at the scene of the crime, not when Ellie needs me.

Ellie...

Love for her bolsters me, gives me the strength to heave my weak body forward, one step at a time. I cradle my injured arm against my chest as a strange numbness seems to permeate my system. I know I should be sobbing, screaming, crying, throwing up, but my body seems to be running purely on adrenaline. Even the blinding pain from before has begun to fade.

I don't even want to think about what that means for me.

I know people can go into shock from blood loss, but I pray that's not the case. I pray it's just adrenaline and endorphins propelling me forward and numbing my body along the way.

I can't die here, not now. Not when my baby girl needs me.

Not when I finally got to taste her.

I remember the way she looked spread out on the top of the grand piano, her shirt bunched around her perfect breasts, her wet pussy on display. And I remember the way she tasted on my tongue—like ambrosia and sin and salvation all wrapped up into one.

For just a moment, she felt like mine.

I want her to be mine again.

I want her to always be mine...even if that's not what she wants.

Pain rears up inside of me, more agonizing than any injury I've just endured, at the memory of her rejecting me.

"I never agreed to be your girlfriend, Ryker." Her sweet voice, filled with vitriol, plays on a loop in my head.

At the time, her words broke me. Or at least, that's what it felt like. I always hated the cliché about having your heart shatter into a thousand pieces, but that's what it felt like when she said those cruel words. I swore my heart broke more thoroughly than the windshield of Landon's car did.

But I've decided it doesn't matter if she doesn't want to be mine. I will be hers—her sword, her shield, her defense and offense, her heart, her soul, her fucking everything. I don't have a lot to give, but what I do have will belong only to her.

I suppose I always knew my ending would lead me here —walking through the nine levels of hell, broken and bleeding, in an attempt to save my girl.

Ellie, baby girl, hang on, I think as I force myself to move, force myself to take step after step as the sun wedges itself behind the tallest pines. *I'm coming for you.*

CHAPTER 2
Landon

I wrinkle my nose as I move through the cesspool of a dive bar on the outskirts of town. Everything is painted in shades of vomit-green with a hint of shit-brown thrown in for good measure. Most of the tables have already been claimed, but fortunately for us, we're not here for the deathtrap they call food.

I lead Dominic and Zane towards the back of the building, where there's a doorway marked Employees Only. A huge man with a shaved head and tattooed arms stands guard, a fierce scowl on his face as he considers the three of us. He only relaxes marginally when he recognizes me at the front of the group.

"Landon." He nods once, and I figure, for him, that's the equivalent of giving me a great big bear hug and a pat on the back. He then turns his gaze towards Zane and Dominic behind me, his eyes narrowing suspiciously. "Who are your friends?"

Zane very subtly—read as not subtly whatsoever—

lowers his baseball cap so his eyes are shadowed. My friend has been banned here more than once for being too "violent" with the other patrons...which is goddamn hilarious, considering where we are.

Dominic simply meets the man's stare with an impassive one of his own. I imagine Dominic, out of all of us, doesn't fit the clientele this man usually sees here. He's practically a goddamn golden boy, with his platinum-blond locks and piercing green eyes. But there's something dark and insidious inside of him, something the security guard can no doubt see the longer he stares at my best friend.

Dominic may be the sanest of us all, but that's not saying much.

He just hides his insanity better than anyone I know.

With only one more passing glance at Zane—who's currently humming "Hit Me Baby One More Time"—under his breath, the man steps away and nods for us to enter.

The door leads us down a long, steep staircase. The air becomes dryer the farther we descend, the combined scents of sweat, piss, and stale beer barraging us from every direction. At the same time, the muted conversations from upstairs transition into raucous laughter, cheers, screams, and taunts.

This... This is where the true party of the night is.

Dominic winces almost imperceptibly and wrinkles his nose.

"This place is fucking disgusting," he murmurs before we even descend the final step.

Zane, on the other hand, looks like a little kid at Christmas.

Or a psychopath in a fight club.

"I just love the smell of blood in the mornings, don't

you?" He inhales dramatically and groans low in his throat, the noise very nearly sexual.

"It's fucking evening, you dumb fuck," Dominic retorts good-naturedly.

Zane shrugs, nonplussed. "It's morning somewhere, is it not?"

Rolling my eyes, I lead the three of us around the corner and push open a second doorway. "Let's just get this shit show over with so we can get back to our girl, okay?"

Zane whoops enthusiastically and pushes past me, practically bouncing inside. Dominic, however, gives me an unreadable look out of the corner of his eye.

"What?" I bark.

He frowns and shakes his head. "Nothing." He takes a step forward, pauses, and then glances back at me. "You just said...our girl."

I did?

My own lips curl down into a frown. I would have to be a blind idiot to not know how my best friends feel about Ellie...but...

Surely, I just meant "our girl" as in...our girl friend. Emphasis on *friend*.

Because the thought of Ellie with any of them...

Of them touching her perfect flesh while I'm forced to stand on the sidelines...

Of them whispering promises in her ear, promises I yearn to make myself...

It takes me an entire minute to realize both Dominic and Zane have already disappeared through the doorway, leaving me behind to stand here like a fucking dumbass.

I shake my head once, twice, three times, hoping that'll be able to scatter some of the cobwebs in my mind. I'm not sure it works—nothing works when it comes to Ellie—but for now, it's enough.

We have a mission to do, and I refuse to allow myself to get distracted, not when her life is at stake.

Somehow, someway, POP and The Divine One were able to get onto Ellie's property, despite the house being equipped with the best security money can buy. Our job is to figure out how that happened—were the security guards paid off?

Or...did Fischer, Ellie's brother, give them the night off?

I don't dare voice my suspicions out loud, but I can't help but wonder...

Shaking my head yet again, I push back my shoulders and enter the huge, dusty room.

There are so many bodies pressed together, the smell of sweat and musk is almost overpowering. I have to bring my arm up to my nose to keep from gagging. The room may be large, but that's nothing when there are over one hundred bodies packed close enough to brush elbows.

The floor is made of dark luxury vinyl tiles—all the better to wipe off blood or at the very least hide it—but the walls are constructed out of distressed wood, so flimsy I half wonder how they manage to stay aloft. Perhaps it's reinforced with concrete or some shit.

To one side of the room is a bar, where the two scantily clad bartenders don't bother to ask their patrons for IDs. On the other side of the room is the fight ring.

Though to call it a fight ring is a severe understatement.

It's nothing but a huge box chalked onto the ground where people can take their aggressions out in the ring. A man in a top hat stands nearby collecting bets, while another sits behind a booth and acts as the unofficial announcer.

A woman wearing nothing but a string thong and bra steps forward and says something that has the entire crowd whooping and cheering. Two men step forward. One is about the size of a semitruck, his entire body hewn from solid muscle. Fuck, he quite literally looks as if he's been carved out of a rock. How can a man be that big? His dark hair is shaved close to his head, and his beady brown eyes hurl daggers at his opponent.

His opponent...

Who happens to be grinning maniacally while wearing a baseball cap and singing a Spice Girls song under his breath.

"God fucking dammit," I curse as Zane tells the lady his name is "Stabby Boy."

"I tried to stop him." Dominic materializes directly beside me, a somewhat reluctant grin tugging up his lips. "But you know Zane..."

"Did you tell him not to murder the guy?" I ask, only half joking.

With Zane, you never know for sure just how far he'll go. The man doesn't have any fucking boundaries...except for when it comes to Ellie. If he's the darkness incarnate, it's only because he spent so long being her shadow. He needs her sunlight like he needs air to breathe, and...fuck this shit. Why the fuck am I thinking about how desperately Zane needs Ellie?

"He won't mess up the mission," Dominic assures me seriously, pushing up the sleeves of his sweatshirt. "He knows how important it is. However, he'll put on a good enough show to keep the crowd's attention while we go find our guys."

"Aaron Smith, Ryan Turner, Seth Clemmons, and Echo

Hugh," I remind him as I scan the crowd, searching for the four faces I memorized.

According to my research, the four of them frequent this joint almost as often as Ryker does.

And they're also four members of Fischer's security team—the team that *should've* been surrounding the house the night it was broken into.

"There." Dominic jerks his chin towards a booth in the corner, where the four men in question sit with girls on their knees that are most definitely *not* their wives. "How do you want to go about this?" Dom asks as he folds his arms over his chest.

Someone bumps into me from behind, sending me stumbling a single step forward, but one narrow-eyed glare from me has them hurrying in the opposite direction with their tail between their legs.

Turning back to Dom, I say, "It depends on how involved we believe they are with POP and The Divine One. If they're innocent and were manipulated, a simple conversation might suffice. But if they're somehow more involved..."

A muscle in Dom's jaw twitches. He hates the idea of them being involved just as much as I do. How often have they been alone with Ellie? Fuck, I'll murder them with my bare hands if I need to. No one—fucking no one—gets away with hurting my girl.

Behind me, the crowd watching the fight gasps in surprise and then bursts into cheers.

Zane's enigmatic voice immediately follows, "The Stabby Boy stabs again!"

His declaration leads to even more cheers, hoots, and whistles.

I don't even *want* to know what the fuck is going on

back there.

"Good cop, bad cop?" Dom suggests with a quirked eyebrow.

I grit my teeth together and sift through all of the possibilities. On one hand, we need information out of them, and quickly. On the other, we can't very well torture them if they're truly innocent in all of this. We need more information before we can talk with them.

"Can you lift that one's phone?" I nod towards the redheaded security guard who's currently sucking face with a petite blonde on his lap.

His phone sits upside down on the table unattended.

Seth Clemmons. I would recognize that fire-red hair anywhere.

Dom's brows crinkle. "You'll need a passcode."

"Don't worry about it. Just get the phone and bring it back here."

Dom still doesn't look convinced, but he nods after only a second.

"All right," he agrees. "Be right back."

He disappears into the crowd, his gray hoodie pulled up over his startling blond hair. A woman attempts to get his attention, plastering her fake tits to his bicep and batting her obnoxiously long lashes at him.

I scowl before I can stop myself.

Why the fuck isn't he pushing her away?

Why is he smiling at her indulgently?

How could he do this to Ellie?

My frown deepens at the direction of my thoughts.

What the hell? Shouldn't I be happy that there's one less man in the competition for Ellie's affections? Shouldn't I rejoice?

Dominic continues to move through the crowd, the girl

still flush against him. It takes me only a second to understand his plan.

The second he reaches the table the security guards are at, he stumbles, forcing the girl clinging to him to fall as well. The redheaded security guard instinctively wraps his arm around her waist to steady her, and the blonde bimbo turns her attention to her savior instead of my friend. Dom, meanwhile, stealthily nabs the phone from the table under the guise of steadying himself. He apologizes and quickly moves back into the crowd.

The security guard is too preoccupied with his newest conquest to notice the stolen phone.

A second later, Dom appears directly beside me with the phone in his outstretched hand.

"You're fucking welcome." Dom shudders and runs a hand down the side of his body the woman touched, as if he's trying to clean her from his skin. "Goddammit, I'm going to need to take a million showers to get her rancid perfume off of me."

I try to keep my tone nonchalant and almost casual when I ask, "So you didn't like her all pressed up against you?"

Dom gives me a look as if I'm insane.

And for some reason...I fucking like that. Mania is a family—me, Beckett, Ryker, Dominic, Zane, and Ellie.

No one is allowed to come between us, not even a woman.

We formed Mania with the sole purpose of protecting Ellie from any and all threats this town has to offer. I want my team to be dedicated to our cause...dedicated to Ellie.

And only Ellie.

What the fuck is happening to me?

I shake the strange thoughts from my head and flip on

the phone. Like Dominic suspected, a passcode is required to enter the dickwad's phone. Fortunately for the two of us, I've picked up a few skills from Beckett over the years.

And hacking some dumb hillbilly's phone? Child's play.

I think through everything I know about Mr. Redhead. Freaking Seth. After a moment, I type in a date.

The phone opens immediately.

"Holy shit." Dominic barks out a laugh, the noise quickly swallowed by the cheering crowd and the chant "Stabby Boy! Stabby Boy!" that echoes through the corrugated room. "What was the passcode?"

"His anniversary," I respond with a grin.

"And those two women clinging to him?"

"Definitely not his wife." I roll my eyes. "I don't understand how men can't be loyal to the women they claim to love."

The thought of being with anyone but Ellie quite literally makes me sick. I've loved her since I was a child, and I'll continue to love her until the day I die. Maybe that makes me obsessive or sick or naïve, but I know true love when I see it. And what I feel for Ellie surpasses anything I've ever felt for anyone in my life.

"Some people just don't deserve love," Dominic murmurs with a ferocity that surprises me.

"Damn right, brother." I turn my attention back to Dickwad's phone and begin to click through his apps.

There are a few recent messages from his very pregnant wife asking when he's going to be home. His response?

In a few hours, babe. Have a late shift.

Lying fucker.

I'm tempted to snap a picture of the cheater at his "late shift" and send it to his wife, but the less Dickwad knows about what we're doing, the better. Hopefully, he'll never realize someone stole his phone in the first place.

None of his text messages prove to be interesting. Even his correspondences with Fischer are all...tame. They're exactly what you'd expect from an employee to an employer and vice versa.

Fischer: *Robert mentioned that you stayed late last night. Thank you for being so flexible!*

Fischer: *Happy Thanksgiving to you and your family.*

I know Robert is Fischer's head of security, but he'll be the hardest to track down and get information out of, mainly because he barely ever leaves Fischer's side. And right now, Fischer is at the state capitol in session. I don't know when he'll be home, but certainly not anytime soon.

Unless he never left in the first place...

I shove my suspicions aside yet again and continue to scroll through the messages and emails on Dickwad's phone.

"I can't find anything," I murmur. "That doesn't mean he's not guilty, though. He might've deleted the messages or—"

"Hey, wait." Dominic, who has been staring intently over my shoulder, suddenly jabs his finger at the screen of the phone. "Stop."

"What? Why? Do you see something?" All I see is...a bunch of games that a grown-ass man should definitely *not* be playing—seriously, is that a My Little Pony simulator?— and what appears to be a dating app.

"I recognize this app." Dom points to the dating app titled *Luminescence—Find Your Match.*

My irritation grows. "Do you have it on your phone?"

"What?" He slides his eyes to me in confusion. "Of

course not. But…" He hesitates before admitting with a grimace, "My bio dad does."

"And you think this is important…because?" I cock an eyebrow as I try to understand the significance of this.

Two slimy, married men on dating apps? Definitely not the strangest thing I've seen in my lifetime.

Dominic forks his fingers through his shaggy hair with a frown. "I don't know, man. What are the odds that both men would have the exact app on their phone?"

"I really don't know a lot about dating apps, Dom, but I'm sure a lot of people have them." Fuck, do I sound condescending? I try to tone it down, just a notch. "Just because we don't—"

Dom rolls his eyes at me and presses down on the app. What appears to be a message board blinks on the screen, and I frown as I scroll through the names. Dickwad has been talking to a lot of people…but nothing that is said makes a lick of sense. There are numbers, random letters, and what appear to be dates.

"What the fuck is this?" Dominic murmurs in confusion.

"I have no idea," I answer honestly.

Does this have something to do with POP and The Divine One? Is this…code? We need to get this back to Beckett, and pronto. If anyone can decipher this, it'll be him.

"Hey!" a low, raspy voice slurs.

A second later, a huge body barrels down on me, his malodorous, practically noxious breath wafting across my chin. He may be tall…but I'm taller.

Dickwad himself glares up at me through heavily slitted eyes, his body swaying precariously in his intoxicated state.

He jabs his finger at the phone in my hand. "Just bhat the wuck are ya doing with my phone?"

CHAPTER 3

Dominic

God, I hate the smell of alcohol, especially on the breath of washed-out beat cops who couldn't make a career in the field, so they had to settle for private security instead. And no, this isn't a diss at every security guard in the world—only Seth Clemmons.

I blanch at the putrid stench of him as he takes a staggering step forward, practically spilling his beer onto my shoes despite his attention remaining solely on Landon.

Landon, for his part, blinks his silver eyes innocently, not a shadow of guilt in his expression. "What are you going on about, sir?"

I have to place my fist over my mouth to keep from snorting.

Sir?

Really?

"Dats my vone," Seth slurs as he points at the silver case in Landon's hands.

Landon's brows furrow. "Um...this is *my* phone," he lies seamlessly, staring at Seth as if the man has lost his mind.

At one point, I may have found that terrifying—how easily my best friend could weave together a lie like a spider spinning its web. He doesn't even have to think about it. Lying comes to him as easily as breathing.

But now, instead of scared, I find myself begrudgingly impressed with his adaptability.

Seth's eyes narrow farther. "You're a bronie?"

Disbelief oozes into his tone, as well as a healthy dose of suspicion.

Landon blinks again. "Excuse me?"

Instead of answering, Seth simply points to a sticker pasted to the back of his phone case. Landon turns it over to see a bright-pink pony staring back at us.

Dude, seriously?

You're a grown-ass man, and you have a My Little Pony sticker on the back of your phone case?

But Landon, always the master at deception, simply flashes a cocksure grin and nods enigmatically.

"I am, actually," he says with a slanted smile. "Are you a bronie too?"

What the actual fuck is happening right now?

Inconspicuously, I grab out my own phone and type in bronie, my brows rising. I had no idea that there's a name for adult men who love My Little Pony. Huh. Learn something new every day.

Seth, in his intoxicated state, clearly hasn't noticed that the sticker on the back of "Landon's" phone is in the exact same location that he put his sticker. The red-haired man's eyes gleam as he launches into a slurred tale about how he first became a bronie and his favorite one.

Landon nods when it's appropriate, laughs when Seth

says something he thinks is funny, offers a pat on the back when Seth begins to sway.

And I can't help but think...

My best friend may truly be a psychopath.

I'm surprisingly not as alarmed by that revelation as I should be.

As Landon and Seth continue to converse, Landon subtly hands me Seth's phone. I take it, place it in my sweatshirt pocket, and then hurry through the crowd.

What the fuck is that app on Seth's phone?

Is it truly a dating app, as the title suggests?

Is it something more...sinister?

And why does my bio dad—gag, I fucking hate calling him that—have the same app on his phone? It could be a coincidence, as Landon said. It's not uncommon for married men to create dating profiles for quick hookups when their wives are away.

Yet for some reason...

My intuition tingles.

"So...are we killing anyone tonight?" a voice whispers in my ear a split second before a tongue lodges itself in my ear canal.

I jump about a foot in the air and whirl around, my fists raised.

Zane stands behind me, looking entirely unrepentant, his dark eyes gleaming and blood dripping from the multiple wounds on his face. He seems to be sporting a black eye, but other than that, he appears relatively unharmed.

"Good lord, man." I shake my head at him as he jumps from foot to foot like a boxer in an arena, still wearing that damn baseball cap. "How the fuck are you going to explain your injuries to Ellie?"

Zane gives me a disbelieving look. "I'm wearing my cap of invisibility. Duh. She'll never notice."

He waggles his fingers in the air as if he's performing some sort of magical spell and then pivots on his heel, spinning in a circle.

"I'm pretty sure your opponent could see you when he was beating your face in," I point out.

"Are you talking about Meat Grinder?" Zane pushes himself up onto his tiptoes and points over the heads of people, towards the mammoth guy being tended to by three nurses—if you can even call them nurses. They probably got those costumes from Party City. "We're good friends now. Isn't that right, Meat Grinder?"

He waves enthusiastically, and the huge, bloody man lifts his head up and spears Zane with a look so venomous, I'm surprised Zane doesn't drop dead right then and there.

Then again, this is Zane.

I'm almost ninety-nine percent positive his middle name is "Batshit Insane."

"I'm pretty sure Meat Grinder wants to grind your face into meat." I place my hand on his shoulder and attempt to steer him away.

"Nah." Zane waves his hand dismissively and gives me a sideways grin. "That's just his version of a love tap." In a louder voice, he adds, "Isn't that right, Meaty Boy?"

"I'M GOING TO RIP YOUR FUCKING DICK OFF, YOU ASS-MUNCHING CUNT!" Meat Grinder bellows at the top of his lungs.

Zane laughs as if Meat Grinder just told the most hilarious joke...but I make sure to move him along more quickly. There's a reason Zane is banned from this place, after all.

As soon as we're in the stairwell and the sounds of the crowd have dimmed to a dull murmur, Zane's trademark smile fades away. He twists so he can face me completely, his features uncharacteristically serious.

"What did you discover? Do we have to kill anybody?"

Sadly, the fucker isn't even exaggerating.

We've killed before to protect Ellie, and I have a feeling we'll need to do it again.

And again.

And again.

"Not sure," I confess as I hold up Seth's phone. "But we were able to nab one of their phones."

Zane takes it from me and twists it to and fro, his eyes snagging on the pink pony in the center of the silver case. His brows arch.

"Seth's a bronie?" he asks excitedly.

"Apparently...and how the fuck do you even know what a bronie is?" I give him a disbelieving look, but Zane shrugs, not answering my question. "Anyway, when we were going through his phone, we noticed an app that...raised suspicions."

"What do you mean?" There it is again—that serious glint Zane gets in his eyes, this cold beauty like the crystalline surface of frost, whenever he's about to dive into an episode.

There's something innately dark about my friend, something terrifying, and I can only pray that his love for Ellie will keep him from doing anything too rash. I have a feeling Zane is a wild, rabid animal on a tenuous leash, and the slightest complication will cause the rope to snap completely.

Who knows what the fuck would happen then?

"I don't know. It's just..." I run a shaky hand through my platinum-blond locks. "I noticed the same app on my bio dad's phone."

"And?" he presses, his voice like the edge of a knife.

God, am I being too paranoid? Creating connections that don't truly exist? Constructing a narrative where my dad is the bad guy, and we'll finally be able to get him out of my life for good? I hate Harvey with everything that I am, and I know the feeling is mutual. He may want me to become the prodigal son, but he'll soon come to learn I'm nothing but a snake hiding within the grass of his own goddamn home. One day, I'll pounce.

And my bite is fucking venomous.

"It's a dating app," I explain. When Zane still appears dubious, I hurry to elaborate. "When I clicked on the app, I didn't see any normal messages. It was just a bunch of random letters and numbers and what I think are dates."

Dark brows dip low over glowering, ice-filled eyes. The juxtaposition from the Zane of a few minutes ago—bursting with chaotic, unfettered energy—versus this man is almost staggering. It's just another startling reminder of how dangerous my friends truly are.

"And you think this app could be connected to POP and The Divine One?" Zane's voice is low and deadly.

There's a promise in his voice, a promise to hunt Seth down if we discover he had any part to play in what happened to Ellie.

"I don't know," I admit. My head feels like it's full of tiny bombs, each one detonating simultaneously. The resulting explosion makes my ears ring. "But the good news is that all four of those security guards live in town. If we need to...*question* them for more information at a later point, we can."

"I like...*questioning* a lot." Zane's eyes gleam wickedly, dark slabs of obsidian in the artificial lighting. "There are so many ways you can...*question* someone, don't you think?

There are burning questions. Sharp questions. Cutting questions. So. Many. Questions."

All I can do is smile and nod, because, really, what can I say to all of that?

"I think Robert is someone else we need to hunt down and...*question*," I continue, really beginning to hate the word "question."

I'm not against Zane's "questioning" methods whatso-ever, but I just ate a burger, dammit, and I'd really like to keep it down.

Never, ever, go into a "questioning" session on a full stomach. You'll wish you hadn't almost immediately, espe-cially if you allow Zane to be in charge of the "questioning."

The man gets brownie points for creativity. I'll give him that. I never knew a...cutting question could be used so effi-ciently.

"That might be difficult while he's at the capitol build-ing..." Zane muses. "But I'm sure Fischer will be home over Christmas."

"Can you believe winter break is only a week away?" I ask, folding my arms over my chest and leaning against the wall as I wait for Landon to return. "It feels like it was only yesterday that we had Thanksgiving."

Zane eyes me suspiciously. "Do you have any plans for the holidays with your moms?"

I hesitate. I've been toying with an idea for a while now, but I haven't actually had the courage to talk to any of them about it. Perhaps Zane should be the first...

"I was actually thinking—"

Before I can finish my thought, the door is thrown open, and Landon stands there, an irritated scowl pulling down his lips.

I push myself off the wall instantly and smirk at him. "Enjoy your bromance time?"

"Shut the fuck up." He shoves my shoulders good-naturedly before giving Zane a quick once-over.

I recognize it for what it is—as the unofficial leader of the group, Landon has deemed himself the caretaker of not only Ellie, but the four of us as well. He's always the first to check us all for injuries, the first to make sure we have a place to go over the holidays, the first to offer us food if he thinks we skipped a meal.

It's why I fucking love that crazy bastard.

"You good?" Landon points towards Zane's eye, but Zane waves away his concerns with a scoff.

"This old thing?" He cheekily smacks at his own face. I can't help but wince in sympathy. "Stabby Boy has definitely endured worse."

"Please don't call yourself Stabby Boy." I pinch the bridge of my nose.

"Stabby...Man?" He cocks his head to the side.

"No," Landon deadpans.

"Stabby Penis?"

"God, no," I say.

"Penis Man?"

"How is that any better?" I throw my hands up in the air in exasperation.

Zane simply cackles and races up the steps in front of us.

Landon hangs back until we're shoulder to shoulder, watching Zane run up the steps like his ass is on fire.

"What's the plan?" I ask.

It's something I always find myself doing, even before we created Mania. There's something about Landon that seems to innately command respect from everyone in his orbit. You can't help but want to listen to him, to learn from him, to obey every order he gives you. It's what made us a seamless unit over the years.

"Grab Ryker and Beckett." Landon flashes me a sideways smile. "Then we'll grab our girl and get to the bottom of this."

There it is again.

Our girl.

Fuck, why do I like the sound of that so much?

My parents died when I was twelve years old.

One would think I'd have a heap of memories considering the age I was when they passed, but that couldn't be further from the truth. It's almost as if a part of me wanted to forget them, wanted to hide from the pain their loss cost me.

Because loss... It can cut you like the edge of a blade, as sharp and brutal as love can. There's no use trying to cauterize the wound. It'll just continue to bleed and bleed and bleed until you're a carcass of yourself, an empty vessel for the wind to howl through.

I knew my mother loved homemade chocolate brownies and that my father would never, *ever* miss a Steelers football game on TV. I knew my mother used to hum under her breath whenever she was doing a household task while my father would sing out loud, his voice gruff and raspy.

But somehow, their faces have begun to blur in my

mind's eye. I can still see their outlines—my mother's petite, willowy frame and my father's sturdy one—but their faces have been erased, touched by a child's clumsy hand.

And now...

Now...

"Dad?" Saying that one word feels like a splash of acid being dropped onto already reddened skin.

I can barely breathe through the tightness in my throat, the razor blades that have become lodged there.

I should be staring at his brown, disheveled beard. His blue-gray eyes. The wicked scar running down the length of his right cheek.

But for some reason, I can't pull my attention off of those damn loafers he wears. They're so shiny I can practically see my reflection in them. I can't remember a time I saw my father in anything other than tennis shoes. Even when he had to go to work, he would insist on wearing this ratty old pair Mom kept threatening to throw out.

My heart trips over itself, inflates, collapses, explodes.

Tension rises like a wave about to break, cresting and then falling, splicing apart against jagged rocks at the cliffs.

Dad...

Dad...

I force my gaze up once more to take in what I missed when the man first walked into the room. His jawline... His jawline is sharper than I remember it being. And his nose... His nose is larger as well, with a slight bump on the tip that suggests it has been broken one too many times.

This man may look like my father, but he's not him.

My blood freezes and then unthaws abruptly.

"Who are you?" I'm grateful when my voice doesn't

shake, doesn't betray the fear roiling just beneath the surface.

Or maybe it's not fear gripping my throat.

Maybe, just maybe, it's *anger*.

The man smiles, and I can't help but think it's a sad one.

Without taking his eyes off of me, he grabs the desk chair I noted earlier and languidly slings his legs over it, sitting backwards. The position is more suited for a casual conversation than one between a captor and his captive.

"Ellie, I'm surprised you don't remember your Uncle Raymond." A tentative smile tugs up his lips, but it's gone in less than a second.

Thank god for that. It looked too unnatural on his face, too out of place on a surface that radiates coldness. I have a feeling this man doesn't smile often, if at all.

"Why am I here? Where's Beckett?" I demand, forcing myself not to back up, not to react.

Don't show your fear.

Don't let him know you're afraid.

Lilly's teachings play on a loop in my head.

"I told you before that the boy is fine." He waves a hand in the air as if he can shoo away my words like one would a swarm of pesky flies. "But I need to talk to you."

Even before he finishes speaking, I'm shaking my head. "I don't have an uncle. I don't know who the fuck you are—"

"You're a smart girl, Ellie." He leans forward until he's able to rest his chin on the top of the chair. "Even you aren't daft enough not to see the similarities between me and your father...my brother."

My heart is pounding so hard in my chest, I half fear it's going to explode out of me and detonate across the pale-white carpeting.

This can't be true.

This can't be true.

This can't be true.

I never knew my extended family. My mother had a falling out with hers when she married my father, and my dad never spoke of his side. Surely, he would've told me if he had a brother.

A brother who looks eerily like him...

"Why are you doing this to me?" This time, I can't stop my voice from cracking, the noise reverberating through the room like an icicle falling from a rooftop and shattering.

Something indecipherable crosses his face too quickly for me to read. In a blink, the expression has vanished, though there's a glint in his eyes that I can't quite read.

"What do you think I'm doing to you?" He cocks his head to the side curiously, a picture of serenity, and I can't help but think that he's too calm right now, too in control, too apathetic.

An act.

This is an act.

"You're The Divine One," I whisper, hating that name with every fiber of my being.

Hating the way it tastes like acerbic poison on my tongue. Hating the way that goose bumps rise on my skin, dusting over my body like skittering fire ants. Hating the man himself for everything he has done, everything he has taken from me.

The man—Raymond, apparently—surprises me by throwing his head back in hearty laughter.

True, genuine laughter that shakes his entire frame.

He holds his stomach and practically doubles over as lungfuls of air escape him.

I stare in disbelief, wondering if I'm dealing with a

goddamn maniac, when he forces himself to sit up and wipe the tears from his eyes.

"Oh, sweetheart," he says around his chuckles. "You got it all wrong."

"Don't sit here and laugh in my face," I warn. I don't even recognize myself anymore. Anger burns white-hot and blistering in my chest, a volcano seconds from erupting. "Don't you fucking dare."

His laughter dries up instantly, and he sits straight up, his lips compressing. Lines bracket his eyes and mouth, though I don't think they're laugh lines. No, those deep trenches on his tan skin are an indicator of his age and all he has experienced.

"You don't understand anything, child." He chews on his lower lip as his gaze remains fixated on mine.

Fuck, those eyes... Those eyes could have belonged to my father, though I can't help but wonder if my fuzzy memory is creating an illusion that doesn't actually exist. Did my dad really have that blue-gray shade of irises, or were they more cerulean? More silver? Those colors begin to merge together until I can't differentiate one from the other.

"Then why don't you explain it to me." I cross my arms over my chest and wait him out. I can practically feel my body vibrating with tension.

A slow, cutting grin takes over his face. "You have a backbone, girl. Your father would be proud."

"Don't talk about my father," I snap before I can stop myself.

I work to modulate my volume, to take calm, patient breaths. I need to remain on his good side in order to keep him talking. I have a feeling that the information he's handing me isn't cheap.

So the question is...

What's the price?

Another emotion I can't quite read flits across his face before his lips settle into a line and he nods once. "Very well." He slings his arms over the back of the chair and studies me as intently as I study him. "But you should know I'm not a part of the Paragons of Prosperity. I'm not The Divine One."

I notice he emphasizes "the" too, as if that word is a part of the monster's name, not an epithet used to describe him. There's an importance in that added "the" in the title he wields for himself.

Anger flares bright-hot inside of me. I find myself taking a step forward before I can stop myself, my hands balling into fists. I can feel the pressure of my fingernails digging into my palms. The sharp bite of pain almost calms me.

"You kidnap me," I hiss, "and bring me who-the-fuck-knows-where. And now you're insisting that you're not the bad guy—"

"All I've ever done is try to protect you!" Raymond abruptly stands, knocking the chair back in the process. He doesn't seem to notice. His chest heaves, and an angry fire bursts to life in those metallic-blue eyes of his. "I promised your dad—"

"My dad never even mentioned you before!" I snap. "I don't even know who you are—"

"We met before." The fight seems to drain from his body like a torrent of rainfall crashing on his shoulders. He practically sags where he stands, wilting like a plucked dandelion. "When you were younger..."

A faraway, distant expression crosses his face before he heaves out a breath and turns towards the door.

"Where the hell are you going?" My fingernails dig even

deeper into my palms. I can feel the beginnings of blood welling.

Raymond doesn't answer at first, but he does pause in the doorway. His hand tightens on the knob for only a second. His shoulders seem to touch his ears before they deflate with his heavy exhale.

And then, in a voice like verglas, he reiterates, "I'm not the bad guy, Ellie. Remember that."

Without another word, he pushes the door open, steps out, and slams it shut behind him.

He may say he's not the bad guy, but when I try the door handle a second later...I find that it's locked.

Leaving me a prisoner once again.

All of the windows have bars.

Clouds float in the sky like cotton balls someone ripped to shreds and then scattered. The wispy white tuffs do very little to conceal the sun, more orange than yellow currently, hanging low behind the boughs of trees despite being midday.

I don't know where we are, but I was right with my initial assessment—we appear to be in some sort of abandoned hotel, nearly twenty stories high. Row after row of windows dot the log siding both horizontally and vertically. The grounds below have been devoured by overgrown weeds just barely poking their heads out through the layer of frost. Huge pine trees surround the hotel, their spindly green needles coated in fluffy snow.

How the heck am I supposed to escape now?

The room itself is modestly furnished, with a queen-size bed dominating the majority of the space. It's flanked by two nightstands adorned with lamps and alarm clocks.

There's not a television, but there is an en suite bathroom, complete with a claw-footed tub and separate shower.

Think, Ellie, think!

I pace the small room as my mind runs a million miles an hour. Fear paints cold lines down my spine as I debate what to do. I don't even know where to begin untangling the gamut of emotions I feel. They break around me like driftwood shattering against huge rocks, leaving me numb.

I know what I *should* feel—confusion, betrayal, and anger—but none of those emotions manage to penetrate the icy wall constructed around me. I know at a later time I'll fall apart, but that'll be after I get myself out of this mess.

After I free Beckett.

Worry for him nearly consumes me. My heart slams against my ribs, and my breaths come out in choppy pants.

What if he's hurt? Injured? Dead?

Fear pounds against the outside of my consciousness, screaming to be acknowledged, like skeletal fingers raking down a window.

I need to get the hell out of here...and fast.

My gaze snags on the air duct and stops there.

I'm small—I know I am. At one point, I would've considered my height, or lack thereof, a handicap, but now...

I consider it for a long moment, noting the screws in each corner.

Am I really going to do this?

Even as the thought solidifies, I'm dragging the desk chair across the room. I position it directly beneath the air duct and then stand on top of it, cursing when it sways precariously. I grapple at the wall for purchase and wait until I'm steady.

Then, I eye the screws with trepidation. I'll need something small and sharp to unscrew it. Perhaps...

Quickly, I remove the ring I wear around my pointer finger. It was a birthday gift from my brother, Fischer, a few years earlier. The diamond stands out starkly in the illumination of the room, the deepening sunset casting its surface in a blood-red light.

Fear slithers through my body as I position the ring in the first screw and begin to twist it.

Please work. Please work. Please work.

My heart slams against my rib cage with such vigor I actually worry I'm in danger of having a heart attack.

If my so-called uncle decides to barge into the room...

If he hears me...

I work to modulate my breathing, to not spiral headfirst into an abyss of panic, as the first screw topples to the floor with a nearly silent thud.

One down. Three to go.

It's slow work, but soon, all of the screws have fallen onto the ground. I just barely capture the vent before it topples as well. It's surprisingly heavy as I discard it on the bed, making sure to not allow it to jangle and make noise. Even still, I find my gaze slipping to the closed door more often than not, engrossed with the light spilling in through the cracks.

Is there someone standing right outside the room now? Could someone be watching me? Are there cameras in this room?

Goose bumps flutter across my skin as I climb back onto the chair.

This is the stupidest decision you've made yet, Ellie, my snide inner voice remarks as I pull myself up into the vent.

Dust tickles my nose almost instantly, and I have to try

not to gag at the pungent, overwhelming scent of dirt and mold. I don't even want to think about when these have last been cleaned. Already, I can feel dust and other unsavory substances sticking to my shirt.

You don't have a choice. You need to get out of here, a second voice comments.

A shard of glass seems to get lodged in my throat as I wiggle like a worm, my arms barely able to fit in front of me. I never considered myself claustrophobic before, but now, I find the air too thin, my breaths too shallow, my heart rate too fast.

I can't do this. I can't do this. I can't do this.

All I can focus on is the scent of smoke in the air. I wonder if hell quite literally opened up beneath my feet, dragging me into its fiery depths.

I almost turn back.

Almost.

But then Beckett's face manifests in my mind's eye, his eyes as fathomless as a starless sky. One as brown as chocolate; the other a forest green. His brown hair had been tousled the last time I saw him, the normally immaculate locks flopping across his forehead.

All of my doubts and worries blow away like dandelion fluff in the breeze.

Beckett needs me.

He needs me, and I refuse to let him down.

"Fuck," I whimper, the curse word slipping out involuntarily as I army crawl forward.

Every inch is agonizing. My body quite literally screams in protest. I'm not unhealthy by any means, but I was never the type of girl who spent hours in the gym on a treadmill or elliptical. I much preferred exercising my mind with books and poems.

Still, I continue forward, praying that "Uncle" Raymond won't barge into my room and notice I'm gone.

Praying that I can find Beckett.

Praying that he's safe and sound.

"Come on. Come on," I whisper to myself as I crawl forward.

I appear to be coming up to a second vent. Dim white light trickles through the metal slats.

My heart lodged in the vicinity of my throat, I peek through the bars to see that it leads down into a hall surrounded by numbered doors. The carpeting is checkered and an ungodly shade of red and blue. It's a stark contrast to the beige-painted walls.

Quickly, I begin the same task from before, my hand twisting at an uncomfortable angle as I attempt to squeeze it through the metal grates in order to unscrew the vent.

God, why is this taking so long?

Tears prick my eyes at the way I'm forced to bend my wrist in order to reach the final corner. Pain races down my arm in a fiery blaze, and I have to bite down on the curse that wants to escape. Finally, after what feels like an eternity, the screw falls to the ground, joining the other three already there.

But this time, I'm not quick enough to catch the vent before it topples to the ground with a drum-shattering clank.

Shit!

I hold my breath, waiting to see if anyone will come running, but when the hallway remains silent, I exhale greedily. I don't know if I just got lucky or some god is smiling down on me, but I thank every deity I can think of.

Wincing, I push myself forward once more...and promptly tumble out of the air vent and land hard on my stomach. My face ricochets off the smooth metal of the broken vent, and pain tornadoes through me.

"Goddammit," I hiss, bringing my hand up to my nose to stem the flow of blood.

Hopefully nothing's broken, but right now, the pain is a distant thing. Worry for Beckett overshadows it.

Where the hell is he?

I debate calling his name but quickly decide against it. That would quite literally be the most idiotic thing for me to do. No, I have to be smart about this, have to think five steps ahead.

I throw my back flush against the nearest wall. Hope blooms in my chest like a rose with thorns—so incredibly beautiful but also capable of slashing me to ribbons.

Beckett's somewhere in this hotel—I know he is—and once I find him...

Is it naïve to believe that everything will be okay?

Hang on, Beckett. I'm coming for you.

CHAPTER 6

Beckett

I ram my shoulder against the door for the twentieth time. Pain splinters up my arm, but the wood does little more than rattle, the noise almost deafening in the silence of the room.

If you can even call it a room.

A closet would be a more apt description.

Shelves line the wall, though the majority of them are empty. Only one is full of folded linens and heavy quilts—nothing I can use as a weapon or picklock.

Not that I know how to pick a lock, mind you. That's not something I was taught across the ocean.

If Landon were here, he would know what to do, how to get out of this, how to save Ellie. Hell, even Ryker, Zane, or Dominic would be a better choice than me. What can I do, except smother our captives to death with my immaculately ironed sweater?

Self-deprecation rears its ugly head as I bang my fist against the door yet again.

"Get me out of here, you bloody wankers! I'm going to fucking kill you all!" Probably not the most creative of insults, but apparently, my British comes out to play when I'm pissed.

And I'm goddamn infuriated.

How dare these bastards kidnap me? Kidnap Ellie?

God, I can't remember a time I felt fear like this before. I always thought of that particular emotion as a massive claw reaching out of the sky to seize hold of you, squashing the breath from your lungs, turning your face blue, breaking all of your bones, pushing out your organs.

Killing you.

Fear's a monstrous entity that you're forced to bear with a smile, even as it crushes you to death.

Where is Ellie now? Is she okay?

If these assholes hurt even a hair on her head, I'm going to skin them alive and then feed them ribbons of their internal organs. They'll choke on their own blood and intestines.

I never considered myself a violent person—that position was usually reserved for one of the other guys, particularly Zane and Ryker. But now, I feel just as bloodthirsty as either of them, just as insane. It courses through my bloodstream, this acerbic and bitter concoction, and siphons the breath from my lungs. Dark specks begin to consume my vision.

They always say that red is the color of rage, but I don't believe that to be true. Black is the true color of anger—this fathomless abyss you lose yourself in, tumbling head over feet, carrying you farther away from shore in a riptide you can't hope to escape from.

Every single person involved will die by my hand if they

have hurt Ellie. I won't even hesitate. Maybe that makes me a complete psychopath, but I don't give a damn. If they hurt her, I'll murder them.

And I won't make it painless, either. No, they'll suffer and scream and cry and beg for me to finally end them, to stick a dagger in their chest and twist it until their heart is a bloody lump of meat at my feet.

A sacrificial offering for my goddess, the ruler of hell's escaped demons.

"Let. Me. Out." I punctuate each word by ramming my fist against the wood.

Bloody hell, what is this door made out of? Concrete?

And then...

"Beckett?"

Her sweet, lyrical voice floats to me as if in a dream. I quite literally feel my breath leave my lungs in a great swooping exhale. My heart bangs against my rib cage, and blood sluices between my ears.

"Ellie?" I don't dare say her name above a whisper, half afraid that if I say it too loud, she'll disappear, becoming nothing but an elusive fantasy, a mirage in the midst of a sandstorm.

"Are you okay?" She sounds as if she's pressed against the door.

"I'm fine," I rush to reassure her. "But are you okay? What the fuck is going on? Is it POP? The Divine One?"

She hesitates. "I-I don't think so, but it's complicated. Just..."

A second later, the lock clicks, and then the door to my closet-slash-prison is yanked open.

Ellie stands on the other side, looking like a goddamn vision with her brown hair disheveled and her glasses crooked. I've never seen anyone more beautiful, more ethereal, more capable of slicing at my skin like the serrated edge of a blade. Fuck, she makes me bleed, and I find that the only emotion I'm capable of feeling is appreciation.

It's only then I notice the blood staining her perfect, cherubic cheeks.

"What the fuck happened?" I demand instantly, pulling her closer and checking her body for any other injuries.

She makes a face, one I shouldn't find as adorable as I do, considering the situation.

"I sort of, maybe, accidentally, um…" A blush paints her cheeks. "Fell on my face climbing out of an air vent?"

The words turn into a sheepish question, and she shrugs helplessly.

"You…climbed through an air vent?" I repeat numbly, already reaching for one of the spare linens I noticed earlier.

Quickly, I dab at her face, cleaning away any and all traces of blood. I'll be the first to admit that it's not just for her. A primitive part of me—the part that fits in with Mania seamlessly—goes absolutely insane seeing blood on her. It makes the anger in me mount and crest, a ginormous wave rising in the air, pulled upwards by the moon itself, and then shattering against the shoreline.

No one, absolutely *no one*, is allowed to hurt our girl.

My girl.

"Well, someone needed to rescue you, didn't they?" she says.

Her lashes bat against her cheekbones innocently, so long and dark they seem to have been charcoaled.

"So I'm the pretty princess in this scenario, and you're my savior? My knight in shining armor?" I ask, only half joking.

Why does the thought of Ellie riding in on a white horse make my dick so hard?

Worst. Timing. Ever.

"I'll buy you a tiara when we get back," she tells me seriously, though her eyes gleam mischievously.

I don't know what comes over me then. All I'm aware of is her—the girl I've loved and desired for far too long.

I suppose I always knew this was inevitable. She's the wave, I'm the shore, and logic dictates that at some point we'll meet in a passionate, intimate embrace.

We crash together like stars colliding, like a meteorite on course to obliterate the Earth. I wouldn't be able to tell you if I reached for her or if she reached for me or if we reached for each other simultaneously. One moment, we're simply staring at each other, my gaze desperately memorizing every smooth line of her face, the flecks of gold in her eyes, the shape of her lips, and the next...

The next she's in my arms, our lips clashing, our souls tangling, our hearts merging. Her kisses rip through me like lightning. I don't know if I've ever experienced something so painfully sweet before—it's a beautiful type of agony, one that rearranges every fiber in my body, reforming me as a new and improved man, one deserving of her love and affection.

Ellie releases a tiny gasp of surprise, and I half fear she's going to push me away. Her hands creep up between our bodies and land in the center of my chest. I imagine she can feel how desperately my heart beats for her, the repetitive *thump-thump-thump* of the organ pounding against my rib cage.

Love for her pulsates through my blood, so potent that I finally understand the meaning of a broken heart. If she pushes me away just now, if she rejects me...

I may just die.

But then her hands slowly, almost tentatively, come up and brush over my shoulders, the softest of caresses, a tease of a touch, and I fucking melt.

I kiss her even harder, tangling a strand of her brown hair in my fist and angling her head where I want it.

This is the way we should be—untrammeled by expectations, by fear, by POP, by The Divine One.

The warmth of her touch sends heat skittering through my body. Her fingers play with the fine hairs at the base of my neck.

I always knew this girl would ruin me. From the first moment I saw her, alarm bells began to ring in my head, and a tiny voice whispered to me, "This girl... This girl will be your end."

Yet here I am, eagerly awaiting my destruction, offering my heart and soul on a silver platter, willingly descending into the madness she creates. If this is my end, then I'll embrace it with open arms.

Ellie's the one who pulls away first. Saliva still coats her lips from our heated kisses, and I can't help but wonder what those pretty, plump lips of hers would look like covered in my cum.

Shock splays across her face as she stares at me with wide, confused eyes. She reminds me of a deer staring down the end of a shotgun—confusion and terror war for dominance.

I track the blush that spreads from her neck to her cheeks. Her glasses have become even more askew, and I lean forward to fix them, my finger lingering on her button nose. Then, I lower it to her full mouth, tracing first her upper lip and then her bottom one with my thumb.

Her breath hitches, and she stares at me with so much confusion, I have to bite down on my grin.

"Do you…? I didn't…? You…?"

"We need to get out of here," I tell her gently.

"But you just…?" A furrow manifests between her brows as she gapes at me.

A tiny sliver of guilt embeds itself just beneath my skin.

"I shouldn't have done that," I confess. "Not now. Not while we're here. But I… I couldn't go another moment without telling you how I feel. Without showing you how much you mean to me."

My heart swells and then begins to bleed when it finds resistance against the barbed wire caging it in.

"You…huh?" She blinks at me, frowns, and then blinks again.

Goddammit, Beckett, I mentally chastise myself. *Why the fuck did you kiss her? You scrambled her mind!*

I don't know if I feel satisfied or horrified by the fact.

But I was being honest before—I shouldn't have kissed her. I don't know what came over me. Maybe my fear for her eclipsed logical thinking. Maybe my time away from her made me realize how short life truly is, how precious every moment together should be. Maybe my love for her is just too fucking strong to be contained.

All I know was that I couldn't go another second without feeling her lips on mine.

She stares at me with eyes the color of a stormy sky. A look of trepidation paves over her expression as her lips part.

"Come on." I try to keep my expression impassive, as if I didn't just kiss the shit out of her. As if my body isn't covered in goose bumps. As if my heart isn't in danger of bursting from my chest. As if I'm not rock-hard and desperate for her. As if my soul isn't crying out to hers, begging her to love me, want me, need me. "We need to get out of here."

I grip her wrist, the contact sending heat fireworking through my entire body, and begin to pull her after me.

I have no idea what we'll face at the end of this hallway, but I do know I'll die with a fucking smile on my face.

CHAPTER 7
Ellie

My lips tingle, and butterflies erupt in my stomach, their wings beating madly.

I stare intently at the back of Beckett's head, my eyes drilling holes into his scalp, but he doesn't turn around to look at me.

As if he didn't just kiss the daylights out of me.

As if he didn't just suggest that he'd wanted to do that for a while.

As if he didn't just turn my world on its axis and make me question everything.

But now isn't the time to think of boys and crushes and kisses that cascade through my veins like magma. First, we need to get the hell out of here. Everything else can wait.

Beckett's fingers are hot around my wrist, almost blisteringly so, and I have to wonder if it's my own body's visceral reaction to him. Everything seems different now. It was like that when Zane kissed me. And Ryker.

Thoughts of those two boys effectively dampen the lust

swirling in my stomach. I have no idea how to deal with all of...*this*. My feelings for them are somehow more terrifying than even POP.

Think about all of this later, Ellie! I mentally scold myself as I follow Beckett down a long, narrow hallway.

Doors line either side of it, with numbers engraved in gold on the wall. It appears we're on the sixth floor.

Six hundred and twenty-one.

Six hundred and twenty-two.

Six hundred and twenty-three.

"Tell me what you know," Beckett whispers as he pauses at a fork in the hall.

He stares intently in both directions, his head cocked slightly to the side as if he's listening to something inaudible to my own ears, before nodding once and hurrying down the left hallway. He's practically dragging me along at this point, my short legs unable to keep up with his long, determined strides.

"A man visited me," I begin, noting—somewhat belatedly—the way he tenses at the word man.

The move is almost imperceptible. If I didn't know Beckett as well as I do, I would've never noticed the stiffening of his shoulders, the way his fingers tighten around my wrist, the clenching of his jaw, the rigidness of his posture.

"A man?" he asks stiffly.

"He looked like..." Swallowing proves to be impossible. It feels as if the air is made of a thousand tiny blades, and I'm swallowing them by the mouthful. They slice, cut, and stab at everything they come into contact with, destroying me from the inside out. Still, I force myself to say the words, to not hide away from them the way the old Ellie might've. "He looked like my father."

Beckett's steps stutter to an abrupt halt. His grip on me is almost bruising as he slowly, almost mechanically, turns back to stare at me. His face has leached of all color, making his multicolored eyes stand out starkly in the dim illumination.

"Your father? He's..."

"It wasn't him," I rush to say, though my heart cracks down the middle just uttering those words out loud.

How many times have I imagined a life where my parents didn't pass away?

How many times have I lain in bed, sobbing my eyes out, praying that death would claim me and take me to them?

The child in me always hoped that they were still alive somewhere, looking for me, waiting to return. The adult knows that the dead can't come back to life, that they can't claw their way out of the ground like zombies.

"Who was it, then?" Beckett's teeth grind together.

It takes me a long moment to realize he's furious on my behalf. I don't know what expression is splayed across my face, but it must be bad enough to elicit this reaction from him. His eyes gleam with a carnal, desperate need for revenge.

He doesn't like that someone hurt me, that someone broke my heart. The knowledge turns the butterflies in my stomach radioactive, as if they've been dipped in green acid.

"He called himself my uncle. My Uncle Raymond." I stitch my brows together in confusion, a reflection of Beckett's own expression.

Those heterochromia eyes of his lock on my face—the brown a shade of champagne flecked with honey gold and the green a bottle of dark chartreuse. His gaze always reminds me of a spring forest, when the snow has melted and the first signs of life begin to erupt through the frost.

His expression darkens even further, a bloated storm cloud moving in front of his face. "You don't have an uncle."

"There's no denying the similarities of that man to my dad," I whisper.

God, they could've been twins. The differences between the two of them are so miniscule it's like looking at a projection from my past.

But there *are* differences, that much is clear. This man's jaw is sharper, his eyes darker, his lips thinner, his nose larger.

I've always considered grief a malevolent monster that lurked above you, constantly watching, constantly waiting, constantly biding its time. When you least expect it, the beast will swoop down with its gnarled, bony claws extended and tighten around your waist. Squeeze you. Throw you around. Push you into the ground.

Sometimes, this monster will hold on to you until you run out of breath, until your body is broken and numb, until the pain threatens to sweep you away in a tidal wave of agony. Other times, the monster will pin you down...and then instantly retreat. Your body will hurt, yes, but the pain will be tolerable. A dull, confusing ache.

It's the former emotion that descends on me now—the type of grief that preemptively steals the breath from your lungs and renders you useless.

All I can see is my father's kind, jovial face.

All I can hear is my mother's laughter as she dances around the kitchen.

All I can—

"Ellie!" Beckett's voice pulls me out of my reverie.

I blink at him in surprise, unaware I tumbled so far down the abyss of my memories.

His hand gently, reverently, carefully brushes against my cheek. Fire licks at my skin at the contact, heating my body.

"Are you with me, sweetheart?" he asks gently.

Like with his kiss from earlier, there'll be a time for me to think about my grief, to lose myself in it. But now...

Now isn't the time.

I force my shoulders back and hold my chin high, emulating a confidence I'm not sure I truly possess. Still, when Beckett's eyes glimmer with pride and a small smile pulls up his lips, I know I made the right decision.

"Let's go," I tell him.

He nods once and continues down the hall. While we walk, I relay everything else Raymond told me—that he's been trying to protect me, that he's not a member of POP, that he's not The Divine One.

I'm not sure if Beckett believes him—heck, I'm not sure *I* believe him—but I can't deny that the revelation supplies me with a tiny smidgen of comfort...and also of despair.

POP?

POP is a threat we know. And while we may not necessarily have a method to stop them, at least it's a threat that's tangible, one we can study and exploit.

But Raymond?

This hotel?

It's an unknown—a factor that none of us prepared for or planned. We still don't know if Raymond is friend or foe, despite his claims. He's a wild card, and that unpredictability makes him immensely dangerous.

We've just turned down a second hallway when Beckett stops abruptly. Before I can catch my bearings, he ushers me back into the previous hallway, pushing my body flush against the plaster of the wall. I cock an eyebrow at him, but he simply places a single finger to his lips and gestures for me to stay.

I stare at him in confusion, but he doesn't need to say a word for me to understand. Less than a second later, a voice reaches me from the end of the hallway we had just been about to travel down.

"No sign of her," the voice says.

That declaration is followed by the murmur of static and a tinny voice I can't understand.

Her?

They can't mean me, right?

But there's no denying the boulder that has just dropped into my stomach. I can't think of any other "her" they would be referring to.

Raymond knows I escaped.

And he's searching for me.

Cold fear trails its icy fingers down my spine. I shiver involuntarily at the sensation as I debate what to do.

Turn myself in and hope Beckett can escape?

I dismiss that idea almost immediately. I know Beckett, just like I know all of my friends. They would never allow me to do that.

Do we go back the way we came from?

Do we—

Beckett lunges from around the corner, in the direction of the stranger, before I can even blink.

I place a hand over my mouth to cover my instinctive yelp of surprise and hurry after him, just in time to see him tackle the man to the ground.

I can't see much of the stranger—only a shock of dark

hair, a gangly body, and a plaid shirt—before it becomes a tangle of limbs and curse words.

Beckett slams his fist into the man's face once, twice, three times. Blood squirts in all directions, painting Beckett's pale skin.

"Holy crap," I breathe, my jaw unhinging.

Beckett remains on top of the man, his shoulders tense, his hand in a fist, his muscular body rigid. He doesn't turn around to stare at me.

"Are you okay?" His voice is unrecognizable—a husky murmur like water flowing over rocks.

"Am I...?" I shake my head in disbelief. "Are *you* okay?"

I rush forward, barely sparing the man on the ground a second look. All I know is that he's unconscious, his face splattered in blood, and that he won't be able to hurt us.

The thought brings me comfort, as macabre as it is. I think the old Ellie would've been frightened of what just happened, of what Beckett is capable of.

The new Ellie is just relieved that it's not Beckett broken and bleeding on the ground, his eyes rolled into the back of his head.

I reach for Beckett and pull him to his feet. He does so, albeit reluctantly.

He still won't look at me.

"Are you hurt? Are you okay?" I ask desperately, searching his body for any injuries.

His brown hair is disheveled, the strands sticking in all directions, and his sweater is stained with blood. I can't help but think Beckett will freak at a later time—he's always so fastidiously clean and immaculately groomed that I imagine he hates this. Hates the blood on his skin and clothes. Hates the bruises already forming on his knuckles. Hates his mussed hair.

His brows draw together as he flicks his gaze down towards the lacquered wood floor, now colored red with pooling blood.

"You're not... You're not afraid of me?" His voice is a mere whisper.

My confusion grows. "Why would I be afraid of you?"

He doesn't say anything, and the barbed wire around my heart squeezes in a way that's almost painful.

"We need to go," I add, gripping his wrist and tugging him down the hall...and away from the unconscious man.

I can't help but notice that Beckett's knuckles are red with blood. His blood? Or the stranger's?

Is it wrong that I hope it's the latter's?

"Ellie..." Beckett begins.

Pain lances his features.

But he never gets to finish that sentence.

At the end of the hallway, standing in front of the stair-case door, is a familiar man. An insouciant smirk plays at the edges of his lips as he considers us.

"Well...you two have been naughty, haven't you?" Raymond's eyes slide to me and stick there. Something I would almost describe as wariness passes his face before he hides it behind an impenetrable mask. "Don't you think we should finish our conversation, niece?"

CHAPTER 8
Ellie

Beckett immediately pushes me behind him, standing up straighter and puffing out his chest. I can't see his expression, not with his back to me, but whatever Raymond spots in Beckett's eyes has him staggering back a step. A look of surprise and fear paves its way across his face before he masks it.

"By the look on your face, you seem to know who I am." Beckett's voice almost sounds conversational, but I can hear the undercurrent of danger and violence punctuating each and every word.

It raises goose bumps on my arms.

"I know who all of you boys are. You. Landon. Dominic. Zane. Ryker." Raymond tentatively touches his waist.

It's fleeting—a brush of his fingers against his waistband—but it sends my heart into overdrive.

"Beckett," I whisper, never taking my eyes off of Raymond. I reach forward and grab the back of Beckett's sweater, my fingers tangling in the soft fabric. "I think he has a gun."

Beckett tenses almost imperceptibly but doesn't turn back to look at me. All of his focus is on the man before us—the man with the uncanny resemblance to my father.

"Are you really going to shoot down a bunch of defense-less, unarmed kids?" Beckett asks, his British accent becoming more pronounced in response to his anger.

A red flush crawls up the back of his neck.

Raymond gives him a dry look. "Of course not. But I know about your reputation. You and your friends will kill me before I even get the chance to speak." Something insidious sparks to life in Raymond's eyes. It darkens his irises, making them look almost obsidian in the dim lighting. "It's why I chose you guys, after all."

"Chose them?" I interject, peeking around Beckett's broad body.

Raymond's eyes flick to me before refocusing on Beckett. Obviously, he's determined that Beckett's the biggest threat here. I should be offended, but I'm not. I know my limitations and capabilities. I've literally only had one self-defense class. Before that, I've never even thrown a punch.

No, if Raymond chooses to attack us, I'm going to be useless.

But that doesn't mean I'll go down without a fight.

Beckett straightens suddenly, the taut string of a bow a second before the arrow flies forward and hits its mark.

"You're... You're our contact?" Disbelief laces his tone. "The man Landon's been in touch with?"

"Took you long enough, kid." Raymond smiles, and I can't decide if it's genuine or not.

Does it meet his eyes? Are there wrinkles around the

curve of his mouth? It's impossible to tell in the dim lighting.

"You've been the stranger helping the guys stop POP?" I clarify, my brows touching my hairline.

Landon told me that he's been in contact with an unknown man. This contact has helped them save numerous people...and get rid of high-ranking members of the cult.

And this entire time, it's been an uncle who I never knew existed?

It seems impossible for me to wrap my head around. I honestly don't know what to say, what to do. Revelations are continually pelting me in the face; there's nothing for me to do but brace myself against the onslaught.

Slowly, Raymond lifts his hands into the air, palms facing outwards, and ventures a single step closer. Beckett freezes as if he's been shot through with lightning and reaches behind him to nudge me farther to the side. All I can see now is the broad, rigid outline of Beckett's back.

"Don't come any closer," Beckett warns.

His accent turns those words into a lyrical growl, a raspy murmur, a discordant piano key.

"I'm not going to hurt you, kid." Raymond sounds annoyed, maybe even insulted. "Everything I've ever done has been to keep that girl right there safe. And I know the same can be said for you and the others."

Beckett begins to move backwards, taking me with him. I still can't see Raymond's face, not with the way Beckett's standing in front of me, but my friend has gone positively rigid, his body hewn from granite.

"I saw something in the five of you, something that intrigued me," Raymond continues. "I've been keeping tabs on Ellie for a while, and when I was told about the five of you...I knew you could help me."

"So you used us," Beckett surmises, fury tinging his words. "You used our feelings for Ellie against us to get us to take down POP. Are you too fucking lazy to do it yourself?"

"It's not that simple, kid."

"Don't call me kid!" Beckett snaps fiercely. "You damn well know I'm not one—not after the things I've done. The things you've made me do. Made *us* do."

What exactly does Beckett mean by that?

What exactly have the five of them done in their attempt to stop the Paragons of Prosperity and protect me?

I find that I don't care about the answer. Not truly. I've always known that my guys have a darkness inside of them, a beast percolating just beneath their flesh, and it never frightened me before. It should—I know it should—but the guys have only ever wielded their darkness to protect me and others.

They're ruthless, wicked demons...but they're not evil. Beckett and the others are inherently *good*.

At Beckett's accusation, Raymond releases a huff of laughter, the noise as acerbic as it is humorless. It coats my skin like sticky tar that no amount of scrubbing and washing will remove.

"I didn't make you do shit. I simply provided you with much-needed information. You kids were trying to save the world and be vigilantes, but you didn't know fuck all about anything." Raymond tsks his tongue. "You guys already had blood on your hands when I contacted you. Why does it matter if I steered you five in the right direction, taking down the men and women who actually deserve to be killed?"

"How do you know so much about the Paragons of Prosperity?" I demand, poking my head around Beckett's bicep.

He immediately tries to shoo me back behind him, but I refuse to hide. Not again.

Raymond's face is shadowed in the scarce lighting. Half of it is nothing but a dark, indecipherable blob. The other is highlighted by gold illumination, emphasizing the downward tilt of his lips, the curve of his brow, the tightness of his jaw.

"All I've ever done is protect you, Ellie," he says, and there's a note of pleading in his voice I've never heard before. It slices at something inside of me. "You're all that matters to me. You know how evil that cult is—I know you've seen firsthand what they can do. They truly believe that they can gain wealth and power by harming others. By *killing* others. The Divine One has warped their minds. But it's more than that—so much more. The cult is nothing but an excuse for the rich and sadistic to do the things they've always wanted to do."

"What do you mean by that?" I ask, somewhat desperately. "And do you know what The Divine One wants with Senator Reece Whipers?"

"Do you know who The Divine One is?" Beckett interjects.

Raymond's jaw clenches. "If I knew who The Divine One was, I'd already be dead." His gaze zeroes in on me like two heat-seeking missiles. "And you'll be dead too if you don't heed my warning."

"And what warning is that?" Beckett demands.

Raymond doesn't take his eyes off of me. "Do what The Divine One says. What POP says. I know you're a member now, and though I never wanted that for you, you have no choice but to fall in line." Darkness sweeps across his face like a velvety curtain being drawn closed. "If you don't, you'll die." He swallows and turns towards Beckett, the movement jerky and unnatural, as if it physically pains him to look away from me. "Go. I won't stop you. But just know that we're on the same side and that I'll be here when you five boys are ready to talk." He reaches into his pocket, retrieves a tiny slip of paper, and then carefully sets it on the ground at his feet. "This is my number. Call me, Ellie, if you ever need anything."

He begins to walk away.

"Wait! We still have questions!" I scream at his retreating back, but he doesn't stop, doesn't slow down, doesn't look my way.

Still, his voice carries to me as if in a breeze, the words raising every fine hair on the back of my neck.

"You're one of them now, Ellie. Play their games, or your life will be forfeit."

CHAPTER 9

Zane

As soon as we return to the dorm, I head straight to the cupboard, perusing the options and humming happily under my breath.

"What the fuck are you doing?" Dominic snipes from somewhere behind me as he and Landon tear off their coats and toss them onto the closet bench.

I haven't even bothered to remove mine yet. Food first.

Food. Always. First.

Except for when it comes to Ellie and her delectable body. Then, it's Ellie first and food second. Or food on *top* of Ellie...

"Fighting makes me hungry." I hum in delight when I find a red box of unmade brownies.

Perfect.

"I thought fighting makes you stabby," Landon interjects, though he sounds absent. His brow is furrowed as he stares intently at his phone screen.

"Fighting makes me hungry *and* stabby," I contend as I

place the box on the counter and then go about grabbing the necessary ingredients and bowls. "I'm a jack-of-all-trades."

"You're a dumbass," Dominic retorts.

That only makes my smile broaden.

"You wuv me, don't you, Dominikins?" I tease in an obnoxiously high-pitched baby voice.

He makes a face at me as he throws himself onto the couch, Sethy Boy's phone still in his hand as he tries to make sense of the strange app. I'm not sure I believe it's important, but I trust Dominic's intuition. Besides, I know his father, and that man is a ripe piece of shit collecting heat from the sweltering summer sun. If there's a way to prove he's involved in all of this nonsense, then I'll be a very happy psycho.

A very happy *murderous* psycho.

Can't forget the "murderous" part of the equation. It's practically half of my identity.

I dump the chocolate powder into the bowl and then go about adding eggs and water. Dominic watches me over the top of the phone as I stir the mixture, singing the Spice Girls at the top of my lungs.

Halfway through, I transition to Celine Dion, but my own edition. "My Heart Will Go On" has never been more bloody and brutal before. Rose and Jack totes would have survived if they had automatic assault rifles and long, sharp katana swords. Just saying.

"You're cooking brownies?" One of Dom's platinum blond eyebrows quirks.

When I first met him, I thought his hair was dyed. I found it unreal that a man had that shade of hair naturally. I'd teased him about it mercilessly before I realized Dominic truly did have luscious, white-blond locks.

Of course, when I tried to tell him that, he simply glared at me and snapped, "Don't call my hair luscious, you fucking weirdo."

So...his hair is most definitely *not* luscious. It's succulent, lush, juicy, ambrosian, scrumptious, and nectarous. Did I spend an entire hour memorizing words from the thesaurus? Yes. Yes, I did.

Do I have any regrets? Nope.

Once the batter has been effectively batter-fied, I grab the entire bowl with a contented grin and move to sit next to Dominic on the couch. He finally tears his attention off of his phone just long enough to give me an incredulous stare, but I simply dip my spoon into the chocolate goodness and take a huge, *scrumptious* mouthful.

A moan of pure ecstasy escapes me—seriously, it sounds as if I'm in the midst of an orgasm, my cock buried nine inches in Ellie—and Dominic's frown deepens.

"That's so unhealthy," he says with a pointed stare.

I wag my spoon of heaven at him. "So is stalking. And you do that in spades with a certain someone..."

I allow my words to taper off ominously, though we all know who I'm referring to.

I'm not an idiot.

I stalk Ellie just as much as the next guy. I know a fellow stalker when I see one, though I much prefer to call it "protecting and serving without the person's knowledge." Stalking just seems like such a...crude term, you know? It conjures up images of perverts hiding in bushes while jacking off their tiny, diseased cocks.

I'm jacking off my large, non-diseased cock, thank you very much.

When Dominic opens his mouth to protest, I wave my spoon back and forth in front of his face, a few droplets of batter splattering his blue jeans. His eyes narrow, but I forge ahead before he can say anything.

"Don't deny being Stalker McStalkerson. I found your stash of…"—I lower my voice to a whisper—"panties."

His nose wrinkles in disgust. "I don't steal Ellie's fucking panties."

"Suuurrre you don't." I give him an exaggerated wink.

"I don't," he insists.

"So you've never, not ever, stolen a pair of little pink panties with a bow at the top? You know, that little white bow?" I gesture to my own nether regions for emphasis, more globs of chocolate batter dripping from my spoon. Oops. "What about that blue- and white-striped pair? Or the one—"

"Shut the fuck up!" Dominic reaches behind him, grabs a throw pillow, and whacks me with it so hard that I nearly drop the bowl of chocolate.

And that… That would be a goddamn tragedy.

"MY PRECIOUS!" I cry in my best impersonation of Gollum. The bowl teeters precariously from side to side before I manage to steady it and hold it protectively to my chest. I caress the porcelain edges the way I would a pussy while hurling daggers with my eyes at Dominic. "Don't you dare hurt Chocolatey."

"You named your brownie batter?" His eyebrows are so high, they practically disappear into that mop of *lush* white locks.

I'm feeling personally attacked right now, and I don't fucking like it.

"I name a lot of things. My cock, for one. Ellie's right boob. Her left. Her pussy—"

Dominic hits me with the pillow yet again.

"You're disgusting," he says, even as a tentative smile flirts with the corners of his lips.

"I'm freaking hilarious," I counter.

"Landon, tell Zane he's an asshole." Dominic turns on the couch to face the man in question, only to frown when he finds Landon's attention still firmly on his phone.

The trench between his brown eyebrows has never been more apparent.

Dominic frowns. "You okay, man?"

"I just checked the security footage we put outside Ellie's dorm," Landon says, his tone stiff and unreadable. His silver eyes are the color of gravestones. Or maybe a better description would be mercury, bright and molten. "She hasn't returned from her self-defense classes with Beckett this morning."

"That fucker probably just took the opportunity to spend time alone with her," I say. And then, in a lower voice, I add, "That's what I would do."

"Beckett hasn't answered any of my messages," Landon continues. Lines of strain bracket his eyes, making him look years older than eighteen. He shakily runs a hand through his dark-brown hair, disrupting the meticulous strands. "You know the rules—when we're alone with Ellie, we have to be on call twenty-four seven until the situation with POP and The Divine One is handled. Beckett knows this."

Concern lances my heart, and I find myself bouncing on the couch with restless energy. It skitters up my spine and then down my arms like an infestation of beetles.

Because Landon's words? They ring true. We have strict rules when it comes to Ellie's protection, and not one of us would be stupid enough to break them.

I try to tamp down my growing fear, try to bury it behind witty humor and stupid jokes. But no words come to me. My stomach twists and tightens like a nest of slithering snakes. My nails dig into my palms hard enough to draw blood.

Darkness encroaches the edges of my mind, tapping incessantly against the translucent windows, demanding to be let in. For so long, I've held the darkness back and was able to keep it at bay.

But now... Now, it's demanding entrance, reminding me that it's the only thing capable of protecting Ellie. That, without it, I'm nothing.

Monsters like me thrive in the dark. We become the shadows to the ones who provide us even a smidgen of light—and that person, for me, has always been Ellie.

"Zane..." Dominic's voice is taut with worry and caution as he stares at me. His eyes are shadowed. "You need to calm the fuck down. We don't know that anything's wrong. Right, Landon?"

Landon finally glances up from his phone and spears me with an unreadable look. Whatever he sees on my face smooths his own features over, the tension tugging at his lips loosening.

He nods once, a stiff jerk of his chin, and says, "We'll just have to beat the shit out of Beckett for worrying us when they get back. Maybe he took her out for lunch and forgot to bring his phone into the restaurant."

It's a flimsy excuse, but it does its job. The anger percolating inside of me, clawing at my defenses, screaming at me like a banshee... It dissipates—an immense tidal wave sweeping over me and carrying it away.

I take a deep, raspy breath and will my body to unthaw. Slowly, incrementally, my muscles begin to relax. First my shoulders, then my back, then my fingers, one digit at a time. Pain radiates from where my nails dug into my palms, but it's a distant sort of pain, easily ignorable.

Dominic eyes me with unveiled concern, his jaw muscles clenching. "You okay, man?"

"Do we have any idea where Ellie could be?" I barely recognize my voice. It's not a growl—not really—but it's something close to it.

I'm not an animal, but when it comes to Ellie and the guys, I turn into something positively primitive. My entire existence is characterized by three words—protect, kill, and destroy.

Protect those I love.

Kill those who hurt them.

Destroy the entire fucking world in a barrage of flames if I lose anyone I care about.

It's that simple.

Maybe that mentality makes me a psychopath. Maybe it just makes me human.

But does it really matter, when the people I'm protecting—the *woman* I'm protecting—deserve my undivided devotion? I'm not doing anything wrong. People have killed others for less. Fathers have shot down intruders to protect their families. Mothers have strangled their abusers in order to save their children's lives.

It's human nature to protect the ones we love, no matter the consequences.

"We can retrace her steps," Landon says, his silver eyes glimmering as he focuses back on the phone screen. "I know where her class was. We can talk to the teacher and figure out when she left."

"We might see something on the way there," Dominic adds. "I can't imagine Beckett took a different route to get home."

"I'm going to fucking murder that British dick if he simply forgot to turn his phone on," I promise.

I'm joking.

Sort of.

Half joking.

Maybe I won't full-on murder the bloke...but I may do a little light maiming. I'm sure Beckett can still design his clothing without a finger, right? Or perhaps I'll take one of his toes...

The pinkie toe is entirely useless. I mean, what's the point of it? It's the size of a goddamn raisin and just...kind of...hangs there. It's the goddamn flaccid dick of toes.

"I don't like this," I say to no one in particular. "It isn't like Beckett to not check in with us. Have you tried texting Ellie?"

"Multiple times." Landon's voice betrays his anxiety.

I can tell he's trying to hold it together for my sake, but I know my friend well enough to hear the barely suppressed fear in his tone. That only exacerbates my own anxiety.

My own darkness.

But I can't... I can't lose myself to it. Not yet. I need to keep a level head if I have any hope of finding Ellie and Beckett.

"Do you think POP...?" I don't allow myself to finish the thought.

Just thinking of the cult tightens every muscle in my body. The need to maim, to hurt, to kill rears its ugly head. It takes every ounce of willpower I possess to not throw myself out of the room, find the nearest POP member, and beat them into a bloody pulp.

"I don't—" The shrill ringing of Landon's phone interrupts whatever he's going to say.

"Is it Ellie?" Dominic demands at the same time I do.

"Unknown number," Landon admits.

And then, hesitantly, tentatively, nervously...he answers the call. He places it on speaker almost immediately for us to hear the conversation as well.

My heart has crawled all the way up my throat and has now become stuck there. I swear my brain is made up of thousands of tiny bombs, and those bombs have been set off one after the other. The resulting explosions have my ears ringing. Dark spots freckle my vision.

"Hello?" Landon's voice is cold—an icicle dangling from a rooftop, just waiting to fall down and impale the unsuspecting victim underneath it.

I don't know who we expect to be on the other end of the phone. A POP member? The Divine One? Beckett? Ellie?

It's none of them.

"Is this...Landon?" a timid, feminine voice asks.

"Yes?" His brows stitch together. "Who is this?"

"My name is Rachelle, and I'm a nurse at North Mercy Hospital. I have your name listed as an emergency contact for a...Ryker Nolan?"

"Ryker?" Landon blinks owlishly at a spot on the wall.

Dominic and I exchange anxious glances.

"I'm afraid there's been an accident," she continues, her voice dripping with sympathy. "Your friend was found facedown in a pile of snow on Highway 19. It looks to be a car accident—we found a few vehicles abandoned a mile from where he was at..."

The nurse continues to babble on, but I barely process a word she says.

A few vehicles?

What the fuck happened to Ryker?

And more than that...where's Ellie?

CHAPTER 10
Ellie

Beckett's fingers are tight on my wrist as he drags me out of the hotel, down a wide staircase, and to a half-paved parking lot directly in front. Loose pebbles crunch under my feet as I struggle to keep up with his brisk, unrelenting pace.

As I stare at my surroundings, I see that we're not at an abandoned hotel as I initially suspected, merely at a half-constructed one. One half—the half we just exited from—is a tall, towering building with eggshell-white painted walls, huge pillars wreathed in vines, and a swooping arcade. The other half is a hollow carcass, nothing but cement lines and windowless squares. A collection of currently abandoned equipment rests beside it—a bulldozer, crane, and forklift, to name a few.

I want to ask Beckett where we are, want to demand answers, but he continues on without pausing, dragging me through the parking lot and towards the stretch of forest surrounding it.

I can't see any buildings, any homes, any landmarks no matter which direction I look. Nothing but tall pines frosted with fluffy snow and semi-frozen dirt and grass border us.

Still, I can't help but look over my shoulder, just once.

Raymond stands in the doorway of the hotel, an unreadable expression on his face. Those gray-blue eyes of his—eyes that remind me so keenly and almost eerily of my father—stare back at me. They seem to be telling me something, but it's like I'm reading a book written in some entirely new and innovative language. There's no translation, no way for me to decipher the words and meaning.

And then Raymond's swallowed by the spindly tree branches as Beckett drags me into the surrounding forest. The cold wind blows across my skin, immediately eliciting goose bumps. I try to hide my involuntary shiver, but it's no use. My body practically shakes with the force of it.

Beckett glances at me in alarm, his dichromatic eyes wide on his face. The green resembles the hint of pine needles peeking through the snow; the brown is the exact same shade as the frozen dirt crunching beneath our feet.

"Are you cold?" He doesn't wait for me to respond, knowing my body better than I do. "Shit, you are!"

"It's not like we had time to grab our coats when we were kidnapped," I tell him with a tiny smile.

I'm wearing my long-sleeved shirt and leggings I had on when I went to my self-defense class. Beckett's dressed in his customary sweater and jeans. Both of our coats have been left abandoned in the car.

"Here…" Beckett immediately reaches for the hem of his sweater and begins drawing it over his head.

Hints of bronze abs reveal themselves to me, making heat rush to my cheeks. Who would've thought that Beckett had a six-pack?

And why am I even looking?!

"No!" I rush to say, grabbing at his arms and forcing his sweater back down. "Are you insane? You'll freeze to death if you walk around shirtless in this weather!"

Even though the thought of Beckett shirtless makes heat pool low in my stomach. That same fire cascades through my veins until I find myself shifting uncomfortably and rubbing my thighs together.

"But—" Beckett's lips purse stubbornly, a retort on the tip of his tongue.

But I can be just as stubborn as him when I want to be.

"No," I reiterate.

I slowly trail my fingers down his wrists until they interlock with his own. It feels...strange to be holding his hands. No, maybe not strange. That word doesn't seem to fit the situation.

Unreal, perhaps?

It's like a dream you've been having every night for years—an elusive fantasy that consumes the entirety of your being, that gives you hope for a better future, a better tomorrow. And then, out of the blue, that dream becomes a reality. It's no longer just beyond your reach but in your grasp.

And god, it feels beautiful.

There are calluses on the tips of his fingers I never would've thought him to have. Not my gentle Beckett who constantly hides away with his notepad of clothing designs. Where did they come from?

What would they feel like caressing the rest of my over-heated skin?

Beckett looks as if he still wants to argue—stubborn fool—but I'm already turning away and peering through the dense foliage.

"Do you have any idea where we are and where we need to go?" I ask, frowning.

Beckett heaves out a breath and reluctantly turns away from me. He squints as he stares in first one direction and then the other. There's no road that I can see—only forest.

That's...not ominous at all.

How the hell did Raymond manage to build a hotel in the middle of nowhere?

Unless he didn't build this hotel but merely decided to use it for his nefarious purposes...

I shove all thoughts of Raymond to the back of my mind. We'll figure out how to deal with him as soon as we find the others. No doubt, they're worried sick about us...if they even realize we're gone. For all I know, they haven't noticed anything's amiss, which would be a relief. The last thing I want to do is worry them.

"There has to be a path somewhere," Beckett tells me, seeming to parrot the direction of my own thoughts. "There's no other way for them to get the equipment to the site without it."

"So we walk in a circle until we find some sort of path?" My eyebrows draw together.

"What else do you suppose we do?" Beckett grants me a sideways smile. "Ask Raymond for a ride?"

"And have him slit our throats? No thanks." I snort derisively.

If there's one thing we both seem to agree on, it's that we don't trust Raymond even a tiny bit. I don't care if he's been helping the guys take down POP. There's something... off about him and his story.

A mysterious uncle I never knew existed?

Who then decided to kidnap me out of the blue, just to talk to me?

Who seems to be squatting at a random-ass, half-constructed hotel in the middle of nowhere?

Who has hired goons working for him?

Yeah. I'll take shady for one hundred, please and thank you.

"Do you think…" I swallow down the lump of emotion in my throat. Beckett's hands are the only things keeping me tethered to the here and now. "Do you think Raymond will come after us?"

God, it hurts to consider. I don't know him…but he's still my family, still my blood. His face is so eerily similar to my father's, it's like looking at a picture of the man I loved and lost. Would he hurt me? Hurt the guys? Is what he said before the truth? Is he trying to protect me?

Why wouldn't he reveal himself to me earlier?

Why now?

So many questions tumble around and around in my brain—ricocheting off each other like loose rocks tumbling down a steep cliffside and landing in the vigorous waters below.

Beckett hesitates, and I have to appreciate the fact that he's actually considering my question instead of rushing to reassure me that everything will be all right. It's one thing I love about him.

The others… The others constantly try to protect me. They see a weak, vulnerable girl in need of being sheltered and coddled.

But not Beckett.

Yes, he wants to protect me, but he seems to realize that I'm not some vintage Barbie doll whose sole purpose is to remain trapped inside a cardboard box. Secrets and deceit are what pushed me away from the guys in the first place.

Their futile attempt to "protect" me only made me resent them.

Hopefully now, things will be different.

"I don't think so," he decides on at last, giving my fingers a tight squeeze. "At least, not yet. I have no idea what his plans are, but he seemed sincere in letting us go."

"Why would he even take us to begin with?" I wonder. "To talk to me? Hasn't he ever heard of a phone?"

"Maybe he was worried about The Divine One getting wind of it?" Beckett suggests, though he doesn't sound convinced.

A tiny crease materializes between his brows, one I always associate with him being afraid or anxious.

"Let's just get the hell out of here."

Another wind rustles through the tree boughs, making me shiver. Beckett immediately straightens, his eyes sharpening on my face and the goose bumps splattering my bare skin.

"There should be *something* nearby. A rest area. A restaurant. A gas station. A house," he says. "We can hopefully find a phone and call the others."

"And get cleaned up." I gesture towards his blood-splattered sweater and my own bloody top. "People will think we were almost murdered."

Beckett's expression darkens almost instantly, though I'd meant for the words to be funny. It's like a ginormous, dark-gray thundercloud blotting out the sun and siphoning all of the light.

"Maybe we were," he says at last.

And for once, I don't have a response to that.

✦✦✦✦✦✦✦✦✦✦

We only walk thirty minutes—the longest thirty minutes of my life—when we stumble upon the first sign of civilization.

A rundown, dilapidated gas station.

There are no cars that I can see, and the pumps appear to be rusted with age. There are two buildings positioned side by side. One is a small convenience store, bright, artificial lighting emanating from the windows. The other appears to be bathrooms.

It's the latter building Beckett leads me to first.

"You're right." A mischievous smile tugs up his lips as he holds the door open for me. "We look like something out of a horror movie right now."

"This *place* looks like something out of a horror movie," I respond as I duck inside.

Surprisingly, the bathroom has been well-maintained and is—dare I say—clean. The sparkling white flooring is a startling contrast to the dreary exterior of both buildings. It's a single room designed for weary travelers who have been driving for hours, even days. There's a sink, a toilet, and a shower.

Beckett immediately pulls paper towels out of the dispenser and hands some to me before grabbing a few pieces for himself.

I place a wad underneath the sink and nearly groan at the hot water caressing my fingers. It burns my chilled skin, but I'll take fire over ice any day.

I begin to dab at my shirt and collarbone, trying to clean off all the bloodstains I can find. The red marring my pale skin comes off easily, but I'm afraid I only smear the blood on my shirt around, the stain enlarging.

We *could* use the shower, but I don't think either of us wants to be soaked to the bone.

And I also don't think we want to get naked in front of each other.

At least, *I* don't want to.

Maybe.

Possibly.

Probably.

No, definitely not.

"I honestly can say I never had to get blood out of my clothes before," I murmur absently, frowning at the huge wet circle near my neckline.

Beckett chuckles dryly, and I automatically slide my eyes to him.

And then immediately wish I hadn't.

Because Beckett...is shirtless, holding his sweater underneath the sink as he attempts to wash it off.

My gaze greedily drinks in the smooth, sinewy lines of his shoulders and chest as that same heat from before clamors up my neck and finds a home in my cheeks. I always considered Beckett the skinniest of my friends, but that couldn't be further from the truth. Every inch of him is well-defined, golden muscles stacked upon golden muscles. My fingers itch to brush against the span of shoulder blades, where there's a tiny dip visible from his spine.

Shit!

I quickly glance away before he can catch me ogling, willing the heat in my cheeks to dissipate. Is it possible to die of embarrassment? Die of overstimulation?

"You know..." Beckett begins, his voice a husky murmur, the sound of a stream trickling over tiny rocks. It has every nerve in my body bursting into flames. "When we were taken... When I woke up in that room alone..." He swallows, the noise deafeningly loud in the sudden silence.

My heart batters against my rib cage, increasing in speed with every second that passes.

"Yeah?" I can't speak above a whisper.

"I realized that I can't lose you, El. I fucking can't. You're not just my best friend... You're a piece of me. You're as vital to me as my heart and my lungs and my fucking brain. Losing you would quite literally kill me. You can't live without a goddamn heart, just like I can't live without you."

His fingers brush my wrist. Tremors rock my body at the connection, menial as it is.

Slowly, my heart somewhere in the vicinity of my throat, I turn to face him.

His eyes are open and earnest, allowing me to see everything, feel everything, be *consumed* by everything.

And I don't even know what that "everything" entails, only that I want it. I want it all.

I want him.

It's not just a want but a desperate, soul-aching need.

He claimed that I'm as vital to him as one of his organs? I'm beginning to believe he's the same for me—him, Ryker, Zane, Dominic, and Landon. My closest friends. My first friends.

My first...loves.

Oh god.

My body is suffused in heat, in fire, in flames that lick and bite at my skin. It feels as if the ground is opening up beneath me and I'm slowly descending into hell. But if this is hell...why does it feel so good? So right?

Why does it feel like heaven?

"Can I...?" His eyes search mine. I feel like prey trapped within a hunter's snare. "Can I kiss you again?"

I can't concentrate on anything but the thundering of my heart.

My mouth moves before my brain can catch up, but I'm not sure a rational Ellie would say anything differently.

"Yes."

Beckett doesn't immediately lean in, despite my permission. Instead, his hand cups my cheek, his thumb leisurely tracing the seam of my lips. That fluttering feeling from before returns with a vengeance. I feel light and buoyant, my stomach fizzing like a can of soda that has been shaken repeatedly and then popped open.

Slowly, his eyes never leaving mine, Beckett brings his lips to my skin.

I can feel the brush of them against my cheek—a mere whisper, a promise of what's to come, a tease of a kiss. I tremble in his arms, and I curl my hands into fists by my sides. I want...more.

I want that "everything" he hinted at before.

He plants another chaste, teasing kiss to my jawline, his fingers expertly moving my chin up to grant himself better access.

"Beckett..."

"I love it when you say my name," he rasps.

I don't know what comes over me then.

Maybe it's the raw, unfettered need in his voice—the one that tells me he desires me just as much as I do him.

Maybe it's my own percolating emotions, my feelings for him compounding with my lust.

Or maybe it's something else entirely, this revelation that I've been waiting way too long to take what I want.

Claim what I want.

Claim *who* I want.

I encircle his neck with my arms as I drag him in, forcing his lips to mine. His brown hair feels like silk beneath my fingers. He kisses me like he's dying, like I'm the antidote to the poison plaguing his body. There's nothing teasing or chaste about this kiss—it's a merging of souls, two stars colliding in an infinite galaxy.

Everywhere he touches me, I feel fire. Flames consume my skin in a way that rolls my eyes back in pure bliss. His five-o'clock shadow tickles my skin deliciously.

I finally give in to the craving that's been bombarding me since I first saw him shirtless—no, longer than that. Way freaking longer.

Very hesitantly, I drop my hands to the width of his broad shoulders, loving the feel of his hard muscles contrasting with his silky-smooth skin. I was right in my initial assessment—he's lean but still muscular, his body reminding me distinctly of Olympic swimmers.

He shudders under my touch, and I feel a surge of power course through me. How is it that I'm able to make a man like Beckett tremble?

"Ellie…" he groans, abruptly placing his arms underneath my ass and hoisting me up. I stifle my gasp of surprise—or maybe he swallows it—as he positions us until my ass is on the edge of the bathroom counter. "God, Ellie."

His tongue licks at my lips, and I open my mouth to him. Pleasure rockets through me as he inhales me like I'm the air he needs to breathe. It's a heady sensation to know that someone desires me that much.

Wants me that much.

Cares for me that much.

"I want to see you," he pants against my lips, pulling away just enough to see my eyes.

For a brief moment, self-consciousness pierces through the haze of lust surrounding me. I know Beckett saw the scars on my arms—the scars I put on myself—but I also know they're not...the sexiest thing in the world. They're a reminder of my pain, my depression, the times that I've stooped so low I thought I'd never be able to climb back out of the hole I found myself in.

Would Beckett really want to see that?

But when I see the look in his eyes—the lust mixed with something else, something deeper, something I'm too terrified to name—all doubts disappear from my head.

I want him to see me, just as I want to see him.

All of him.

My pulse skitters in nervous anticipation as I whip my shirt off over my head. His eyes heat with a banked fire as I pull my sports bra off next, my breasts springing free. I can feel the warmth in my neck and cheeks, and I have the irrational urge to cover myself, to hide from his prying gaze.

Then he whispers, "You're so beautiful, love. So fucking beautiful."

His hand slowly, reverently, reaches upwards to cup one of my breasts, testing the weight in his palm. My eyes roll back in my head as he flicks his thumb over my pointed nipple.

"Beckett..."

Beckett releases my breast, and I immediately open my mouth to protest. That protest dies on my lips when he grabs my arm gently and brings it up to his lips.

I swear my heart is seconds from bursting free from my chest as he lightly kisses the very first scar marring my flesh.

"I need you, Ellie," he whispers as he kisses the second scar. "*We* need you. Please don't do this to yourself. Please. I'll do whatever you ask of me—be whatever you need. But you can't... You just can't... Please don't hurt yourself anymore." When he moves to kiss the third scar, I see that his eyes are glimmering with tears. The green and brown look positively luminescent.

"Beckett…"

"Please, Ellie. Please." His voice is choked with emotion as he continues to kiss the scars on my wrist, one after another, his lips feather-soft against my skin.

I want to tell him that I won't hurt myself again. I want to make that promise I see he so desperately needs, but the words get caught in my throat right alongside my breath.

Because depression isn't just a switch that I can flip on and off. I'm taking the steps to heal myself…but what if I sink back into a hole I can't escape from? What if I'm not strong enough to resist the allure of the darkness?

"I…" I open and shut my mouth repeatedly as a single tear trickles down my cheek, catching on the top of my lips.

Beckett leans forward to kiss it away.

"I'll show you," he whispers, his breath heated on my skin. "I'll show you what you have to live for. You have me and my love for you, and that may not be enough…but maybe it'll help. Maybe it'll give you enough strength to fight."

Love?

Before the thought can fully form, Beckett leans forward and kisses me once more.

CHAPTER 11
Ellie

All thoughts flee as I lose myself to Beckett's kiss, to the way his lips meld with my own, to the way his tongue tangles and dances with mine.

I've heard people say before that fireworks explode behind your eyelids when you're kissing your soulmate, but I never believed that to be true before.

But now...

I've felt it three times.

With Zane. With Ryker. And with Beckett.

They explode in my vision, a light show of garnet red, cerulean blue, and emerald green. The colors twirl and dance in the night sky—each configuration accompanied by a loud, deafening boom that has my ears ringing.

That's what it feels like to kiss my guys. To be in their arms.

Beckett's lips leave my own, but only to travel down the hollow of my throat. I arch my neck eagerly, desperate to feel his lips on every inch of my skin. My shyness from before has seemed to dissipate, burning away like dry tinder in flames. Maybe it's because I trust Beckett so irrevocably to take care of me and protect me. There's not a shadow of doubt in his intentions.

He pauses when he reaches the swell of my breast, and his teasing kisses turn into long, languid flicks of his tongue. He swirls it around one of my nipples, hardening it to the point of pain, before licking between the valley of my breasts and capturing my second beaded nub between his teeth. He stares up at me through his fringe of dark lashes, his eyes hooded and burning with desire.

"Ellie..." he moans as he pulls away from my breasts to kiss me again.

I rake my fingers through his chocolate-brown hair, loving the way he groans at the contact. He pauses to briefly untie my shoes and then pulls them—and my socks —off. I feel like a reverse Cinderella, suffused in his love for me.

Every kiss...

Every touch...

Every lick...

It's a promise.

One of his hands continues to fondle my breast while his other inches towards the waistband of my leggings. Heat grows in my abdomen as I lift my hips up, allowing him access to drag the skintight material down.

He does so with a reverence that leaves me breathless— I heard what he said before, that whispered L-word, but I dismissed it as the mindless chatter of a man in the heat of passion. But there's no denying the way he looks at me, the way he touches me, the way he runs his fingers over the curves of my body as if he wishes to memorize them through touch alone.

He touches my skin like it's his notebook and I'm his newest creation he wants to paint and draw. I can almost pretend that his fingers are the whiskered ends of a paintbrush, creating long, swooping lines that color my skin, that mark me as his.

My panties fall to the ground next, and I find myself completely bare before him.

"My god, Ellie," he breathes in awe. His throat bobs as he swallows. "You're so bloody gorgeous."

A blush crawls its way up my cheeks. "You keep saying that."

I duck my head until my brown hair cascades forward, obscuring him from view.

He grips my chin instantly and forces my eyes back to his.

"And I'll say it every goddamn day until you believe it." One of his fingers teases my sensitive pussy, running up and down the slit, glistening with the evidence of my arousal.

I'm so wet for him already, so needy. The ache between my thighs is almost painful.

"Beckett," I whine as I bring his lips back to mine.

"Tell me what you need, love," he says against my skin, his breath fanning across my face and eliciting another round of delicious goose bumps. My hard nipples brush against his bare chest as he inches even closer to me. "Tell me what you need."

In answer, I thrust my hips up against his finger, wanting more. Desperate for it.

His chuckle is low. Carnal. Sensual. The fine hairs on my arms stand at attention.

"I need your words, darling," he says silkily, the words practically a purr that digs its way into my soul.

"I want..." I push past my instinctive embarrassment and finish with, "Your fingers inside of me."

He smiles against my lips as he slowly inches one of his fingers inside of my tight channel.

"You're so wet for me, Ellie. So fucking wet. So perfect. I can just imagine what you'll feel like wrapped around my cock."

His dirty words have my cheeks heating and my hips thrusting upwards.

Out of all the guys, I'm less certain about Beckett's past. He never really talked about what his life was like before he transferred to the States. Did he ever have a girlfriend? Has he done this with other girls before?

A fierce wave of jealousy crashes over me at the thought, as ridiculous as it sounds. Here I am, lusting after five separate guys, and my vision turns green at just the thought of them with another woman. Am I really that selfish?

But as a second finger joins Beckett's first inside of my pussy and his tongue continues to tangle with mine, I decide that...yes. Yes, I am.

I want him.

And I want the others as well.

I push all of my selfish, irrelevant thoughts to the side and instead lose myself to the sensation of Beckett's fingers inside of me, scissoring back and forth, stretching my channel. He plays my body like a guitar—strumming and plucking in a way that has music cascading through my veins.

Sweat glistens on my skin as Beckett tugs on one of my nipples, twisting it in such a way that pain momentarily eclipses the pleasure. But then that brief stab of pain transforms into something *more*. I find that I want him to do it again, to do it harder.

Is it wrong of me to like pain with my pleasure?

Is that normal?

Those thoughts fade to the distance as Beckett's thumb begins to flick my clit excessively, these back-and-forth swipes that have sunbeams exploding behind my eyelids. Pleasure ripples through me as an orgasm tears my body apart and then rebuilds it in its glorious image.

"Fuck!" The swear word slips out without conscious thought as my fingernails dip into Beckett's shoulders, no doubt leaving tiny, crescent-shaped indents in his skin.

Through my orgasm, Beckett holds me to him, whispering soothing words against my flushed skin, kissing my shoulders, my cheeks, my lips.

I tremble and shake in his arms as pleasure tornadoes through me, leaving absolute destruction in its wake. When I finally come down from my high, I'm putty in his skilled hands. I lower my head against his shoulder and work on regulating my breathing.

Beckett's hand follows the pathway of my spine as he kisses the top of my head.

"How are you feeling, my love?" he whispers.

"Like my soul just jumped out of my body and found a spaceship to Mars," I murmur drowsily.

His chuckle is rife with masculine satisfaction. "I take it that's a good thing?"

"It's a *really* good thing," I assure him with a tentative smile, pulling away.

I dip my gaze down to his jeans and the hard outline of his cock.

I want...

I want to take care of him, the way he just took care of me.

Beckett notes the direction of my gaze, and his brows draw together. "Ellie, you don't—"

"I want to," I whisper, a wave of shyness blowing over me. "I just... I haven't done it before."

He swallows. "You haven't? Not with Ryker or—"

"Not that." I nod towards his pants to indicate what I mean.

God, I feel like my cheeks are on fire. You could cook an egg on them.

He swallows again, his jaw twitching convulsively, his pupils dilating. "I can walk you through what to do...if you want. I can tell you what I like."

"Have you...?" I almost don't want him to answer that question.

Almost.

"No." He shakes his head adamantly. "I never allowed anyone to touch me like that. And I never touched anyone like that either."

Am I mistaken, or is Beckett actually blushing? His cheeks have taken on a distinct rosy hue that loosens the knots in my stomach. It's almost as if I'm seeking comfort in his nervousness, in his inexperience.

I want this to be something we learn together.

"But I've done stuff...with my own hand," he confesses, the red in his cheeks deepening until he looks like a ripe tomato.

"How... How should I start?" I can't pull my attention off of the bulge in his pants.

It seems to twitch under my attention, and god help me, that only amplifies my own lust.

"You… You get on your knees." He stumbles over the words, an adorable furrow manifesting between his eyes.

Still, the arousal in his eyes is unmistakable.

He wants this—wants me—even if he'll never admit it to my face. He wants this to be my choice; always my choice.

I drop down immediately, grateful for the soft surface of his sweater against my knees. I stare up at Beckett through hooded eyes, naked, vulnerable, and desperate for him. Desperate to please him.

His hand shakes in a way it didn't when he pleasured me as he fumbles with the waistband of his jeans. Slowly, he unzips them and then pushes them down his muscular thighs.

My breath stutters at the sight of tight boxer briefs that mold to his figure, leaving very little to the imagination.

"Ellie, are you sure? I don't want you to think you have to just because—"

My hands are surprisingly steady as I reach for the waistband of his underwear and push it down. His cock springs free instantly, already rock-hard and a tiny bit of precum glistening on the tip.

Beckett hurriedly steps out of his boxer briefs and jeans, awkwardly removing his shoes and socks in the process, and then turns to face me.

Naked.

Completely and utterly naked.

I drink in the sight of him—the sharp planes of his chest, the trail of hair leading down to his hard cock, the powerful muscles of his thighs and calves.

I've never seen a cock in person before, and heat travels straight to my clit at the sight.

Beckett's is long, a shade lighter than his naturally tan

skin. The mushroom tip has a single line down the middle, where white liquid resides.

"Can I...touch it?" I ask nervously, afraid I'm overstepping, that I'm making him uncomfortable.

His voice is a mere rasp when he says, "Please do."

Hesitantly, I trail a finger over the tip, smearing the precum. Beckett's hips jerk forward instinctively, though I can tell he's trying to stay still. Trying to restrain himself for me.

He stands there, naked and vulnerable, allowing me to blatantly peruse him. I'm overcome by the enormity of my emotions for this man, as fathomless and as deep as the ocean itself.

Never taking my eyes off his face, I run my fingernails gently down the vein on the side.

"Fuck, Ellie," he groans, his eyelids fluttering shut, dark shadows against his cheekbones.

I pull my hand back instantly. "Did I hurt you?"

"No." His eyes snap open, and he spears me with a look that has an indecipherable sensation swarming in my stomach like gnats. "Fuck no. God, the feel of you touching my dick... Seeing you on your knees before me naked... Is this even real? Am I dreaming?"

"It's definitely real," I whisper as I wrap my hand around the base of his cock and begin to stroke him.

The texture... It's strange. Silky smoothness over solid muscle. I've never felt anything quite like it before. I wonder what his cum would taste like...

"I've had so many dreams about this," Beckett rasps out. "So many fucking dreams of you touching my cock. Stroking it. Sucking it." He groans and thrusts his hips, matching the rhythm of my hand. "I dreamed about fucking those perfect tits of yours, watching them bounce."

A flush spreads across my entire body at the vivid image he paints.

"I want to...taste you." I tremble as I stare up at him. "Can I?"

"Are you sure, sweetheart?" Even as he says that, his cock jerks in my head, his appreciation for my words abundantly clear.

I lower my face to the head of his dick and give in to the desire riding me. I flick my tongue out and lick the tip of his dick, tasting the precum gathering there. It's...musky. I'm not sure it's entirely pleasant, but it's definitely not the worst thing I've ever tasted. And besides, it's a part of Beckett; it seems to make him feel good, too, if his moans are any indication.

I utilize what I've learned from reading smutty romance books and open my mouth wide, hollowing my cheeks. I have no idea if I'll be able to swallow him, but I want to try. I want to taste him, to feel him in my mouth, to know that I'm the catalyst for his pleasure.

"Fuck, baby, fuck!" His long fingers tangle in my hair, pulling the brown strands away from my face in a makeshift ponytail.

My glasses become askew, but I suppose that doesn't matter. Nothing matters but him.

"Graze your teeth down the edge of my cock, darling. Yes...just like that," Beckett praises as I do as he instructed. "Fondle my balls."

Tentatively, I reach forward and begin to play with them, unsure if I'm even doing it right but loving the groans and praises that leave his mouth. It fills me with a sense of satisfaction, probably similar to what he felt when he made me orgasm.

"I'm going to come, love." He tries to move out of me,

but I dig my fingers into his muscular ass and hold him steady.

With a roar, his hips jerk forward, and he shoots ropes of salty cum into my mouth. I try to swallow every last drop of it, but when I begin to gag—the white liquid dripping down my chin—Beckett immediately pulls out of me.

"Ellie, sweetheart, are you okay?" he asks anxiously, his eyes scouring my face, searching for any sign that I'm upset, that I regret what happened.

His cum continues to drizzle down my chin and lands on my breasts.

"Was that...? Was that okay?" I whisper, unsure if I screwed everything up by being unable to swallow all of his cum.

"Was that *okay*?" Disbelief laces his tone as he stares at me incredulously. "Fuck, Ellie..." He gathers me against him, but this time, it's not to kiss me senseless. He merely places my head against his sweaty chest and holds me to him, stroking my hair. "You're fucking perfect."

"I'm not," I respond instinctively.

"You are to me," he whispers.

And for the first time in forever...the darkness of my own brain doesn't consume me.

CHAPTER 12
Ryker

For years, I was haunted by the same nightmare.

Ellie stood on the street in front of the rundown, dilapidated shack my mother called a house. Overgrown weeds surrounded a single oak tree that teetered precariously to one side, threatening to topple completely and demolish our home—though I could never consider the structure anything but a prison.

The painted white walls were beginning to flake, and the wooden floor beams of the porch were covered in mold and mildew. I knew for a fact that the very top step creaked in a way that made alarms unnecessary, even in a town such as this.

I'd always been so damn embarrassed of my home, of my upbringing. It's why I refused to allow any of the others —especially Ellie—to visit my house. Visit my goddamn street, even, with the garbage lining the cracked road and the vandalized, graffiti-painted buildings.

In this particular nightmare, Ellie was staring blankly

ahead, her brown curls swaying in the light breeze. Her eyes appeared almost gray in the mist that curled around her like smoke. Low-hanging, black storm clouds dominated the sky, cloaking the sun.

I stood opposite her, chained to a huge wooden pillar I knew didn't truly exist in reality. It seemed to pierce the sky —pierce heaven itself, the tip disappearing amongst the bloated clouds. Cold metal dug into my skin from the chains surrounding me as I struggled futilely, but I knew I couldn't escape. I was a prisoner, trapped and utterly useless.

The first few years I had this dream, I never recognized the figures who surrounded Ellie. They were merely blurs, these hazy, indistinct outlines that resembled a child's smudged drawing. But over the years, their features began to sharpen, their lines becoming more defined, their hair glistening with color, their bodies hardening.

One was my mother. I would recognize the vapid bitch anywhere, with her dark hair so similar to my own and lightly tanned skin. Her dealer stood beside her sporting a cold, malevolent grin.

More and more people joined those two—Dane, the douchebag bully from the academy, and his evil stepsister.

Catarina Loukas who bullied Ellie all throughout middle school.

Miles Burgerson who asked Ellie out in eighth grade... and then began spreading awful rumors about her when she rejected him.

Mr. Moreau.

Dominic's dad.

I never understood why this nightmare scared me so badly. These people... They never hurt Ellie. They simply surrounded her, their gazes zeroed in on her face despite my screams for them to leave her alone, to focus on me. Some were angry; others lecherous; still others were enamored.

Now, my dreams have changed.

There's only one person standing beside Ellie.

A figure cloaked entirely in red.

A figure wearing an intricate, jewel-encrusted mask.

A figure with a tinny, mechanical voice that sounds like two rocks scratching against each other.

The Divine One.

And in this dream, all I can do is watch as he extends a gloved hand...and Ellie puts her own into his.

She doesn't put up a fight as he pulls her away.

••••••••••

"Ryker? Can you hear me?"

Bright sparks dance behind my closed eyelids, amplifying the pounding in my head.

"He seems to be responsive."

"What's his BP?"

"One twenty over eighty."

"Did we get his head CT back yet?"

"Came back normal."

Voices...

One male. One female.

I don't recognize either of them.

"Sir. Sir. You're okay." It's the woman who's speaking now as panic bursts through my system like errant sunbeams.

My eyes snap open instantly.

The first face I see obviously belongs to the woman. She has a grandmotherly vibe that should put me at ease but only magnifies my trepidation. White, curly hair is pulled back into a sleek ponytail, and wrinkles bracket blue-gray eyes and bushy eyebrows. A taut frown tugs at her lips as she stares at me.

There's a stethoscope around her neck, and she wears a white, flowing lab coat.

Doctor.

She's a doctor.

Slowly, I flick my gaze in the direction of the second voice—the man.

Mussy brown hair. Fox-like features, with a pointed nose and hollow cheeks. Blue scrubs.

Nurse.

"W-where am I?" My voice sounds rough and raspy to my own ears, this prolonged, out-of-tune note. I clear my throat and try again.

The last few hours seem like a blur—everything indistinct and insubstantial, nothing but flimsy memories that slip through my fingers like water.

And what's this around my neck?

A fucking neck brace? Why would they put one on me?

"You're in the hospital," the woman says kindly. "You were found unconscious on the side of the road a couple hours ago. You were nearly hypothermic. You also had extensive wounds on your body, as well as a broken arm. We found your car a mile or so away. Did you get into an accident, son?"

Accident.

Accident.

Accident...

Like when I first woke up in that car—groggy, hurting, and bleeding profusely—Ellie's face flashes across my vision, a burst of sunshine in the darkness.

That same panic from before begins to beat anew within me. Terror fizzles in my blood like poison.

"I need... I need to go." I reach across my body to remove the IV they injected into my hand, pain splintering up my broken arm.

It's been haphazardly placed in a splint, but I know they haven't fixed the break. Not yet. But that doesn't matter. Nothing matters except getting Ellie back.

I reach for the damn neck brace next, tear it off of me, and toss it onto the ground at the doctor's feet.

"Ryker—" the woman begins, her tone rife with concern. Her face is white as chalk.

I freeze at the use of my name before realizing she probably found my ID in the abandoned car.

"I need to leave," I stress again, kicking my legs over the side of the bed.

The cool, linoleum tiling is cold beneath my bare feet. It feels like ice—the same ice I just traipsed through for over a mile before falling unconscious.

Fuck, why do you have to be such a failure, Ryker? You had one goddamn job to do. One! And now, who the fuck knows what Ellie is going through?

I search the room for my discarded clothes—at some point, they must've changed me into a scratchy, uncomfortable hospital gown, a shade of vomit-green—and my tennis shoes. I don't even see my damn coat anywhere.

It doesn't matter.

I'll go like this if I need to.

There are a few bandages on my skin—two on the arm that isn't broken, one on my neck, and five on my face—but I don't know if they gave me stitches or not. There's a painful tightening sensation whenever I speak, but that could just be from my swollen face and the plethora of bruises that now decorate it.

As soon as I find out who ran me off the road, I'm going to hunt him down and kill him.

"Sir—" the doctor tries again, reaching placatingly towards me.

I level her with a glare capable of cutting through bone, muscle, and sinew. "I'm eighteen fucking years old. You can't keep me here against my will," I growl out, hoping she can see the sincerity in my eyes.

There's no way in hell she can get me to change my mind, not while Ellie's still out there enduring god only knows what.

I need to call the others, and together, we can come up with a plan to get her back.

I'll do whatever it takes—even bleed to death, painting the snow a violent shade of red.

The doctor's thin lips purse, making the lines on her face even more pronounced. The deep grooves around her eyes resemble trenches.

"You're right," she says at last, her tone as stiff as a rubber band pulled taut. "We can't keep you here."

"Doctor Marsha—" the nurse begins in disbelief.

She holds up a hand towards him, and he silences instantly. "I'll have someone come in soon with forms for you to fill out. But understand... If you leave against medical advice, I can't promise what will happen to you. The hospital will in no way be liable—"

"Yeah, yeah, yeah." I grunt as I force myself to my feet completely, grateful when I don't wobble. Even still, I imagine this is what sailors mean by "sea legs." I feel unsteady and adrift, as if even the slightest gust of wind will blow me over. "Give me the damn forms already."

"A police officer is here waiting to take your statement as well," she continues. The furrow between her brows deepens.

Fucking police.

I just need to call Landon, and he'll take care of it for me. He always does. There's a reason the entire school—no, the entire *town*—fears him, and it's not just because he's the self-proclaimed king of the academy.

It's because he's immensely powerful and rich and lethal. He has more connections than most politicians, is more resourceful than most world leaders. He's cultivated this intricate network of powerful men and women who fear him, desire him, and want to become him. The power he already wields at such a young age would terrify me if I didn't trust him explicitly to do what needs to be done.

Blackmail, extortion, murder...

Landon will do them all if it means protecting the ones he loves, even a no good son of a bitch like me.

"Send the damn officer in." I give the room a second once-over. "And where are my damn clothes?"

••••••••••

APPARENTLY, they threw away all of my clothes when they had to cut them off of me.

Instead, I'm issued a pair of gray sweatpants and a matching sweatshirt, both of which have the hospital logo prominently displayed.

My arm twinges painfully—the pain meds doing very little to ease the ache now that I'm actively using the limb—but I try to compartmentalize it, to bury my pain in an impenetrable iron vault that no one, not even me, knows the combination for.

Still, tears erupt in my eyes as searing, agonizing pain radiates up my arm and all the way to my shoulder. It feels as if every nerve ending is alive, sparking, exploding, erupting. I place a palm against the bathroom door and cradle my injured arm to my chest, working to get breaths out past the tightness in my throat.

Deep breath in.

Deep breath out.

Deep breath in.

Deep breath out.

"Come on, Ryker. Come on," I mentally chastise myself. "Ellie needs you, you worthless piece of shit."

On the other side of the door, I hear footsteps in my small hospital room. No doubt, it's either registration checking me out or the police officer Doctor Marsha mentioned. I hope it's the former. Perhaps I can convince him or her to allow me to use the phone and call Landon.

I take another deep, jittery breath, feeling as if I've just jumped out of an airplane hundreds of miles in the air and landed in the Arctic Ocean. I don't know if the cold will kill me…or the impact, the feeling of every bone in my body snapping, every organ rearranging, every limb compressing.

My heart jackhammering in my chest, I push open the bathroom door.

Only to instantly freeze, my blood turning to ice.

Horror rushes through me before it's tampered by another emotion—one slightly more insidious and volatile.

Anger.

"You son of a bitch," I seethe, racing forward.

But I'm weak and hurt and fucking useless.

The Divine One simply chuckles darkly as he stealthily steps out of the way, his red cloak trailing behind him like a goddamn wedding train made of blood.

Vomit creeps up my throat, acerbic and bitter, as he turns his masked face to stare at me.

We don't know for sure he's a male, not with the cloak obscuring possible curves from view, but we've always assumed he was. It's not that women can't be evil—they definitely can be; my mother is a prime example of that—but there's just something about this particular demon...

His golden, ostentatious mask glimmers in the white lighting of the hospital room. The gemstones, each one intricately placed, shimmer in shades of red, blue, and green, a kaleidoscope of colors that should be pretty but instead just appear threatening.

"Ryker." His artificial, mechanical voice scratches at my skin like the claws of a lion. Jagged scars are left behind in their wake. "I heard what happened."

That golden face of his lowers until it almost feels as if he's staring at my broken arm.

I can't detect any emotion in his voice, any inflection, but I almost believe he sounds...amused, as if he finds my pain hilarious.

Sick fucking bastard.

"What did you do with Ellie?" I demand, worry for her eclipsing the fear I have for myself.

He can do whatever the fuck he wants with me if it means getting Ellie back, safe and sound.

The Divine One cants his head slightly to the side, oddly resembling a besotted dog waiting for commands from his master. Those orifices where his eyes are supposed to be are nothing but dark, fathomless holes.

Black holes—capable of sucking you in and sending you tumbling head over feet until your entire existence is characterized by nothing but unrelenting darkness.

Would I be able to lunge across the room and strangle this sick bastard?

No. Not while he has Ellie.

She comes first.

She always comes first.

"Ellie's safe." One of The Divine One's gloved hands comes down to the tiny table flanking the hospital bed. He places a single finger on the surface and then lifts it up, as if inspecting it for dust. "For now."

The world seems to shift underneath my feet. Or maybe it's just *me* who's shifting, *me* who's swaying from side to side. Dark spots fleck my vision as my knees shake, threatening to give out.

The Divine One continues to twist his finger to and fro, watching the way the artificial lighting reflects off the dust particles. The curtains of the room are currently pulled closed, but through a tiny gap, I can see the sun beginning to set, splashing blood-red over the surrounding treetops. It also highlights the side of The Divine One's mask in a way that has goose bumps skittering across my skin and the tiny hairs on the back of my neck standing at attention.

"What are you going to do with her?"

Please, not Ellie.

Please.

Oh god.

I won't be able to live in a world that doesn't have her in it. I can't. I fucking refuse. From the first moment I set eyes on her, I knew I was a goner. Maybe I should see a psychiatrist about my obsession with her, but I don't think it will help. No pills or therapy sessions will cleanse Ellie from my system. If she's a drug, then she's one I'll take willingly, happily, with a huge-ass smile on my face.

She may be the sputtering airplane with fire licking at

the wings, but she's also the parachute capable of keeping me alive while the world goes up in flames around me.

"You love the girl, don't you?" The Divine One finally drops his hand back to his side and gifts me his full attention.

I'm not sure I like that. It's unnerving to be the sole focus of his gaze, even with the mask firmly in place.

I don't bother responding to him.

If he's been stalking the five of us as long as we've been stalking him, then he already knows the answer to that idiotic question.

"Why are you here?" I growl out. "To taunt me? To threaten me?"

I bare my teeth at the murderous asshole as blind, insidious rage cascades through me. It's nearly overwhelming.

This is a man who has hurt so many people, sacrificed so many innocent women. And for what? For a goddess that I'm not even sure he truly believes in? For wealth and riches? For a gaggle of mindless followers who do whatever he says, whenever he says it? He's nothing but a dictator with an army at his back.

And if history taught me one thing, it's that dictators, no matter who they have backing them, don't stay in power long. There's always someone opposing them, someone fighting back, someone resisting.

Someone like...Mania.

Someone like me.

"What would you be willing to give up in order to save your precious Ellie's life?" Once again, his head cocks to the side as if he's studying me just as keenly as I am him, dissecting me through his gaze alone. "Your friends? Your family? Your *life*?"

There's not an ounce of hesitation when I respond. "Yes. I'd give it all up."

"Admirable." Why does it sound like The Divine One is smiling beneath his mask? That my answer somehow pleases him? "How about I make a deal with you, my dear Ryker?"

"Fuck you," I spit vehemently, hatred for him seeping from my pores and permeating the room. It's so thick and cloying I'm practically choking on it.

Choking on my loathing for him.

"I would listen, Ryker, unless you want something to... happen to your sweet Ellie." He gracefully glides around the side of the bed until he's able to stand directly in front of me.

Surprisingly, we're the same height, though he feels taller than me. More imposing. There's just something about the way he holds himself that makes me think he's used to being the most powerful person in the room. I imagine it's a similar pizzazz that politicians and royals and celebrities possess.

"Don't you fucking hurt her," I warn. "If you do, I'll blow up your entire organization. I'll destroy you. You know what Landon has on you—"

"But the girl you love will still be dead," The Divine One counters. "The Paragons of Prosperity can rebuild, even if I'm no longer in the picture. But you can't rebuild a dead girl, now can you?"

It takes every ounce of willpower I have not to wrap my fingers around his neck and wring it until his body falls to the ground limp.

Who will be staring at me beneath the mask?

Fischer?

Mr. Moreau?

One of Ellie's roommates?

Someone I've never met before?

My heart batters against my rib cage with increasing speed. I ball my hands into fists, ignoring the searing, blistering pain that climbs up my nerve endings from my broken arm. But the pain is a distant thing, second only to my overwhelming fear for Ellie.

"Your life...in exchange for hers," The Divine One says.

His gaze is steady on my face—those pinprick black orbs never waver, never falter, never look away. He holds himself utterly still, a predator hiding in long grass and waiting to pounce on the unsuspecting prey.

I may not be unsuspecting.

But just then, I *am* prey.

His prey.

"What...? Why the fuck do you want my life? What does it do for you?" God, I can't hear anything over the pounding of my own heart. It sounds like a snare drum inside of my head.

"Does it matter?" The Divine One still doesn't move. Not even his long, gloved fingers twitch. "What the goddess wants is none of your concern."

"You don't even believe in your own damn goddess," I snap with a derisive sneer. "Don't pull that shit with me."

"Oh, Ryker..." A low, humorless, mechanical chuckle echoes from inside of the mask. It slides over my skin like sticky tar. Just as quickly as it began, his laughter cuts off. "The deal will only last for the next minute. Your life...in exchange for Ellie's."

"How do I know you won't kill her? How do I know—"

"Because I won't kill you now." The Divine One takes a graceful step forward, his body moving like a poltergeist roaming a haunted house. "I'll give you time with the girl you love. I won't interfere." Another step puts him directly in front of me, so close I could reach for the mask, grab it, see who's standing underneath it... "But on December sixteenth, you will die by my hand. And in exchange, I promise not to harm Ellie, now and forever."

Almost belatedly, I realize that the day he gave me is the same day he gave Ellie in regards to Reece Whipers, the senator The Divine One wishes to meet with.

What's the importance of that date?

But all of that is a distant thought—the crashing of thunder miles and miles away. Lightning streaks across my vision, brilliant, jagged white lines that explode before my eyes, and all I can hear is the pounding of rain.

I'm in the eye of a fucking hurricane, and no matter where I look, I see nothing but death and destruction.

"You won't hurt her." I can barely raise my voice above a whisper. "Ever?"

"Ellie will be safe from the Paragons of Prosperity," The Divine One vows.

"How do I know you won't go back on your word?" I demand.

Tha-thump. Tha-thump. Tha-thump.

How have I never noticed before how deafening my racing heart is? How obnoxiously loud?

"You don't really have a choice, do you, Ryker?" The Divine One says simply. "We can kill her right here and now—"

"No!" I lunge forward instinctively, the fingers of my good hand wrapping in the fabric of his cloak, blood-red against my tan skin. "I'll do it. I'll fucking do it."

Swallowing proves to be impossible. Razor blades scratch at my throat, drawing blood.

"On December sixteenth, you'll come to me with Reece Whipers," The Divine One says.

I have the distinct impression that I played directly into his hand, that he skillfully moved the pawns on the board until he was able to capture all of my pieces.

"And then, you will die."

Die.

You will die.

You will die.

But there's one thing The Divine One is forgetting.

The most important piece on the chessboard is the queen.

And if I have to sacrifice myself to keep her alive?

Then so be it.

CHAPTER 13
Landon

I'm across the parking lot in six quick steps and then pulling the disheveled girl into my arms.

"Kitten…" I murmur, breathing in her natural lilac scent tinged with something almost bitter.

Coppery.

Bloody.

Ellie's arms come up instinctively to wrap around my waist as I press my nose into her wet, brown hair.

You can imagine my shock—and fucking glee—when on the way to the hospital, Ellie called. I swear the storm raging inside of my stomach settled at the sound of her sweet, lyrical voice. The winds died down, the rain cleared away, and the sun poked through the clouds, yellow rays dancing over my suddenly overheated skin.

"I'm okay," she whispers. Her breath wafts across my skin, setting off another wave of goose bumps. I swear those fuckers are always around whenever I'm in her presence, as if my body is alive and responds to her proximity in a way that's almost visceral. "*We're* okay. But there's a lot we need to tell you."

Before I can respond or even demand an explanation, I feel something sharp press against my back.

A blade.

A goddamn motherfucking blade.

I tense automatically and slowly twist my head until I'm able to see over my shoulder.

Zane stands directly behind me, his eyes wild, crazed, unhinged. The irises have practically been swallowed by his dilated pupils as his chest heaves and his hands shake. His dark hair stands at attention on the top of his head, almost as if he stuck his finger into an electrical socket.

He doesn't need to say anything for me to get the hint—he needs Ellie right the fuck now, or he's going to lose his shit.

I always knew that Zane was a ticking time bomb whose fuse had been lit years ago. I just assumed I had enough control over him to talk him down from any of his... more *eccentric* ideas. I thought I would be able to save him from himself when he inevitably imploded.

However, I'm beginning to believe no one—not even Ellie—can tame this volatile beast. He's a predator through and through, a lion prowling in a semiarid African desert, just waiting to pounce on the defenseless gazelle.

I step away from Ellie with great reluctance, and the bastard pockets the knife before Ellie can see it. I bite down on my lower lip hard enough to draw blood as he scoops Ellie into his arms, her feet an inch off the ground, and begins to rock her back and forth.

"*Princesa. Princesa. Princesa,*" he whispers repeatedly, that single word blurring together until it begins to sound like an elongated P.

Ellie rubs his back soothingly, saying something to him that's too low for me to hear, and I turn my attention towards Beckett instead.

It's hard—it's really fucking hard—to peel my gaze off of Ellie, even for a second. She feels like an elusive mirage, one that will disappear at a moment's notice. I fear if I blink, she'll dissipate in a cloud of smoke.

"Where's Dom and Ryker?" Beckett asks, no doubt noticing their absence.

I imagine he's stunned that the two of them aren't crowding around Ellie as well, desperate to soak up every inch of her attention like a flower arching towards the sun.

I take a step closer to him until our shoulders brush.

"Ryker's in the hospital. Dominic's going to visit him." I keep my voice low so it doesn't reach Ellie.

I'll tell her the truth—we agreed that we won't have any more secrets between the six of us—but I know Zane needs this moment with her. He's practically shaking in her arms, his body rocked by violent shivers.

His fear is one I can relate to.

When I realized Ellie was missing…I almost lost my damn mind. The only thing that kept me going was the drive to find her, save her, pull her into my arms where she belongs.

Beckett scrubs a hand through his wet hair, the strands almost black in the dim lighting of the convenience store behind us, and releases a muffled curse.

"What the fuck happened?" he demands.

"Car accident, apparently." My voice is acerbic and bitter, even to my own ears.

But come the fuck on. Can you blame me? I don't believe for one second that Ryker's accident wasn't intentional.

Obviously, he was following Ellie and Beckett—I know for a fact that crazy fucker put numerous trackers on her—so there's definitely more to the story than what we heard.

Who else knew he was in the area?

Why did they kidnap Ellie and Beckett but try to kill Ryker? Because he was close to rescuing them? For some other nefarious reason? Or were the people who took Ellie and Beckett different from the ones who hit Ryker?

These questions will drive me fucking insane.

"I'm surprised Dominic didn't want to see Ellie," Beckett murmurs with a sideways glance at me.

I snort and cross my arms over my chest. "Trust me. He was *not* happy when I kicked him out of my car and told him to get an Uber to the hospital. But one of us needed to check on Ryker and make sure he's okay—and tell him what happened with Ellie. If he discovers she's still gone before we can get to him and say we found her..."

I shudder at just the thought.

Zane's darkness is unpredictable and eccentric—a flickering candle flame that can sway from side to side, be blown out, and then be relit within seconds. Burning, blistering, and red-hot.

But Ryker's darkness...

It's a cold gust of wind in the middle of winter, the kind that kicks up snow and obscures your vision with white flurries. There's no shelter, no warmth, no survival, just ice that seeps into your body and freezes you alive.

I imagine Ryker's already freaking out, knowing what he does about Ellie and Beckett. The only thing that will calm him is seeing Ellie with his own two eyes and knowing that she's safe and sound. I doubt even Dominic will be able to get through to him, but it doesn't hurt to try.

"What the fuck happened with you two? Where have

you been? What did Ellie mean when she said you were fucking kidnapped?" I ask now, craning my head back to stare up at the darkening sky.

Wispy, white-edged clouds roll in over a brilliantly blue sky. The setting sun illuminates everything in shades of red and orange, framing the ragged edges of the clouds with light. It seems almost...surreal that it's still light out. I would think everything would be dark as pitch after everything we've been through—the fear for Ellie compounded with our worry for Ryker.

Isn't that where bad things usually happen?

In the dark?

"I think Ellie should tell you this story," Beckett says, scratching absently at the shadow of a beard on his chin.

He's usually so clean-shaven that the sight of him with a five-o'clock shadow actually makes me do a double take.

"I'm just so fucking grateful she's okay." My throat closes as the enormity of my emotions for her crashes over me.

Just staring at her pumps helium into my blood; I feel light as air.

Zane finally—reluctantly—releases her, though I notice he doesn't let her go completely. One of his arms remains twined around her waist as he practically pushes her back against his chest.

Not that Ellie seems to mind.

A small, contented smile plays at the edges of her lips as she glances up at him.

But then she turns towards Beckett, and a blush darkens her cheeks.

Interesting.

She awkwardly tries to step away from Zane, but he

merely tightens his grip on her, refusing to allow her to move even a step away.

"No, *princesa*," he rasps in her ear. "I need to feel you with me. Feel you against me."

He trails his fingers down her side until he's able to fiddle with the hem of her long-sleeved shirt. He lifts it just enough to caress her bare skin, the porcelain flesh claiming my attention like a blazing beacon.

Her cheeks look like they're on fire. The blush is striking on her naturally pale skin—brushstrokes of red.

It's goddamn beautiful to witness.

"We should get going." I raise my voice to be heard over Zane's continuous whispers in her ear. "We have...a lot to tell you as well."

Understatement of the fucking century.

Beckett eyes me with concern but nods once.

Both of us have no idea how Ellie will react to the news about Ryker. A needle drives into my heart at just the thought of her fear and panic. I hate that I have to be the bearer of bad news, but I know I'm the only one who's capable of it. It's my job as the leader, as the glue for this fucked-up family.

The weight of my responsibilities has never felt so heavy before.

Zane scoops an arm underneath Ellie's ass and—ignoring her squeal of surprise—begins to carry her bridal style to the car.

As he buckles her in, I turn towards Beckett and place a hand on his arm to stop him before he can move towards the passenger seat.

"Why are you two wet?" I ask, nodding towards his hair, the strands appearing almost onyx.

"We showered," he replies nonchalantly.

Too nonchalantly.

I narrow my eyes in suspicion.

"Together?" I hiss, though I find that I'm not appalled by the idea.

Not at all. If anyone else were to do that with Ellie, I'd rip their heads off and shove their eyeballs up their assholes. Hell, I'd even make them eat their own castrated cocks. I may not be as prone to violence as Ryker and Zane, but I'll do what I need to for Ellie.

But the thought of Beckett—a man who I know loves Ellie just as much as I do—with her, washing her perfect body, caressing her porcelain tits, flicking her hard nipples, rubbing at her pussy...

Fuck.

"No," Beckett refutes immediately, gaping at me in horror. "Of course not! We showered one at a time."

I tighten my grip on his arm and stare at his face intently, gauging his sincerity. His different colored eyes peer back at me, not a hint of deception in them. But...

"Did you do *something* with Ellie?" My voice is a whisper —I don't want Ellie to overhear and think I'm mad at her.

Or worse...that she did something wrong.

She did nothing—absolutely *nothing*—wrong, and I'll kill anyone who tells her differently.

Beckett's normally pale face drains of all color, and he staggers back a step. I don't release his arm, however, as he scrambles to come up with an excuse.

But I can see it clear as day in his eyes.

The pounding of my heart feels almost violent— someone slamming against a door, demanding to be let in, screaming and crying and punching the wood.

I search inside myself for any anger, any jealousy, any hatred... And while there is definitely jealousy, the anger I thought I'd feel remains suspiciously absent. There's not even a trickle of any ill will towards the man in front of me, only envy that he got to touch her.

That he got to touch *my* girl before I did.

Our girl.

Our...girl.

Fuck.

"Get in the car," I say, releasing him and turning away. "We'll talk about this later."

Beckett nods immediately, his head lowered like a kicked puppy, and I instantly feel like shit.

But how can I possibly explain the gamut of emotions percolating inside of me?

The strange and exhilarating jolt that cascades through my veins at the thought of him with her?

The knowledge that a solution to all of our problems has been glaring us in the face for years...and that we've been too stupid to notice it?

I shake off the beginnings of my idea before it can fully form.

Later.

I'll think about it later.

But now... Now, we need to get to Ryker.

✦✦✦✦✦✦✦✦✦✦

ELLIE SPENDS the first few minutes of the car ride telling us everything that went down with her "Uncle" Raymond.

I grip the steering wheel so tightly my fingers turn an ashen shade of white. Every muscle in my body is locked tighter than a nun's asshole. I can tell Zane isn't faring much better, especially when Ellie describes her tumble out of the air vent and her bruised nose. He looks as if he wants to rip Beckett a new one for allowing her to get hurt in the first place.

That darkness from before manifests in his eyes, and his fingers are practically claws around Ellie's petite waist while she sits on his lap.

But then she begins to rub at his hands, the lightest of caresses, and I watch his body relax incrementally. The tension seeps from his shoulders like a heavy torrent of rainfall being poured over him. The darkness dissipates from his dark-brown eyes as his lashes flutter closed, a soft sigh escaping his lips.

Maybe...

Maybe I was wrong before.

Maybe Ellie *is* capable of wrangling Zane's monster.

But fuck, what are we going to do about this so-called uncle of hers?

I've done extensive research on Ellie and her family and never, not once, stumbled across a goddamn Raymond. Is he truly her uncle? It sounds as if Ellie believes he could be—the resemblance, apparently, between him and her father is uncanny.

But where has he been all these years?

Why isn't there any record of him?

What does he want with her?

And to learn that he's the mysterious man who's been helping me take down POP...

Cleaning up crime scenes for me and the guys...

What the hell does he even want?

Fuck.

The conversation takes a drastic turn when I tell Ellie about Ryker.

She immediately lets go of Zane's fingers and bolts upright. Her face turns ashen, almost chalky, and I suddenly realize how tired she truly looks. Dark, prominent circles rest beneath both of her eyes. Her cheeks are abnormally thin as well, almost sickly looking.

When was the last time she ate? Had a cup of water?

"Oh my god." She places a hand to her mouth in horror. "Is he...?"

"The doctor said he's okay. Dominic's with him at the hospital now." Or the bastard should be. I haven't heard from him since I forcibly removed him from my car—despite his protests and threats—and drove away.

But I also knew he wouldn't complain too much. Out of all of my friends, he's usually the most levelheaded and calm. It's why I chose him to check on Ryker. If I were to pick Zane...I imagine he would go on a fucking murder spree and wear the doctor's skin as a lab coat and their organs as stethoscopes.

Fucking psychopath.

I love him, but he cray-cray.

Ellie lurches forward. "We need to go to him! We need to—"

"We're almost there, darling," Beckett assures her from the passenger seat.

He swivels to stare at her. Even from my periphery, there's no mistaking the love emanating from his eyes.

How have I never noticed it before?

Or... Or maybe I always did. Maybe a part of me knew just how deeply my friends have fallen for her, but I was too consumed by my own feelings to acknowledge theirs.

Selfish.

You were being a selfish bastard.

I tap my fingers against the steering wheel as I turn into the parking lot of the hospital.

Ellie doesn't bother to wait for me to park, practically

jumping out of the car as soon as I'm near the sliding glass doors. I curse and slam on my brakes, but she's already racing inside, Zane only a few steps behind her.

Beckett throws me a helpless glance and then quickly unbuckles his own seat belt, hurrying after her.

Fuck.

I watch the three of them disappear inside the bright building. Only when they're no longer in sight do I place my forehead against the steering wheel and take a deep, jittery breath. It feels like I'm sucking in daggers. My throat aches fiercely with every inhale I take.

I know I should park the car, but I can't seem to get my body to work, my brain to function.

A mysterious uncle we never knew existed?

A car accident?

The Divine One?

The Paragons of Prosperity?

Just what the fuck have we gotten ourselves into?

And how am I supposed to protect everyone I love, when I don't even know who—or what—we're fighting against?

CHAPTER 14
Ellie

I don't know why I thought everything would go back to normal after I called the guys and told them to pick us up, but I stupidly—and naïvely—did.

But now...

Now...

Fear for Ryker is a noose around my neck, and I just know the floor is going to drop out from under me at any second.

What if Landon's wrong, and he's in worse condition than we suspected? What if he's...?

No. I can't think like that. I refuse to consider that even a possibility.

I skid to a stop in front of the receptionist desk, where a kind-faced, older woman stares up at me from her computer. White-blonde hair falls forward into her eyes as she smiles compassionately at me.

Her gaze momentarily drifts to the men flanking me on

either side—Beckett and Zane both standing like silent sentries—before refocusing on me. "Are you okay, dear?"

Terror sizzles through my blood like poison as I work to get my thoughts in order.

"Ryker..." I can't breathe, can't speak, can't do anything but gaze at her with tear-filled eyes. I clear my throat and try again. "Ryker Nolan. He's here. He's been admitted. He's—"

The pitying expression on the woman's face doesn't waver as she types something into her computer. If anything, it becomes more pronounced as a frown touches her lips. "Unfortunately, only family is allowed to visit him. But—"

"It's okay, Tanya. They're with me." Dominic hurries from around the corner, his hands shoved into the pockets of his baggy, gray sweatshirt.

His eyes home in on me immediately, and relief physically cascades through his body, dropping his tense shoulders.

"Dom..." I'm across the room in only a few strides, and he pulls me into his arms with an audible exhale.

All I'm aware of is the spicy scent from his cologne and the flowery one from his laundry detergent. The ache in my soul lessens at his touch.

"Don't you ever fucking scare me like that again," he rasps, planting a kiss to the top of my head.

I don't bother with a response. The last thing I want is to be kidnapped again, but I seem to be a magnet for the dark and depraved. Maybe I'll promise to always carry a knife on me so I can stab first, ask questions later? Though, knowing my guys, they'll just become paranoid that I'll accidentally stab myself. Ye of little faith.

"Jesus, sweetheart, you're freezing." Dominic pulls

away and stares at me in alarm—his gaze flicking over my thin, long-sleeved shirt and skintight leggings.

He reaches for the hem of his sweatshirt, and before I can argue, pulls it over his head.

The dark shirt he wears crawls up his toned abs in the process, giving me a glimpse of his chiseled stomach, before he straightens and the shirt slides back down. Silently, he hands me his gray sweatshirt.

I take it without complaint, knowing that Dominic, more than any of the others, likes it when I wear his clothes. It brings him...comfort, I think, though I can never understand why.

Either way, tingles rush through my nerves and set my skin aflame.

I give him a tiny, grateful smile as I slide the sweatshirt on. It practically engulfs my small form, the sleeves completely covering my hands from view and the hem stopping just below my knees. I feel so small in his clothes, so precious, so vulnerable.

And...I love it.

Every time I inhale, I catch a waft of his spicy and flowery scent. You would think that the two scents wouldn't combine well, but the overall result is positively decadent. I could breathe him in all day long.

Not that I would admit that out loud...

"How is he?" I ask desperately as Dominic places his hand on the small of my back and begins to walk me down a long hall lined with individual rooms.

I don't even ask how he was able to get special privileges to go and visit Ryker. These guys are capable of just about anything when they set their minds to it.

"He's..." Dominic forks his fingers through his platinum-blond hair, causing a few strands to fall forward into his eyes. His golden face seems pale in the bright, fluorescent lighting. "He's fucking out of his mind," he admits at last. "He doesn't seem to believe me when I told him that you're safe. He keeps insisting that he needs to go after you, needs to find you."

It feels as if a vacuum just drew all the air from my lungs.

"Shit." I quicken my pace instinctively, desperate to see him.

If I could just pull him into my arms and whisper in his ear, everything will be all right. It has to be.

Oh, Ryker...

"What was he even doing out and about to begin with? He didn't come with us to Ellie's self-defense class," Beckett inquires from behind me.

The heat from both his and Zane's bodies seeps through Dominic's sweatshirt and warms my skin. I'm keenly aware of their presence the same way I am of my limbs—of my fingers curling into fists, of my legs propelling me forward, of my shoulders stiffening until they nearly touch my ears.

These boys are a part of me.

They always have been, and hopefully...they always will be.

"I think he followed you guys." Dominic slyly casts his gaze in my direction before focusing straight ahead once more. "To your self-defense class, I mean." This he directs at me, a sheepish smile tugging at his lips. "But he doesn't know who hit his car."

I ignore the first part of his statement and focus on what matters. "Do you think it was on purpose?"

Did POP do this?

The Divine One?

Raymond?

Dominic's vibrant-green eyes darken, until they almost resemble the needles of a pine tree. "I'm beginning to think that nothing that happens in this town is a coincidence."

Any response we may have had to that ominous statement is interrupted by raised voices in the distance.

"You already said I can fucking leave! Just give me the damn forms, and let me get out of here!"

Ryker.

I'd recognize his raspy voice anywhere, though I'm not sure I've ever heard him speak so many words in a sentence that wasn't to me.

My pace quickens until I'm practically sprinting down the hall, ignoring a nurse's startled cry and her warning for me to slow down.

I skirt around the corner and nearly plow headfirst into the figure standing there.

He's dressed in a pair of gray sweatpants and a matching sweatshirt—two things I would never see Ryker wear normally—but the rest of him is unmistakable and so painfully familiar I could cry.

His ice-blue eyes peer down at me with no small amount of surprise, a startling contrast to his tanned face and shock of dark hair. His chapped, pink lips part, but not a sound escapes him.

He just stares at me as I do the same to him.

Tears fill my eyes as I take in his state.

Bruises—most beginning to darken to a hideous shade of black and blue—mar his cheeks, chin, and forehead. Small bandages are positioned intermittently across his skin as well, a few already red with blood that has soaked through. Numerous cuts that haven't been bandaged litter his bronze skin. And his arm...

It sits in a splint, but I can tell it causes him immense

pain to move. He keeps grimacing and flicking his gaze towards it. The agony in his eyes is impossible to miss.

"Ryker..." I step away from him and place a hand over my mouth.

The last thing I want to do is hurt him more.

"Don't do that," he rasps, still staring at me in disbelief.

I wonder what thoughts are going through his mind right then and there. It almost feels as if he's looking at a ghost, as if I'm not real to him.

"God, Ellie... Fuck. Fuck. Fuck."

He wraps his good arm around me and squeezes me tightly against him. I can feel the hard ridges of his muscular body against my smooth curves. He fists his hand in the back of Dominic's sweatshirt as he lowers his forehead to my shoulder, great, heaping sobs escaping him.

It takes me a moment too long to realize...Ryker's crying.

Ryker, a chiseled mountain of male perfection, is actually crying.

For me.

I tentatively wrap my arms around his waist, making sure not to apply too much pressure in case he's injured there. I'm distantly aware that we've garnered an audience —a white-haired doctor, a few nurses, and the other guys, including Landon who has come to join us—but they're hazy to me, layered in a metaphorical fog.

I feel adrift just then. Disembodied. A dandelion seed floating in the wind.

"Can we...?" I sniffle and continue rubbing soothing circles into Ryker's back. "Can we have a minute?"

I don't know who I'm addressing the question to, but surprisingly, it's the kind-faced doctor who answers.

"Of course. We'll give you a few minutes." She nods towards the nurses, who scatter immediately.

My guys are a little more reluctant to leave, but another glance at Ryker in my arms has them nodding once.

"We'll wait here," Landon says.

Zane opens his mouth as if to protest, but Dominic places a hand on his shoulder and frowns up at him.

Zane's lips snap closed immediately.

"Thank you," I whisper as I slowly untangle myself from Ryker's arms.

He makes a strangled sound in the back of his throat—a mixture between a plea and a cry that breaks my heart—but I simply squeeze the fingers of his good hand and pull him back into the small hospital room.

The scent of bleach immediately assaults my senses. It's so overwhelming that I find myself wrinkling my nose instinctively. The stark white walls and tiling are probably supposed to appear cheerful and comforting, but they make the entire room look like something plucked straight out of a horror movie—you know, the type of room where you tie up innocent victims and torture them to death.

Perhaps I've been watching too many horror movies with Zane...

"I thought you were dead," Ryker whispers brokenly as he collapses onto the bed.

He immediately wraps his arms around me once more and presses his head against my stomach.

"Ryker, your arm..." I warn, but he doesn't seem to hear me, too lost in his own thoughts, his own fears.

Tentatively—still terrified I may hurt him—I bring my hands to his dark, short hair and begin to rub my fingers through it. It feels strange to indulge in a fantasy I've had for so long when he's so vulnerable. It conjures up memories of his face between my legs as I sat on the grand piano...

"I saw the car. The abandoned car, I mean. I knew that something had happened to you. I knew that POP got you, that The Divine One got you. I tried to help you, tried to save you, tried to—"

"Ryker." I gently grab his cheeks, mindful of the bruises and lacerations, and force his gaze up to mine. This Ryker frightens me in a way I can't articulate with words. I'm not afraid for myself...but for him. There's so much self-loathing in his gaze that my heart compresses in on itself, shattering into razor-sharp shards. "Everything's okay. I'm okay. You're okay. There's nothing you could've done. All we need to worry about now is fixing you up. I can't beat you in an arm-wrestling match if you don't have a working arm."

I offer him a small smile, one he doesn't return.

Why is he doing this to himself?

Why is he taking on so much blame?

"What did those sick bastards do to you?" he whispers, the sound torn from his throat. Raspy. Broken. Hollow.

"POP didn't take me," I rush to reassure him before his mind can create macabre fantasies that didn't truly happen. "It wasn't The Divine One."

His brows scrunch together, a bit of coherence seeping into his icy gaze. "What?"

Quickly, I recap everything that happened at the hotel —from waking up in the room by myself, to meeting "Uncle" Raymond, to freeing Beckett, to our final confrontation with Raymond before he allowed us to leave.

Ryker listens to my spiel without interruption, though his face turns ashen with every word I say. His throat bobs as he swallows convulsively. God, I wish I could read the expression on his face. It's unlike anything I've ever seen before.

"POP...didn't take you?" he whispers. His chalky complexion begins to tinge green, and a bolt of concern shoots through me at the sight. "The Divine One never had his hands on you?"

"I don't think so. Unless Raymond is secretly The Divine One..." But no, that doesn't seem right. I don't know what role Raymond has to play in all of this, but it sounds as if he's as against POP as the six of us are.

Ryker abruptly pushes away from me and lunges towards the trash can in the corner of the room.

"Ryker!" I call in alarm as he grips the edges of the can and begins to vomit.

His back heaves as he leans over the metal container, awful retching sounds escaping him.

I drop to my knees behind him and place a hand on his back. He shudders at the contact but surprisingly doesn't push me away.

"Ryker, baby, talk to me," I plea, the term of endearment slipping out before I can think better of it.

Fortunately, Ryker doesn't seem to notice my slip.

"I fucked up, Ellie. I fucked up. I thought... I thought he had you... I thought..." His body continues to shake as if jolts of electricity are currently coursing through him.

I've never seen him like this before, and my own trepidation ratchets up a dozen notches.

"What do you mean, Ryker?" I begin to rub his back more urgently, as if I can transfer comfort to him through touch alone. "What happened? What—?"

But he doesn't get the chance to answer.

His eyes roll into the back of his head, and he collapses to the ground at my feet, unconscious.

CHAPTER 15

Ellie

"You have two weeks' worth of pain meds," the grandmotherly doctor says to a grumbling, pale-faced Ryker.

His jaw sets as he scowls at her, though it lacks any of his usual ire.

It's been a week since he passed out and was rushed into surgery. A horrible, agonizingly long week where the rest of us were forced to go back to the academy and continue classes as if nothing were amiss.

As if bombshell after bombshell hadn't just been dropped on our heads, detonating one after the other.

I moved from class to class mechanically, barely paying attention to the lectures. My three roommates and friends —Jane, Piper, and Victoria—noticed my deadened state, but they didn't question me on it. The entire school knew that Ryker was in the hospital.

By the time the week ended and winter break came around, I was practically bursting with unfettered energy, desperate to see Ryker again. The one-hour visits every day after school weren't enough.

The doctor told us that he passed out from overstimulation—that there hadn't been any internal bleeding as they initially feared. They *did* have to reset his arm, though, hence the bright-blue cast currently decorated with all of our names written in black permanent marker.

Zane wrote, *LONG LIVE THE SEX GOD.*

Beckett's said, *From your favorite Brit in the whole wide world. I know you love me.*

Dominic and Landon just wrote their names.

I wrote Ellie in swooping cursive across the inside of his arm. And then, in smaller letters, my face aflame, added, *I heart you.*

I don't know what came over me, and I still haven't been able to look at Ryker directly since I wrote those words on his cast. His entire face had lit up, however, as if breaking his arm and being in the hospital for an entire week was worth it just for those three little words.

And for the one millionth time, I pray for the floor monsters to swallow me whole.

"Make sure he takes his meds," the doctor instructs me, casting an annoyed look at Ryker.

I imagine that he wasn't their most...model patient.

"I will," I assure her as I take the bottle from her hand.

Ryker mumbles something too low for me to hear before he stomps down the hall, towards the sliding glass doors.

"Hey, Rykey!" Zane calls, cupping his mouth with his hands. A shit-eating grin explodes on his face, one that instantly makes me uneasy. A mischievous Zane is a scary Zane. It usually means he's up to no good. "Do you need a wheelchair to leave here?"

Ryker simply offers Zane the middle finger over his shoulder before storming outside.

Zane, who has already grabbed said wheelchair, frowns and then shrugs.

"Suit yourself," he says to no one in particular as he throws himself into the seat and begins to wheel himself towards the door. "WHEELCHAIR RACE!"

Thank god the hospital is virtually empty in this particular wing.

"Somebody stop him, please," Dominic deadpans with a tired sigh.

He stands shoulder to shoulder with Landon, both of them looking eerily like twins despite their difference in looks.

Same stance—arms crossed over their chests while their legs are shoulder width apart.

Same expression—reluctant love intermingled with annoyance and agitation.

Same brows—a slight furrow between them, though Landon's is deeper than Dominic's.

Same hands—currently curled into fists, even with their arms crossed.

I can't help but think they resemble night and day. Landon's dark locks of hair are juxtaposed by Dom's golden ones. His silver eyes, the color of pure mercury, remind me of the night sky and the stars twinkling inside of it. Dominic's green ones resemble the rich forest floor as the sunlight beats down, painting everything in shades of palest white and gold.

"I'll get him," Beckett says now, drawing my attention to him as he hurries down the hall after Zane.

Nurses and doctors alike jump out of Zane's way as he

barrels forward, his arms working like crazy as he spins the wheels.

"YEE HAW! Ride 'em, cowboy!" Zane hoots.

"Slow the fuck down, you big idiot," Beckett calls back as he jogs to catch up.

The two of them disappear around the corner.

A second later, Ryker's gravelly voice snaps, "YOU JUST RAN OVER MY GODDAMN FOOT!"

"Oops!" Zane sounds entirely unrepentant.

I wince in sympathy.

"Ryker's going to be a bear this holiday break," I say with a slanted smile at Dominic and Landon, thinking of the pill bottle in my hand.

I imagine I'll have to wrap the damn pills in cheese to get him to take them.

And that's... That's when Dom's and Landon's personalities shine through. Dominic almost immediately offers me a tentative smile, one that softens the harsh angles of his face and makes his eyes glimmer like gemstones. He looks like a freaking angel.

Landon, on the other hand, takes my words at face value. His frown grows even deeper as he narrows his eyes at the exit Ryker just disappeared through.

"He shouldn't be alone," he agrees.

"None of us should," Dominic adds. He throws me an unreadable look before focusing once more on Landon. "That's actually what I was going to bring up the other day—"

"ZANE!" Beckett hollers from somewhere in the distance.

Dominic, Landon, and I exchange worried glances before hurrying towards the door and into the chilled morning light.

Laughter gets caught in my throat when I spot Zane facedown in a pile of snow, the wheelchair lying abandoned on its side beside him, one of the wheels still spinning. Ryker stands near the side of Landon's car, and though he's not laughing, I swear I see a tiny smile playing at the edges of his lips.

Beckett, meanwhile, doesn't have such qualms. He's gripping his stomach as he falls apart in raucous laughter, the noise blowing through me like a summer wind and thawing the ice in my body.

Zane slowly pushes himself to his hands and knees and shakes his head from side to side like a wet dog—though I don't dare say that comparison out loud. We all know about Zane's...*phobia* of pups.

"You fucking bastard—" Zane seethes, abruptly lunging to his feet with a ball of snow in his hand.

Beckett tries to run away, but he's laughing too hard to do anything but stagger back a few steps. Zane grabs him by the sweater and shoves the entire blob of snow down it. Beckett yelps in pain and jumps a foot in the air.

"Okay, guys," Dominic says with a roll of his eyes, moving to stand between the two of them.

Beckett jumps from foot to foot as he attempts to shake the ice and snow out of his sweater. Zane, meanwhile, is still scrubbing at the snow across the front of his body, including his face and hair.

"Not in front of a goddamn hospital," Dominic warns them.

Zane pouts. "He started it! He pushed me into the snow while I was wheelchair-boarding. It's like snowboarding... but in a wheelchair."

"I did not, you bloody idiot." Beckett gives Zane a look that suggests he's sincerely questioning his sanity. "You got the wheel stuck in a damn lump of ice. I tried to help your dumb ass."

"Liar, liar, pants on fire."

"Real mature." Beckett scoffs.

"Oh, for the love of..." Ryker instinctively lowers to a crouch in front of the car—a position I constantly find him in. He holds his broken arm against his chest as he volleys his gaze between his two friends. "Zane, Beckett didn't push you into the snow, though he definitely tried to. You just happened to trip over a lump of ice before his hands could make contact with the back of the chair."

His raspy voice makes the butterflies in my stomach do running dives and backflips. Maybe it's because it's so rare I get to hear it for more than a few seconds. Ryker doesn't talk much, if ever, but the last few days...

I swear every time I've come to visit him in the hospital, he's had a new story to tell me, a new tale to spin. I half wonder if there's something going on with him that I don't know about, but whenever I question him, he simply dismisses my words with a wave of his hand.

And I swear... I freaking swear...that he's smiling more too.

This time, I'm definitely not mistaken when he flashes me a tiny smirk. It makes those damn butterflies turn freaking radioactive.

When was the last time I've seen him smile like that?

Unbridled and free?

The sight of his smile should infuse me with a sense of happiness, but instead, all I feel is despair. It's a sinking, tugging sensation in the center of my gut, almost like I've been shoved down an elevator shaft, my scream carrying in the breeze as I plummet to my death.

There's something going on with Ryker.

Something I can't quite pinpoint.

And I'm more determined than ever to figure out what it is.

⬥⬥⬥⬥⬥⬥⬥⬥

THE GUYS DROP me off at my dorm, though Landon insists on staying with me. I don't even bother to argue with him. After everything that went down with POP, The Divine One, and then Raymond, we can never be too careful.

I doubt my one self-defense class will be enough if either group chooses to attack me. I'm still learning how to form my hand into a fist without breaking all of my fingers, thank you very much.

The rest of the guys have returned to their own dorm to finish packing up for break, and we'll meet them there as soon as I've grabbed everything I need.

"I should be just about done," I tell Landon now as I shove my key into the lock. "I've spent the last few days packing everything up. It was either do that or go insane, so…"

"We already have enough insanity in this group to last us a lifetime," Landon says dryly as I push open the door. "We don't need any more of it."

"Any more of what?" Piper balances on a chair near the back of the living room as she attempts to grab down a photograph she hung on the wall a couple months back.

In the photo, Piper's dressed in a strapless black gown, her vibrant hair in wild curls around her shoulders. She has her arm slung around Blair—a petite, gorgeous girl with elfin features and light blonde hair.

They took this particular picture at the beginning of October, a few weeks before Blair's death. I can see the tell-tale signs of autumn in the background, from the collection of orange, red, and yellow leaves littering the ground to the flush on their cheeks from the early October wind.

Blair's death was officially ruled an accident.

A car crash.

Of course, Piper doesn't know the truth about what happened to Blair...

I wait for that familiar pang of guilt I always feel when I think of Blair, but it never comes. At some point, I must've come to terms with the fact that I had no part to play in my friend's death.

There's only one person responsible, the man who pulled the trigger and then covered up her death—The Divine One.

Even thinking of the bastard tightens my stomach into one giant knot. He sought to push me down, destroy me, ruin what little good I had in my life.

What he doesn't realize is that I'm a phoenix rising from the ashes of a fire I set myself. He didn't break me—he *forged* me.

Piper scrubs a hand through her pitch-black hair streaked with purple and red. Her aquamarine eyes, heightened by thick, violet eyeshadow and dark eyeliner, flick in our direction as we step farther into the spacious dorm—a small kitchenette, a living room, and four bedrooms.

"We don't need any more of your ugliness," Landon quips good-naturedly in response to her question.

Piper casts him a dry look and says, "Ha, ha, ha. Very funny, turd bag. You're just jealous you'll never have my naturally stunning good looks."

I have to turn my face away to hide my growing smile.

Usually, it's only Zane who dares to antagonize my roommates, but over time, the other boys have joined in on the fun as well. Most girls may feel a little bit jealous that their crushes are becoming friendly with other girls—especially ones as gorgeous as my roommates—but I know none of the guys see them that way and vice versa.

Jane once confessed to me that the five of them remind her of the big brothers she never had and honestly doesn't want. And Victoria just said she would rather eat a pussy than go near them with a ten-foot pole—and considering how boy crazy Victoria is, that's saying something.

"Can you use your muscles for something other than throwing Ellie on a bed, and come help me?" Piper snipes, folding her arms over her chest and jerking her chin towards the photograph.

Landon sighs and gestures for her to step down from the chair. She does so instantly, her black and red skirt flaring around her thighs as she moves.

She smiles at him sweetly and bats her lashes. "Thank you. You're a dear. I'll make sure to mention this in my evaluation of you."

Landon pauses with his fingers halfway extended towards the framed photograph of Piper and Blair.

He frowns. "Evaluation?"

"To give Ellie, of course. She's definitely going to need help deciding which one of you hunks of man meat to date." She waggles her eyebrows suggestively as I wait for the ground to swallow me up whole.

Where, oh where, are the floor monsters when you need them to eat you? Why can't this be a sexy monster romance novel?

"I mean, you five are already losing points from me for not having tits and a vagina."

"Piper!" I squeal, swatting at her arm. My cheeks feel as if they're on fire.

She stares at me innocently—or as innocent as she can be, considering she doesn't have a guileless bone in her body. She's like Zane in that respect. Maybe that's why they became such close friends.

"What? I think Landon can agree there's just something...riveting about playing with a girl's nipples while fingering her pussy. Am I right, or am I right?" She extends a hand upwards as if waiting for him to high-five her.

Floor monster, oh floor monster, where art thou?

Landon, for the first time in his entire existence, seems at a loss for words. His cheeks have turned a shade of red I didn't think was physically possible, and his gaze flicks between Piper's face...and my breasts. He looks away so quickly that he almost falls off the chair.

"I think I broke him," Piper whispers conspiratorially to me as Landon continues to gape, struggling to maintain his footing.

"I'm going to grab my stuff and pretend this conversation never happened." I whirl on my heel and begin to hurry towards my bedroom.

But not before I hear Piper ask, "So...how often have you imagined Ellie's boobs?"

And Landon's response of, "Jesus."

Oh my god.

I'm going to kill her.

Or him.

Or both.

A little homicide has never hurt anyone, has it?

I push open my bedroom door only to freeze at the sight of both Victoria and Jane already inside of my room.

The latter is perusing my collection of books—my *new* collection of books, considering the old one was destroyed during one of my...episodes. Her brown, frizzy hair is held back by a bright-pink headband, and she wears a flowered dress that stops just below her knees. She fingers one of the titles before moving on to the next book on my shelf.

Victoria reclines on my bed, looking like a walking contradiction. As always, her beauty takes my breath away—long, voluminous red hair, pouty lips, and a body encased in a skintight black skirt and red blouse that matches her lipstick. But while she may look like a super-model, she's lying on my bed as if she's a dude with a pair of balls that are too big for her to function. She's practically sprawled spread-eagle, showing a glimpse of translucent panties as her skirt rides up.

"Girl, close your legs." I toss the nearest object I can find—a balled-up shirt—at her.

She laughs and immediately does as instructed.

"Don't be such a prude, Ellie," she taunts in her lilting French accent.

This time, I throw a pillow at her, which she gracefully catches out of the air as she sits upright.

I move towards my suitcase and half-packed duffel bag resting on the floor. Most of my clothes have already been packed, but I want to grab my songwriting book as well.

A lot of my instruments had been...destroyed in what I'm now referring to as Hurricane Ellie, but I'm more deter-mined than ever to get back to playing. There's something immensely calming about creating music, about losing yourself to the notes and lyrics, to becoming one with the melody and harmony.

I need that in my life.

I need it more than just about anything else.

"My mom is picking me up in a few minutes," Jane says as she finally pulls her gaze away from my bookshelf. "I wanted to say goodbye before I left."

"And her mom is also dropping *me* off at the airport," Victoria adds.

Jane's brows crinkle in concern as she surveys me. Of all my new friends, I always get the distinct impression that Jane sees me more clearly than the others. I sometimes feel as if her eyes are dissecting me, pulling away skin and bone, peering at the parts of me I wish would remain hidden. It's an uncanny sensation...but I'm not sure it's particularly unpleasant.

"How are you doing, sweetie?" she asks gently. "How's Ryker?"

"Home from the hospital," I say, ignoring her first question. "Cranky as all can be."

"Ryker? Cranky? I never would've guessed," Victoria says with an exaggerated roll of her eyes.

"And you?" Jane presses, apparently determined not to let this go.

Am I mistaken, or does her gaze dip to my arms, where my scars are currently hidden by Dominic's red sweater I put on this morning?

"I...I'm going to be okay," I say simply, though I'm not sure who I'm trying to convince. Them...or myself. It freaking sucks when your own mind is against you. "I think this break will be good for me, especially after what happened with Ryker."

The girls don't know the truth about POP and The Divine One, and that's the way it has to be. For their own protection. Right now, they just think my disembodied state has been a consequence of Ryker's car accident, and they can't know the truth. Not ever.

That would make them a target, and if something happened to the two of them because of me...

The *three* of them...

Just the thought has poison coursing through my veins.

"Are you going to be by yourself over break?" Victoria stares at me in concern—which is a huge red flag.

Victoria really only has two emotions: sarcastic and even more sarcastic. So for her to be anxious? I must look like complete and utter shit.

My stomach turns over itself and twists into a pretzel.

"My brother will be home over Christmas—" I begin.

"Come with me to France," Victoria interrupts, her eyes alighting at the prospect. She practically bounces on the edge of my bed in excitement. "I'm sure we can find you a plane ticket, and you'll be able to meet my family—"

"No need." Landon's voice comes from directly behind me.

I have no idea how long he's been eavesdropping, but I find that I'm not upset by it.

He takes a few steps farther into the room and ropes an arm around my shoulders. Both Jane and Victoria fixate on where he touches me, and matching, mischievous grins light up their faces.

"Oh?" Victoria cocks a perfectly manicured red brow in his direction. "Are you going to be...shall I say...taking care of Ellie over break?"

There's no mistaking the sexual innuendo in that seemingly innocent question.

"I can assure you that Ellie won't be alone and that she'll be *well* taken care of," Landon says, ignoring her quip. Or maybe joining in on it? Crap. I have no idea. "But thank you for the offer. You guys truly have been good friends to Ellie."

"We don't really have a choice," Piper jokes from where she stands behind him in the doorway, the framed photograph hugged tightly to her chest. "We're kind of stuck with her."

"It would be really awkward if we hated her guts and were forced to share a dorm with her," adds Victoria, flashing me a red-painted grin.

"You're lucky I don't have anything else to throw at you," I tell her.

And as the three girls laugh, there's a lightness in my chest that I've never felt before, not even with the guys.

Is this what it truly means to have...friends?

CHAPTER 16

Dominic

I place my finger to my chin as I study the board placed in the center of our living room.

It used to be a chalkboard—one of those old, green monstrosities that boomers tell their kids about—but it has been repurposed to fit my needs.

Distantly, I hear Beckett, Ryker, and Zane rummaging through their rooms as they finish packing things up, but I don't focus on them. My entire attention is consumed by the damn board and the secrets it holds.

"Still studying your murder board?" Zane asks cheerfully as he reappears in the living room, his duffel bag slung over his shoulder.

He throws himself onto the couch behind me and then positions his body so he's dangling off the edge, his feet in the air. His dark hair grazes the ground as he balances himself upside down.

"It's not a fucking murder board," I grumble, squinting at the pictures tacked to the green surface.

"Um...I've seen my fair share of murder boards over the years, and that is definitely a class-A mur-dur board." He pops his lips together...and then begins to choke on his own spit since he's still upside down.

"It's not a goddamn murder board!" I throw my arms into the air with a huff of irritation.

Beckett, drawn in by our arguing, sticks his head out of his bedroom door and frowns. He flicks his gaze in my direction.

"Sorry, mate," he says. "Definitely a murder board."

"For the love of..." Ignoring the two idiots, I focus back on my greatest creation.

Is this what it's like to be a parent?

The past week—while Ryker was in the hospital and the rest of our group slowly began to lose their minds with worry—I gathered all of the information we received about the Paragons of Prosperity, The Divine One, and good old Uncle Raymond. Every clue, every secret, every revelation has been meticulously tacked to the green chalkboard with white lines connecting one thing to another. I've even included pictures of some of the...men and women we've taken out over the years.

Ranking officials of POP.

And people Raymond sent us after. His own personal lackeys. Guard dogs. Hit men. Serial killers. However the fuck you want to classify us.

That familiar surge of anger rushes through me, pouring through my veins like magma.

What is Raymond *really* after?

Was everything he did truly just to protect Ellie, his niece?

I find that hard to believe. It's not that Ellie isn't lovable —she most definitely is—but I doubt a virtual stranger would devote time and money towards murdering anyone who threatens her.

Not everyone is as psychotic as the guys and I.

"Are you bringing that thing home with you?" Beckett asks nonchalantly as he leans his hip against the doorframe. "Might be kind of awkward to carry an entire murder board with you across campus."

"Not a fucking murder board."

"He could just say it's a science project," Zane refutes. He begins to sway from side to side like the pendulum on a grandfather clock—with his head being the fucking pendulum. "The science of murdering crazy fuckers."

"Not. A. Murder. Board." I level my glare at each of them, but they both smirk at me, entirely unrepentant.

"I see at least ten people on there that we've killed," Beckett counters, pointing. "Hell, I even see the man we killed a few months ago. Remember? Zane used his head as a basketball—"

He stops talking abruptly when the door opens and both Landon and Ellie step inside. Landon carries behind him a flowered suitcase. A pink duffel bag has been slung over his shoulder.

Ellie's eyes immediately zero in on the chalkboard, a furrow materializing between her brows.

"Do you have...a *murder board* in your living room?" she asks in disbelief.

Motherfucker.

"Ha!" Zane gracefully rolls his body so he's able to somersault-slash-flip off the couch. He lands on the carpet on his back with a shit-eating grin on his face. "Vindicated!"

"Vin-di-ca-ted," Beckett agrees, purposely dragging out every syllable.

"Does anyone here even know what a murder board is?" I throw my hands up into the air.

Children, I tell you. A bunch of unruly children.

Ellie ignores my outburst and tentatively steps forward. I suddenly find myself...anxious. So unbelievably anxious. I'm practically on pins and needles as I gauge her reaction with bated breath.

I know Ellie isn't completely oblivious to the demons inside of me and the other guys. It's what drew us to her in the first place—she sees the darkness inside of each and every one of us, but she doesn't shy away or cower. Her light is exactly what we need to keep us from going too far into the abyss. She's practically the sun embodied. We've spent way too long in the dark that we're desperate to soak up its heat.

But to see the truth of our sins firsthand?

To know the extent of our depravity and darkness?

Zane has gone completely frozen on the ground, only his eyes shifting to focus on Ellie's face, much the same way I am. Beckett's as taut as a bowstring a second before the arrow is let loose, and Landon seems to be holding his breath.

Out of my periphery, I notice Ryker emerge from his room and crouch down in the far corner, clinging to the shadows. His ice-blue eyes peer back at me from the hood of his gray sweatshirt.

God, is this when Ellie runs?

When she screams in terror and declares us too insane to deal with?

But she doesn't do any of that.

Her tone is rife with anger and indignation as she jabs her finger at one of the pictures taped to the board.

"What the hell is my brother doing on the board?" she demands, her body trembling with the force of her rage.

Oh…shit.

Kind of forgot about that.

Written in large, block letters are the words THE DIVINE ONE. Surrounding it are numerous pictures of men and women we think could be the murderer himself…or herself.

Mr. Moreau, the pervy English teacher, who Ryker beat the shit out of. He conveniently skipped town the very next day after turning in his resignation…but that doesn't mean shit to us. He very well could still be involved.

My father, a horribly disgusting prick of a man.

His Barbie-like wife.

His two idiotic sons.

Paulina, Dane's stepsister, who also left town after her stepbrother mysteriously…disappeared.

And Fischer.

Ellie's finger continues to tremble as she keeps it fixated on the smiling face of her brother, with his shaggy brown hair and light eyes.

"My brother is *not* involved in this," Ellie snaps, her tone a type of poison that seems to inject itself straight into my bloodstream.

"Ellie…" Landon begins carefully.

"No, Land." Ellie shakes her head and pushes up on her tiptoes to remove the tiny photograph. "I know my brother. I promise you—I swear on my life—that he's not a part of POP. And he's certainly not The Divine One."

I exchange a wary glance with Landon, but he shakes his head nearly imperceptibly, signaling for me to drop this conversation. I clench my jaw tightly but do as he instructs.

Besides, there's no way for any of us to explain our

suspicions to Ellie. If we're wrong, she'll hate us for accusing her brother.

But if we're right...

The thought of Ellie alone in that fucking house feels as if the Grim Reaper himself is trailing his ice-cold finger down my spine. I don't quite know if the shiver that comes over me is from the chill...or my own fear.

I clear my throat once, garnering all of their attention to me.

Ellie glances up from where she's staring intently at the photo of her brother, frowns, and then folds it up and places it in her back pocket.

"I was thinking about this long and hard—" I begin, feeling oddly shy.

"Like my cock," Zane interrupts like the thirteen-year-old boy I know he is.

Both Beckett and Landon throw something at his head —Landon, an apple off the table, and Beckett, his entire backpack.

"Oww! Ellie! They hurt me." His lower lip begins to tremble as he sniffles exaggeratedly. "Can you kiss my booboo and make it feel better?"

A muscle in the corner of her mouth begins to twitch, but she doesn't allow herself to fully smile. Probably, I assume, still pissed at us for accusing her brother.

"I'm sure Dominic will be more than willing to kiss all of your booboos away," she quips with a pointed look in my direction.

Almost immediately—goddamn unerringly—Zane turns his attention onto me.

"No." I back away. "Don't you dare."

Zane jumps to his feet and extends his arms. "Come

here, Dominikins. I think I broke my ass. I really need a kissy to make the booboo better."

He continues to advance on me while I move backwards and stops when I'm directly in front of a laughing Ellie.

"I will cut off your balls and feed them to the sharks," I warn severely.

"Do you own any pet sharks?" Zane cocks an eyebrow. "No? Didn't think so."

"You don't need to own a shark to feed balls to one," Beckett points out cheerfully.

And Ryker adds, "I know a shark guy. He'll help you."

A broad smile erupts on my face. "Thank you both."

If I thought Zane would be perturbed by my threats, I was sorely mistaken. If anything, that malevolent smirk on his face seems to grow, stretching until he resembles the damn joker. Honestly, I believe Zane may be just as insane as him— the Heath Ledger version, not the shitty Jared Leto one.

"Don't make me do this," I threaten, subtly reaching behind my back.

"Do what?" he taunts, thrusting his hips forward and then shaking them from side to side. "My cock is all yours, baby. Do with it what you will."

He takes another step closer...

And I reach behind me, grab Ellie, and spin us both so she's in front of me.

"Dom!" she squeals around her laughter. "Are you seriously *sacrificing* me?"

"Sorry, sweetness." I hold her up so her wiggling feet are suspended an inch off the ground. "You're my human shield."

Beckett brings his fist to his mouth and winces in feigned sympathy. "Damn, man. That's cold."

"Ohh! This just got more interesting!" Zane singsongs, bouncing on the balls of his feet.

His dark-brown eyes home in on Ellie in my arms. His smile this time around is positively lascivious—a starving man desperate to take a bite out of the only apple in the field.

"I REFUSE TO BE A HUMAN SHIELD!" Ellie bellows.

And then, in a move that surprises the shit out of me—and turns me on like nothing I've experienced before—she takes my hand in hers then lifts it...and bites down.

She just motherfucking bit me!

Lust seems to transmit through my body from the space where her teeth drill into my skin. I feel hot all over. Blood rushes straight to my cock, leaving me oddly light-headed as I drop her instinctively. She cries out in triumph, pumping a fist in the air, but all I can focus on is the image of her teeth biting down into my neck as I thrust into her.

Fucking hell.

Landon begins to chuckle, obviously sensing the direction of my thoughts, and Ellie flashes me a smug grin, obviously *oblivious* to them.

"Sorry." She grants me a mocking pout, one that makes me ache to close the distance between us and nip her plump bottom lip. "I guess you're on your own. I really hope you like kissing ass, Dom."

"I like eating ass. *Your* ass," I murmur...but too low for her to hear.

I'm not quite ready to traumatize the poor girl.

Even still, my pulse thunders like a roaring drum in my ears. Lust for her cascades through my veins until my entire body is attuned towards hers in a way that feels almost supernatural.

Carnal.

Exquisite.

"I still need someone to kiss my booboos," Zane sings. "And since Dominic isn't game…"

Before Ellie can protest, he scoops her into his arms and walks them both backwards until he's able to sit on the couch with her in his lap. She wiggles in a way that has my cock twitching in sympathy—and envy. Lucky bastard.

But Zane just looks unperturbed as he grins down at her.

"I'm not kissing your ass," she warns.

Goddammit.

The words "kiss" and "ass" leaving her mouth make my dick jump to attention. The damn bastard goes from being half erect to full-on, full-steam-ahead hard.

Maybe it's because Ellie is usually so innocent, so naïve…that the sound of her saying such crude terms has me spiraling. It's not as if I've never heard Ellie swear before, but it's extremely rare when she does.

What would she say if I were to spread her out on the couch and eat that perfect cunt until she's weeping?

Fuck?

Hell?

Shit?

Dominic?

All of the above?

"I'm not going to have you kiss my ass," Zane protests, blinking his long lashes innocently. "Unless you want to, of course. I'm an ass of all trades."

Ellie's cheeks turn crimson. Before she can respond, however, he points to his cheek, just below his eye.

"It hurts here."

Ellie gives him an exasperated look but obediently

stretches upwards to kiss the skin he indicated, her pink lips lingering.

"And here." This time, his finger lands on the tip of his nose.

Ellie obliges with a grin that alternates between annoyed and amused.

"And here." He touches the edge of his lips.

Ellie twists her face, a banked fire flickering in her eyes, and Zane swivels his head at the last second, capturing her lips with his.

The kiss lasts for less than a second, but during that time, I feel as if my entire world has just rearranged itself. The magnetic poles have reversed, north is now south, the sky is now the ground, and I feel as if I've just been stabbed with a javelin.

What the fuck?

Are we allowed to do casual kisses with Ellie now?

Is that a goddamn thing?

Why wasn't I informed?!

Zane smiles like the cat that ate the canary, while Ellie's cheeks turn a shade of red I'm not sure scientists have a name for.

Subtly, I search the other three men's faces, gauging their reactions.

Landon just seems amused, his arms crossed over his chest and an indulgent grin on his face. Beckett simply shakes his head and rolls his eyes. Is that jealousy flicking to life in his brown and green gaze? Envy? Anger? I'm usually the second best at reading these guys after Landon, but just then, I've forgotten every goddamn word in the English dictionary.

And Ryker...

His hand clenches on his knee where he's still crouched

in the shadowy corner of the room. A scowl distorts his features as he fixates on where Ellie sits on Zane's lap. A dozen emotions pass across his face, all of them too quick for me to comprehend.

My tension ratchets up a dozen notches as I wait to see how he'll react. Will he explode in anger? Beat the shit out of Zane? Take his anger out on Ellie?

But after a moment of glaring, Ryker takes a deep, jittery breath—one that makes his bare, scarred chest heave—and then forces himself to relax. He begins to fiddle with the zipper of his open sweatshirt, pulling it up and down, up and down, up and down. The repetitive motion seems to calm him, and I watch with bated breath as his shoulders drop an inch and his frown settles into a straight line.

Landon clears his throat, once again ensnaring all of our attention. He does it with an effortless sort of grace that once made me jealous of him. Everything he does...he does with ease. One look into his metallic eyes is capable of commandeering an entire army. One sharp, domineering word from him has men and women alike falling to their knees at his feet, asking what he needs. He doesn't even need to think about it to take control of an entire room.

It's what makes him a leader—one who will no doubt rule the entire fucking world someday.

"We should probably discuss winter break," he says, pulling the attention off of Zane and Ellie's kiss and onto him.

Smart man.

A frown tugs on Ellie's lips as she shifts on Zane's lap to face us. Her cheeks are still tinted red, but the color has begun to fade, gradually turning a shade of light pink instead of crimson.

"What do you mean?"

"The Divine One and POP have been abnormally quiet the last week," Landon begins, his eyes sweeping over the room. "But I don't believe that they're done with us...done with you, Ellie."

This he addresses to the girl who has captured each and every one of our hearts.

The goddess capable of wrangling five beasts.

"So you don't think it's safe for me to be alone," she deduces, not bothering to voice it as a question.

"I don't think any of us should be alone," Landon counters gravely.

"That's actually what I wanted to talk to you guys about." I shove my hands into the pocket of my gray hoodie and take a step forward. This new position doesn't put me in front of Landon, only shoulder to shoulder with him. "My mothers have a cabin up in Pine Lake—a cabin that no one knows anything about. Momma Cheryl uses it when she needs to get away and write without distractions."

Momma Cheryl is a *New York Times* Bestselling Author... and one of the most popular fantasy authors in the world, currently. Her latest series has been opted for a major motion picture deal. Because of that, my parents have a few locations that they have chosen to keep off the grid— homes and cottages they've paid for entirely in cash that no one aside from the three of us knows about.

"I already talked to my moms about it," I continue. "They said we could use the cabin over break. No one knows its location. Absolutely *no one*," I stress.

I don't know why I haven't thought of this before. It's a goddamn gold mine.

"So we'll be hidden from POP, The Divine One, and

Raymond?" Ellie whispers tentatively, her voice suggesting this all sounds too good to be true.

And hell, maybe it is. This particular mine could be made up of nothing but fool's gold, but it's worth taking the chance.

"For the time being, I believe so. I doubt it'll stay secure for long, but hopefully, it'll give us enough time to figure shit out." I shrug. "Beckett still hasn't been able to get anything off that damn app on Seth's phone. And we still need to decide what we're going to do about Senator Reece and the deadline The Divine One gave us."

Landon claps me on the back, causing me to stumble forward a step. "That's a damn good idea, Dom. But Beckett, Zane, and I won't be able to join you right away. We have...things we need to take care of."

His eyes flick to Ellie and then immediately shift away, but my girl doesn't let it go that quickly.

"What things do you need to take care of?" Her pink lips purse with irritation. "Remember. We said no more secrets."

Landon forks his fingers through his dark-brown hair and heaves out a breath. After a long moment of silence—during which I fear he'll decline answering—he confesses, "We plan to do some recon on Senator Reece Whipers. If you truly need to bring him to The Divine One..."

He allows his words to taper off, but the meaning remains clear.

If we need to sacrifice one senator to save Ellie's life, then we'll do so without any complaint or hesitation.

Maybe that makes us calloused monsters...or maybe it makes us human beings driven to protect those we love.

Ellie's face turns a sickly shade of green as she fiddles

with the cords of my sweatshirt. "I don't want to hurt him if he's innocent. I'm not... I can't..."

"Please don't worry about it, Ellie," Landon says gently.

He exchanges a long, eloquent look with me, one that makes words unnecessary.

Ellie may not be willing to hurt him...but we certainly are.

We'll be her swords in this battle so her hands remain free of blood.

Isn't that the whole point of monsters?

"And all three of you need to go?" She turns towards Zane first, whose face is uncharacteristically grave, then a somber Beckett, before finally facing Landon.

He chews on his bottom lip as he considers her. "Unfortunately."

"I told him I'd rather stay with you, *princesa*." Zane nuzzles his face against Ellie's neck, seemingly only half paying attention to the conversation.

Then again, the crazy bastard is smarter than anyone would suspect. His sharp mind is no doubt focused on everything all at once—dissecting every word and reaction the way a scientist would a corpse in the morgue.

His dark eyes, the color of a freshly dug grave, lock on her face. "But don't worry. I'll send you lots of dick pics to remember me by."

She shoves at his shoulder instantly, even as her cheeks turn magenta. "Be serious."

"We *are* serious," Beckett interrupts. "We're the best men for this job. But we'll be quick. It should only take us a day or so. Hopefully sooner."

Landon claps his hands together. "And Ryker and Dom will stay with you—"

"Just Dom." Ryker cuts Landon off, his tone as sharp as icicles falling from a roof. And just as icy too.

Landon stares at him, momentarily taken aback. "What?"

"I have something I need to do," he says stiffly. He focuses on his scarred hands as if they hold the secrets to the universe.

"Something more important than protecting Ellie?" Zane scoffs, but I detect a hint of what we refer to as his "darkness" in his voice.

The fine golden hairs on the back of my neck prickle in warning.

If a fight were to break out...

Ryker's scowl is so severe that it creates wrinkles on his face—prominent lines that make him look decades older. His eyes frost over, promising death, and I take a step forward instinctively—

"Enough!" Ellie chastises, glaring at Zane, who immediately pushes his lower lip out and whines like a kicked puppy.

The darkness in his eyes recedes as if it's never been there to begin with.

She ignores him and turns towards Ryker. Her expression considerably softens when she stares at the scarred, silent man. "You do what you need to do, Ryker. I trust you."

A look of wonder and awe flits across his face before he conceals it behind his trademark scowl.

Fuck, that man is an absolute goner for her, isn't he?

"This cabin..." Ryker's gravelly voice slashes through the air like a racing bullet. His face has taken on an ashen, chalky quality, and his eyes are unreadable—icy-blue orbs that seem to refract the darkness surrounding him. "You truly think it'll be safe from POP? You think we'll be able to hide from The Divine One there?"

I can't read the inflection in his tone.

"There's no way in hell he knows about it," I promise.

Something flashes in Ryker's eyes, but once again, it's there and gone too quickly for me to decipher.

What the fuck is going on with him? What can be more important to him than protecting Ellie?

He lowers his gaze to where his hands dangle between his legs. His head falls forward, razor-black hair cascading into his eyes. For a long moment, he doesn't speak, his entire posture rigid—chiseled from limestone, a puppet held up on taut strings.

"All right," he rasps at last. Only his eyes are visible through the darkness of his hood as he shifts his head to stare up at us. "I'll be back by tomorrow at the latest. But what I have to do... It's important."

I have a thousand questions I want to ask but manage to hold my tongue. Trying to get Ryker to divulge his secrets is how I imagine it would be to train a cat. He hisses, bites, and scratches at you if you dare to get too close. However, if you give him his space, allow him to come to you...

We just need to wait until he's comfortable opening up to us about whatever's bothering him.

Landon's hand turns into an iron vise on my shoulder, his fingers gripping it tightly enough to leave bruises.

"It's just going to be you and our girl tonight, Dom." The words are said cheerfully, almost casually, but I can hear the warning beneath it all.

The reminder of what we're fighting for.

Who we're fighting for.

"I'll protect her with my life," I vow softly.

The tension riding his body seems to seep out of him at my words like water being wrung out of a sponge.

He gives my shoulder another squeeze before releasing me. "I know you will, brother. I just hate being away from her."

"I'll stick to her like glue," I reassure him.

Only then does the full realization of what's about to happen hit me like a goddamn freight train.

Me...alone...with Ellie.

For an entire fucking night.

In a cabin.

In the woods.

Fucking hell.

◆◆◆◆◆◆◆◆◆◆

THE GUYS HAVE ALREADY LEFT when my phone rings.

Ellie sits on the sofa in our dorm, nibbling on some popcorn I made for her as I finish packing up my clothes.

And yes, I'm bringing the murder board, dammit, though I still think that's a misnomer.

I fumble my phone out of my pocket and press Accept before I even look at who's calling me.

"Hello?" I balance the phone between my shoulder and ear as I work to zip up my suitcase.

"Dom!" My bio-father's cheery, exuberant voice sends a cold chill racing down my spine.

Fear courses through my bloodstream like poison as I tense, every muscle in my body locking tightly.

Ellie glances my way in concern, slowly rises from her seat, and ventures a step closer to me.

"Harvey," I say stiffly.

Not Father.

Never Father.

"I heard that Grove Academy's winter break started today," he says.

Fear taps against my brain like the claws of a three hundred pound, six foot beast.

"Yes." I don't bother to give him more than that.

Ellie's face pinches with worry as she takes another step towards me.

"Perfect! I was hoping you can stop over tonight for family dinner. I never got to talk to you last time." He chuckles, but the noise holds a type of darkness I can't begin to comprehend.

It's different from Ryker's or Zane's or even my own, though I can't pinpoint why. Either way, my consciousness fragments, and black dots dominate my vision.

"I can't," I find myself saying, my mouth moving before my brain can catch up. Reality slowly, agonizingly, begins to reassert itself around me. "I have plans."

"Oh?" Harvey's voice is a splash of acid on red, peeling, bloody skin—acerbic, bitter, and cruel.

A part of me wonders if I should take him up on that offer. Perhaps I can take a peek at his phone and the fucking dating app I noticed there. Maybe then we'll be able to solve one goddamn puzzle.

But even as the thought begins to form, a knife wedges itself into my chest.

I can't leave Ellie.

I fucking refuse to.

"I actually have plans with Ellie," I find myself saying.

And then I inwardly curse, hating myself for my unintentional slip.

Fuck. Fuck. Fuck.

"Oh, bring her with you! I haven't seen the girl in way too long." Harvey's voice is laced with glee.

"I'm not sure—"

"I'll see you both at seven," Harvey finishes.

Before I can mount a protest, he hangs up, and all I hear is the hum of a dial tone.

Fuck.

Fuck. Fuck. Fuck!

The guys are going to murder me.

And maybe... Maybe I'll just let them.

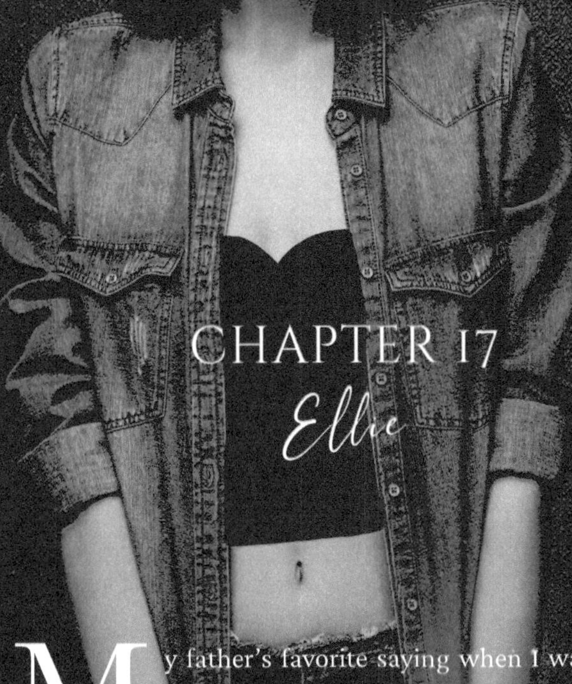

CHAPTER 17

Ellie

My father's favorite saying when I was a child was an overexaggerated and extremely dramatic, "It's the end of the world!"

He would place the back of his hand to his forehead and collapse onto the nearest available surface—the couch, the bed, the table, and sometimes even the floor.

Mom would shake her head with a sly smirk on her lips, while Fischer and I would giggle at Dad's antics.

As Dominic paces in front of me, I can't help but remember those moments with my parents and brother.

"It's the end of the world!"

He's certainly acting as if the world is ending—as if the sky is falling down and crushing us both beneath its immense weight. As if the fluffy clouds are made of poison capable of seeping into our bloodstreams. As if the sun is radioactive, burning our skin straight from our bones, melting it like ice cream in an oven.

His fingers repeatedly scrape through his platinum-blond hair as he wears a hole into the carpeting with his bare feet. Incoherent mutterings escape him, though I can't make out a single word he says.

"Dom..." I begin slowly.

He doesn't seem to hear me; he doesn't seem to even *see* me, his glossy green gaze distant and unfocused, fixated on a spot on the wall.

I didn't have to hear the conversation he had with his father to deduce what happened.

Harvey Rollins, Dom's biological father, has invited us both to his house for dinner tonight.

I know how much Dom hates the man. He dreads every forced encounter he has with him and his self-centered, perverted wife. I've seen his sunken cheeks and the purple shadows beneath his eyes more times than I care to admit after a dinner with them. His green eyes always look significantly darker at just the mention of his sperm donor.

The Divine One may be my personal devil, but Harvey... Harvey is Dom's.

"Dom." I'm across the room before I can think better of it, capturing his face in my hands.

His golden cheeks feel hot beneath my palms, flushed, almost as if he has come down with a fever. His unfocused eyes flit back and forth across my face without sticking to any feature in particular.

"Dom."

"Ellie..." He leans forward until his forehead presses against mine. His lashes flutter shut, charcoaled twigs against his high cheekbones.

Of all the guys, I've always considered Dominic to be the most traditionally handsome. Angelic, even, with his blond hair, gemstone-green eyes, and the smooth, sensual curl of his pink lips. He's my golden god—this statue displayed inside of a church that people ogle and awe over.

For a moment, I simply marvel at the sheer beauty of Dominic Black and my ability to touch him without repercussion.

Has any girl ever placed her hands on his cheeks before? Has any girl ever drawn lazy circles with her thumbs, just to the sides of his closed eyes?

A knot forms in my stomach at just the thought.

"What do you need?" I whisper, my fingers unconsciously beginning to stroke his face.

I swear I have no control over them; they seem to have a life of their own.

Slowly, his breathing begins to even out, though he still doesn't open his eyes. I watch the rise and fall of his chest, the muscles straining against his thin gray T-shirt.

"You're not going to my dad's house," he whispers at last.

His eyes finally snap open and immediately home in on my face. Heat sizzles through my veins almost instantly, as if his gaze itself is capable of setting me on fire.

"Dom..." I begin tentatively, hesitantly, slowly...keenly aware that I'm on a tightrope thousands of miles above a turbulent ocean. One wrong move will send me toppling off the edge. I continue stroking his cheeks, my thumb tracing his prominent cheekbone. "You know that we have to go."

"Ellie, *no*—"

"If you think that Harvey is involved in all of this, what better time to look for clues?" I become more animated with every word I say.

If this man has even a small amount of information about POP, The Divine One, or even Uncle Raymond...

"Maybe we'll be able to nab his phone," I continue as

his eyes shutter with a plethora of unreadable emotions. "Then we can see for sure if he has the same app as Seth on it...and if they're somehow connected."

"Ellie, it's dangerous."

I can tell Dominic is wavering, though. He's never been able to resist me for long. The other guys may put up more of a resistance, insisting that my safety comes first, but not Dominic. Never him.

"I'll have your back, and you'll have mine," I reply firmly, jutting my chin out in indignation. "We're a team, Dom. All of us. If we don't go together, then I know you're going to try and go alone." I narrow my eyes at him, but he doesn't bother to deny my claim. Damn stubborn man. "Besides, it's just dinner, Dom. Not a freaking murder orgy."

"Jesus Christ, Elle." He places his hand overtop mine where it still rests on his cheek. "Are you trying to get me killed? You do realize the guys will murder me and use my bloody skin as a fucking flag if I bring you to my father's house for dinner."

"Better to ask forgiveness than permission," I singsong, triumph already tingling through my veins. And then, in a more serious tone, I add, "Nothing will happen to either of us. You'll protect me, and I'll protect you."

He's so close I can see the splatter of darker green flecks in his eyes—various trees in springtime all clustered together, rolled in rippling dunes.

His gaze flicks to my lips for a fraction of a second, and I wonder... What would it be like to kiss him? Would his kiss be as brutal and claiming as Zane's? As fiercely possessive as Ryker's? As sweet and loving as Beckett's?

Is it wrong that I want to breach the distance between us and see for myself?

Oh god. The last thing I want to be is a cheater. Am I

dating one of the other guys? Surely, we would've had a conversation about it if we're in a committed relationship...right?

But then I remember Ryker's crestfallen face when I denied being his girlfriend.

My heart feels like a bird that flies into a window, collapses to the ground, and then gets a second burst of strength, allowing its glossy wings to ruffle and take to the air again.

Change the subject, Ellie! Stat!

"Zane left me, what he calls, his stabby knife," I whisper to Dom, trying desperately to reclaim the brain cells that fled the second he focused on my lips.

"Do you mean that literally, or...?" He cocks a blond brow at me, and I playfully swat his shoulder before reaching into my—his, technically—sweatshirt pocket.

The tiny pocketknife is bedazzled with pink gemstones.

"Stabby knife," I say gleefully.

"Good lord... We're making you into a little psychopath, aren't we?"

The smile on his face suggests he doesn't mind either way.

••••••••••

Harvey Rollins and his family live in a five-story mansion planted smack-dab in the middle of nowhere. The nearest house is over two miles away, and only trees surround the opulent brick building. Long, rectangular windows domi-nate the largest wall adjacent to the garage; through them, I can see an elegantly furnished living room and a door-less frame that leads into a kitchen.

There are no outdoor lights on, but the copious amount

emanating from inside illuminates the perfectly planted perennials lining the walkway and the colorful, hanging plants near the front door.

It's surprisingly...homey, something I didn't expect from the man Dominic despises so much.

"Have you ever imagined what hell looks like before?"

I glance at Dom out of the corner of my eye, wondering if his thoughts went down the same direction as mine.

His fingers are white where he grips the steering wheel, and a muscle fluttering in his jaw commandeers my attention. It draws my gaze to the golden hollow of his throat...

A throat I can't help imagine sinking my teeth into.

I blush uncomfortably at the direction of my thoughts and focus on his words instead.

Hoping to diffuse some of the tension permeating the car, I say, "Feet."

A golden brow rises as he turns to stare at me incredulously. "Feet?"

I shudder. "I hate feet. They just look...weird. Like, their angles aren't perfectly straight, but they're also not curved. It's almost like...an indent."

Dom continues to look at me as if I've lost my mind. "An *indent?*"

"And toes... Don't get me started on toes. What is even the purpose of them? They just look like chopped-up sausages. You could totally survive without your toes."

The corner of his lip twitches into the makings of a smile. Tentative...but a smile all the same.

"So you have a feet phobia." His fingers tap against the steering wheel as he focuses once more on the grand house before us. "Noted."

"They're weird-looking," I contend. "And smelly."

"How many feet are you sniffing, baby girl?" He flashes

me a teasing smile, and my heart jumps at the casual term of endearment.

"It's a phobia and a kink," I tease. "Don't judge."

He makes a face. "I once walked in on my half brother licking Dana's feet," he confesses.

"Your stepmom?" My mouth drops open. I know Dana isn't technically related to any of Dominic's brothers—they're a product of a hookup with a prostitute in Vegas—but still.

"Don't even get me started on the things I've seen..." He gives an overexaggerated shudder and then flashes me another one of those timid smiles.

He finally removes his hands from the steering wheel and places one overtop mine.

Heat explodes where he touches me, traveling directly to two places—my cheeks and my core. It's almost embarrassing my reaction to him.

"Are you sure you want to do this, Ellie?" His frown deepens. "We can turn around right the fuck now and head to my moms' cottage. Harvey will be pissed, but he'll get over it and—"

"Dom." I put my hand overtop his until it's a damn hand sandwich. The thought almost makes me smile, but I squash it before it can fully manifest. "We're a team, remember? I have your back."

"And I have yours." His lashes are long and charcoaled against the sharp lines of his cheekbones. "You ready to descend into hell, baby girl?"

"With you?" I reach for my door handle. "Always."

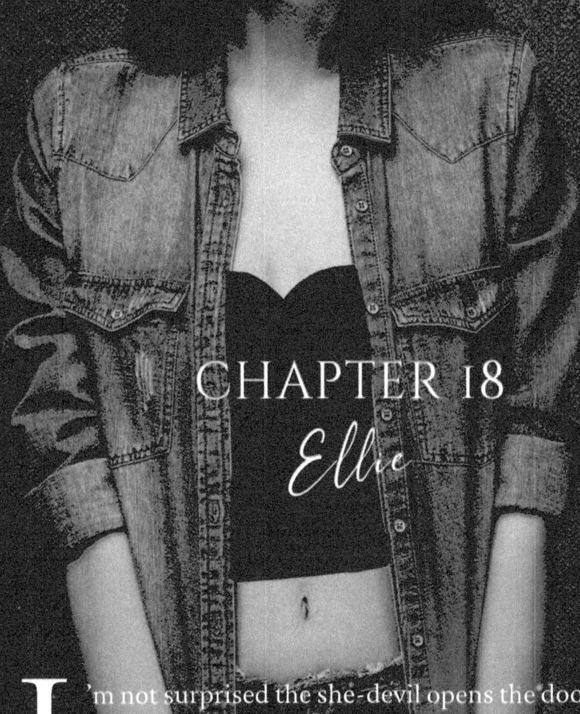

CHAPTER 18

Ellie

I'm not surprised the she-devil opens the door.

What does surprise me, however, is the fact she's only dressed in a red bathrobe, her stringy blonde hair with the black roots mussed.

Her mouth pops open in feigned surprise, and her hand flutters to her chest like a fainting maiden from Victorian times.

"Oh, Dominic! You're early! I didn't expect you yet."

"I'm a half hour late, Dana," Dominic responds dryly.

"Silly me." Dana releases a lilting laugh, one that sounds like a screech of a hyena. "I must've lost track of time."

She shifts slightly, and her bathrobe slides down. And all of a sudden, I'm face-to-face with a watermelon-sized breast with a dusky nipple.

Dom keeps his attention squarely on her face. "Can we come in, please? Harvey's expecting us."

"Oh, Dom!" She giggles again and takes a step closer,

her hand clamping down on his bicep. "You know you can call him Dad!"

Dom glares down at the offending limb as if he's visualizing cutting it off. I have to admit...I'm right there with him. Anger thrums through me, a low and steady rhythm, at the sight of her paws on his flesh.

Dear god. Does Dominic have to deal with this every time he goes to this house? I had no idea it's this bad.

My hatred for this woman increases exponentially.

Dana continues to ignore my existence as she bats her fake lashes up at Dom.

"It's so good to see you again. I had the cook make your favorite and—"

Dom doesn't even spare her a glance as he shoulders past her and enters the foyer. He stops there and extends a hand for me to take.

I smile gratefully, accepting the proffered hand. Heat dances across my cheeks as he very gently helps me remove my winter coat.

I've chosen to wear a cute, gray dress with a sweetheart neckline and a black belt tonight. The outfit's complete with a pair of black dress boots. I pinned back my brown hair in a stylish bun, leaving a few tendrils down to bounce around my face. I even chose to wear contacts instead of glasses and applied a small amount of makeup—blush, lipstick, mascara, and eyeliner.

I know I made the right choice to dress up when Dominic's eyes flare hotly and sweep down the length of my body. His gaze feels like blistering flecks of ash landing on my cheeks. He swallows heavily, and for a long minute, he doesn't speak. He simply examines me as if the rest of the world has faded away, and all he has left is this one moment in time.

I imagine I'm studying him much the same way.

God, is it even possible for Dominic to look more like a male model? The green shirt he wears is a shade darker than his eyes, creating a startling and sexy contrast.

My hands go sweaty the longer I stare into his eyes. Is this what people mean when they claim they get butterflies in their stomach? When they say fireworks explode all around you?

"Shall we go?" Dom extends his arm for me to take, and I do so without any hesitation.

His corded bicep feels warm beneath my fingers. I swear I see goose bumps fluttering across his skin at my touch.

"Dom!" Dana's shrill voice cuts through the moment.

I completely forgot she's here, too caught up in Dom and his eyes and his smooth skin and his—

Crap.

Head. Out. Of. Gutter.

With a sly smirk over my shoulder, one that would make Victoria proud, I say to the she-devil, "Thank you so much for your hospitality, Mrs. Rollins. And I'm not sure if you know this, but..." I wince in feigned sympathy, even as her eyes narrow with an almost incandescent fury. "I think your tit is hanging out."

Dom laughs loudly as he leads me towards the dining room.

✦✦✦✦✦✦✦✦✦

Dominic gives me a brief tour of the house, making sure to point out every location and the benefits they have for...feet.

Cheeky bastard.

"And this is the movie room. Pretentious, isn't it? But at

least all of the armchairs can recline. Perfect for putting your feet up." He throws me a saucy wink, and I shove him with a laugh.

"And this is the kitchen. Do you see that cheese grinder on the counter? Perfect for getting dry skin off the bottom of your feet."

"This is the bathroom. It comes with a personal foot-stool...to help with bowel movements. Dana read that somewhere in a magazine. No idea if it's true or not."

"This is the sitting room—not to be confused with the living room. Apparently, they're two entirely separate things. You see this fireplace? It's perfect for you to put your feet next to and warm up all of your little toes."

By the time we return to the dining room, I have tears in my eyes from laughing so hard, and Dom's sporting an easygoing grin.

But that grin dies a quick and vicious death at the sight of the four people already sitting around the long, wooden table. There are only two chairs left—one between his two half brothers and the other directly beside his dad, who's at the head of the table, and across from Dana.

"Dom! Ellie!" Harvey rises from his chair and spreads his arms exuberantly in either direction, as if he wishes to give us both a hug. "Welcome!"

"Thanks for the invitation, Mr. Rollins," I say pleasantly as I hover in the doorframe with Dom's hand on the small of my back. I take comfort in the warmth his palm seems to emit, seeping through my gray dress and setting my skin on fire.

"Please. Call me Harvey." He offers me another smile, one that shows a little more teeth than I'm comfortable with. "When did I last see you? Two years ago? Three?"

Honestly, I don't have an answer to that question. Dom

never invited me to his bio father's house before. Every interaction I've had with the domineering man has been at school events or functions.

It always struck me as odd how short Harvey Rollins truly is—maybe because he embodies a god complex that makes him appear feet taller than his actual height. He also has a paunchy belly that suggests he spends too much time drinking whiskey instead of going to the gym. His platinum-blond hair and vibrant-green eyes, however, are eerily similar to his son's.

"We saved you two seats," Harvey continues without giving me a chance to respond. He nods first towards the chair between the two twins and then at the one beside him.

"I was sort of hoping I could sit by Ellie," Dom says diplomatically, his hand tensing on the small of my back, his fingers digging into the fabric of my dress.

"I'm sure you can handle not fondling the poor girl for one hour," Dana retorts dryly, pursing her bright-red lips.

She's gotten dressed since I last saw her, though I can't say the tight red number is any better. Her breasts are practically spilling over the top, the fabric straining against her flesh. Her stringy blonde hair has also been straightened, the strands falling around her shoulders like corn silk. A rope of rubies curls around her throat like a bloody scar.

Dom looks as if he wants to protest, but one glance from me snaps his lips together. He nods his chin once and reluctantly moves away from me, heading towards the seat Harvey indicated. He looks more as if he's walking to his execution than a family dinner.

My heart pinches at the sight, and I'm suddenly desperate to erase the deep line between his brows, to see him smile and laugh the way he did only a few minutes earlier.

Dustin and Doyle both grin at me lewdly as I claim my seat between them.

Unlike Dominic and Harvey, both brothers have light-brown hair styled the same way—shorter on the sides than the top—and muddy-brown eyes. I honestly can't tell the difference between the two of them. I believe the one in the gray jacket is...Dustin. And that would make the man in the brown jacket Doyle. Maybe.

As Harvey attempts to reel Dominic into conversation, Doyle and Dustin turn their attention to me.

"So how is our little brother treating you?" the man I believe to be Dustin asks candidly. He gives me a slow, salacious once-over, and I feel thousands of beetles skitter across my skin at the unwelcomed glance.

"Is he...fulfilling all of your needs?" Doyle places his elbow on the table, nearly knocking over his glass of water.

I ignore both of them as one of the kitchen staff—an older woman with black- and gray-streaked hair—hurries forward to serve us the first course. It appears to be some kind of soup, and the enticing combination of smells wafting from it makes my mouth water.

I suppose if there's one good thing that will come out of this evening, it's eating like a queen. At home, Fischer had an army of servants and maids, but I much preferred to do things on my own...even if it meant having pizza rolls and Hot Pockets every night.

I only pick up my spoon when I see everyone else at the table doing so. Then, I take a huge gulp of the creamy, salty goodness. I still can't tell what type of soup it is, but I detect the taste of chicken and some vegetables. There may even be some gnocchi in it.

"How's the soup, Ellie?" Harvey asks with a beaming smile directed my way.

I startle at being addressed directly, and Dominic offers me a sympathetic glance. "Amazing, sir."

"Ellie...I told you already to call me Harvey," he gently reprimands, that darn smirk never leaving his face.

Both Doyle and Dustin shift on either side of me, apparently uncomfortable with their father's informality with me. I remember Dominic telling me that the two of them are immensely jealous of what they perceive as preferential treatment from their father towards Dominic.

I just think Harvey knows that he has two idiots living under his roof. If he hopes to continue his so-called family "legacy," he'll need to take Dominic under his wing and mold him in his image.

As if that'll ever happen.

"Harvey," I contend with a small smile of my own.

Does it look as fake as it feels?

My cheeks actually begin to hurt with the force of holding it.

Dana scoffs and begins to stir her soup slightly more aggressively.

"So how is school?" Harvey focuses once more on his soup and takes a small mouthful.

Dominic, who hasn't even touched his food yet, folds his hands on top of the table. "It's going well. Thank you for asking, Father."

I can tell it pains him to call the man that. Harvey Rollins is nothing but a sperm donor. Dominic's true parents are the two women who raised and loved him since he was a baby.

"I heard that you're keeping up your grades. That's good, son. Very good."

Doyle and Dustin exchange an indecipherable glance over my head.

Dustin leans forward eagerly. "Father, I actually wanted to—"

"And Ellie?" Harvey cuts Dustin off before he can finish his thought. He turns towards me, his lips curling into a rictus grin. "How is school going for you?"

"Oh." I blink at him, momentarily surprised at once again being the center of his attention. Dominic's frown deepens. "Very well. Thank you, Harvey."

"Are you still getting A's in all of your classes? You always were such a smart girl, Ellie. Your parents would be proud."

Something strange takes over me then at hearing Harvey Rollins talk so casually about my mother and father.

As if he knew them.

As if he were intimately familiar with them.

As if he had enough knowledge of who they were as people to come to this conclusion.

My heart plays leapfrog in my chest, and my hand suddenly turns to ice where it still grips the spoon. I'm not sure if anyone would be able to remove it from my ironclad grip. Blood sluices between my ears as I stare at the man who just dropped an atomic bomb in my lap...and then ran away with a giddy, gleeful smile on his face.

"You knew...my parents?" The words are a croak, a whisper, a hushed murmur—the silent pitter-patter of rainfall against a vaulted roof in the middle of the night.

Harvey glances up in confusion. "Of course I did. It was a shame what happened to them."

Doesn't he know that my life's imploding?

That I'm seconds from tumbling straight off the tallest

skyscraper, soaring through the air and splattering across the asphalt hundreds of feet below?

Dominic clears his throat somewhat desperately and forces the attention back onto him. "So, Father, I wanted to ask how work was going..."

The conversation resumes all around me, but I can't focus on that. I can't focus on any of that. Their voices enter through one ear and immediately leave through the other. Even Dustin and Doyle give up on trying to engage me in conversation, focusing instead on Dominic and Harvey, their eyes drilling holes into the former's head as if they wish they could kill him through looks alone.

Harvey...a suspected member of POP...

Knew my parents.

And was friendly with them.

Does that mean my parents were members of POP too?

What the hell am I supposed to do with this information?

The name and phone number in my purse—*Raymond's* name and phone number—has never felt heavier.

After dinner, Harvey insists I meet him in the office. I want to argue, but I know it will be futile. What Harvey wants, Harvey gets. I know he's already furious with me for skipping out before we could meet during the last family dinner.

I hate to abandon Ellie, especially after the revelation that her parents knew Harvey, but she promises me she'll be fine.

"Go," she says softly, giving me a pointed stare that would be impossible to miss.

Go...and figure out everything you can.

This may be our only chance.

I don't want to leave her alone with Doyle and Dustin, but Ellie promises me she'll be careful.

With no choice but to trust her, I follow Harvey down the long hallway and into his office.

To call it ostentatious would be an insult. It's the most extra thing I've ever seen in my entire life. A huge mahogany desk dominates the center of the room, and behind it rests a wingback black chair. Shelves of books line the right wall, but I know for a fact that Harvey hasn't read a single one. They're just for show, to make him seem more important. Smarter. Well-educated. The opposite wall has heads of deer with engraved plaques underneath.

Harvey Rollins has never gone hunting in his life.

It's a sham—everything about the proud, pretentious man is.

Harvey gestures towards the seat opposite the desk, and I sit at the very edge, ready to spring up and away at a moment's notice.

If Harvey notices my unease or even cares, he doesn't let it show. Instead, he reaches behind him and grabs a glass tumbler full of a dark-brown liquid—whiskey, more than likely. His drink of choice.

Surprisingly, he pours two glasses and hands me one. There's a twinkle in his green eyes I've never seen before.

"I know you're not twenty-one yet, boy, but if you're old enough to vote, you're old enough to drink."

After a moment of hesitation, I grab the drink and wrap my hand around it. I have no intention of actually drinking the damn alcohol—I need to keep my wits about me and have a clear head—but Harvey doesn't need to know that.

I watch the old man languidly sit in his chair, his small stature somehow seeming to dominate the space like a king in a grand hall. The power he exudes almost reminds me of Landon—but while Landon rules by instilling fear in people and exhibiting a cunning sort of ruthlessness, Harvey does so with arrogance and deceit. There's not a damn thing about Harvey Rollins that's genuine. His office only proves that.

"You're probably wondering why I keep insisting to

meet with you, son," Harvey begins, swirling the liquid around in his glass.

He takes a slow sip, his eyes never leaving mine over the rim.

I pretend to take a sip as well, but the vile liquid never touches my tongue.

"Father-son bonding?" I ask dryly.

He lets out a bark of laughter. "I suppose you can call it that..."

He absently begins to rub at the whiskers splattered across his chin. It's not a beard...but it's also not a five-o'clock shadow like Beckett has. It almost appears as if he superglued a bunch of blond pubes to his face.

"What do you want, Harvey?" I try to keep the impatience out of my tone, but all I want is to finish this conversation and get back to Ellie.

I know my girl can handle herself, but I hate having her out of my sight, even for a second. What if The Divine One kidnaps her while I'm preoccupied with this bastard? What if Dustin and Doyle try something? What if—

"You've proved yourself to me over the years," Harvey begins. He focuses on the swirling brown-red liquid in his hand, staring at it so intently that his eyes glaze over. "You're a smart boy. Powerful." At that, his gaze slides towards me, the emotion in it unreadable. "I know what type of men you surround yourself with, Dominic. Landon, for example..."

My heart beats painfully at the mention of my best friend.

"What about Landon?" I ask.

"The amount of power he's able to wield at his age... It's exceptional. He has captured the attention of a bunch of important players. Very, very important players." He casts me a pointed look then, one that I still can't read. I may as well be staring into a brick wall with all of the emotion he displays. "But so have you and the others."

I hesitantly lick my lower lip. "I'm afraid I don't understand."

Harvey doesn't beat around the bush but instead goes straight to the point. He's a man equipped to deal with lightning-fast decisions—does he buy or sell? Invest or pass? Open or close? He doesn't have time to deal with pleasantries, not with things he deems as important.

"There's a...club, so to speak, that I think will benefit from members like you and Landon and Zane Lorenzo. Hell, even that British kid would make a fine addition."

A club?

He couldn't be talking about...?

I straighten almost imperceptibly as I will my heart rate to slow the fuck down. Something bitter paints the back of my throat, and every time I swallow, it feels as if I'm chugging down battery acid.

"Of course, you'll have to prove yourselves. Take out the trash. Convince the club you'll be—"

I lean forward, effectively cutting Harvey off. "What do you mean? What is this 'club' you speak of?"

I decide that playing it dumb is probably my best course of action.

Hell, it may be my *only* action.

Harvey begins to swivel in his chair—back and forth, back and forth, back and forth. Through it all, his green eyes, the shade so similar to my own, never leave mine.

"All of that will come in time. But if you're interested..."

A part of me is appalled by what he's suggesting, but a larger part of me sees the benefit in his twisted words. Ellie is, for all intents and purposes, a member of the Paragons of Prosperity. If I can find a way to infiltrate the club, to join, then maybe I can keep an eye on her. Protect her from the inside.

I have no doubt The Divine One knows where my allegiance truly lies, but maybe… Maybe The Divine One doesn't know who all of the members are. They all wear masks, don't they? If my father can find a way for me to join, perhaps The Divine One will never discover I'm a part of his ranks—a lion prowling through tall grass, just waiting to strike at the unsuspecting zebra.

Or maybe this is all a trap, and I'm about to step directly into it.

Either way, Harvey is offering me information on a silver platter. I don't have an option but to accept it.

"I… I want power," I whisper, the words tasting like flaky ashes on my tongue. But I know it's what Harvey wants to hear. What *all* the members of POP want to hear. They worship a goddess who doesn't truly exist for exactly that. "If you can offer me more of it…"

"I can offer you the world, my son." He stands then, all five foot six of him, and crosses the room until he places a hand on my shoulder. Why does his grip feel like a branding iron, scalding the skin where he touches? "But you'll need to be patient. Everything takes time."

I force my lips to curl into a smirk I've seen Harvey wear way too many times—a mockery of a true smile, cold and malicious.

"I've worked with the guys to build an empire while I was just in high school. I know that shit takes time."

Harvey gazes at me as if I've just gifted him everything his heart desires, as if all of his hopes and dreams ride on my shoulders.

It's a bit...discombobulating, if I'm being completely honest.

How often as a little kid did I dream I'd make my father proud?

How many times have I sought his approval only to come up short?

I hate that a part of me craved his love...and I hate even more that a diminutive part of me still does, even when I attempt to eradicate that piece from existence.

"That's all I needed to discuss with you today." Harvey moves to sit back down and clasps his fingers together on the top of the desk. "You should probably get back to your girl before your brothers steal her away."

He chuckles, but the noise lacks any genuine humor.

Even still, the reminder of Ellie—and more specifically, the company she's keeping—has an ice cube skidding down my spine.

I jump to my feet immediately and offer my birth father what I hope is a respectful nod. "Thank you. For everything."

"Don't forget what I said, son." His penetrating eyes cut through skin and bone, baring me to his inspection. I wonder what he sees when he looks at me. A savior...or a massive disappointment. "Take out the trash."

"Of course."

It's only when I'm halfway out the door that I begin to wonder... What trash is he referring to?

There are five people I spend all of my time with—Ellie, Landon, Zane, Beckett, and Ryker.

Harvey mentioned three of them.

So who is the trash?

Ryker...or Ellie?

I DON'T KNOW if luck is smiling down on me tonight or if I'm just an idiotic rabbit walking straight into the trap hidden skillfully beneath a foliage of leaves.

As I hurry back to where I left Ellie, I notice something resting on the kitchen counter, directly next to the sink.

My heart hammers like a snare drum as I hurry forward and touch the object in nervous anticipation.

Harvey's...cell phone.

Fuck.

What are the odds that he would leave it behind? In plain sight?

My birth father is a lot of things, but an idiot isn't one of them. There's a reason he climbed to power and managed to remain there all of these years. He may be a small, insignificant man, but sometimes, they're the ones with the most influence.

My heart writhes madly in my chest as I stare, just stare, at the seemingly innocent phone.

There's no goddamn way I can take it.

But...

Icy coldness drips down my spine at the realization of this phone's purpose.

It's a trap.

My father is testing me to see what I'll do, where my loyalties lie. He's a smart man. He must know that he can't take my word at face value, so he set a trap for me to see if I'll fail or not.

Nerves rubbed raw, I take a tentative step closer, my mind churning a mile a minute as I think through what I could do. Maybe... Maybe I could call Beckett and ask him if he has a way of cloning phone data. Then I wouldn't need to take my father's phone at all.

I dismiss that idea almost instantly.

No, that would take way too damn long.

Maybe I could...

An idea begins to form—an idiotic idea, but an idea all the same.

Quickly, I pull my own phone out of my pants pocket and remove the blue phone case. Then, I grab my father's phone off the counter and place the case on it. By some miracle, we both have a silver back and no cracks on the screen. My phone should pass as his...for now.

On closer inspection, however...

Gunfire rips through my chest as I wait in the middle of the kitchen, waiting, waiting, waiting...

On cue, I hear the sound of footsteps, and my father enters directly behind me.

I pretend to be oblivious to his phone as I spin around, allowing my brows to crinkle. "Father, do you have any idea where Ellie is? I left her in the sitting room, but she's not there."

Harvey's gaze immediately flicks to the phone, and a tingle of triumph runs through my nerves.

Ha! I was right! It *is* a test.

Fucking asshole.

"I believe she's in the parlor with Dana and the twins," he says.

Once again, as if unable to help himself, he turns his attention to his phone. I wonder if a part of him suspected I'd fail this so-called test.

If a part of him secretly hoped I would.

I follow the direction of his gaze. "Oh. Do you want your phone?"

I grab it and begin to move towards him. Every step closer makes my heart rate spike.

One more step…

Just one more…

My foot connects with the edge of the counter, and I fall forward, gripping the sink to steady myself. At the same moment, I drop the phone into the sink…and straight down the garbage disposal, which has been left on by the staff, who are still in the process of cleaning up after dinner.

The phone makes a strange whirring and crackling sound as my father shouts in horror.

I eye the destroyed phone in wide-eyed horror— genuine horror, too. My poor, precious phone. I'm just grateful I backed up all of my pictures to the cloud. There are hundreds and hundreds of Ellie over the years.

"Shit. Shit. Shit. Shit," I murmur, blanching.

Hesitantly, my heart in my throat, I turn to face my father.

His face is red with rage as he volleys his glare between me and the phone, me and the phone, me and the phone. Slowly, that red hue never dissipating from his skin, he moves to flick the switch to turn off the disposal. The shattering sound immediately stops.

Now, this…

This is where my entire plan could go to hell.

I reach into the sink and grab the mangled phone. Just before I give it to Harvey, however, I click the buttons to see if it'll turn on.

It doesn't.

Relief washes over me, almost painful in its intensity, but I don't let it show on my face as I extend it towards my father.

Hopefully, this means the SIM card is destroyed too. Because if it's not…

Shit. Don't think about that.

"I'm so fucking sorry. I'm so—"

"Don't worry about it," Harvey snaps…though his tone suggests I definitely *should* worry about it.

The vitriol emanating from his eyes is impossible to miss.

"You can use my phone, if you want…" I fumble with the phone in my pocket—his phone, technically—and he eyes it with a dismissive glare.

"I think it's time you and your girlfriend left for the evening, Dom." He stares down at the destroyed lump of metal in his hands, a forlorn expression on his face. "It was lovely seeing you."

I don't need to be told twice.

Without waiting for the volatile bastard to change his mind, I hurry towards the parlor where Ellie sits cramped on the couch between Doyle and Dustin. All thoughts of phones and fathers flee my brain as I zero in on where their thighs are pressed against hers.

Dana sits opposite them on the one-seater, a similar expression of anger marring her face as she glares at her two stepsons. And lovers. I imagine the cunt is jealous they're giving someone who isn't her their attention.

Ellie flashes me a grateful, relieved smile as I hurry into the room and extend a hand for her to take.

"Dominic." The glare disappears from Dana's face, replaced by a simpering smile. "Are you leaving so soon?"

"Yeah, Dom. We just started getting to know your little friend." Doyle gives Ellie a look that has me visualizing carving his face up with Ellie's bedazzled stabby knife.

I imagine it would look quite good covered in blood. Definitely an improvement.

He should just be lucky Ryker or Zane isn't here to see the way he ogles her.

He wouldn't have survived the next few minutes.

"Unfortunately, we need to get going," I say as I practically push Ellie towards the front entrance and help her into her coat.

"Where are you heading?"

Dustin, Doyle, and Dana have followed us. The two twins stand on either side of the bitch, matching leers on their faces. It's Dustin who asked the question, though I don't turn my attention away from Ellie to give him a response.

"It was nice seeing you," I lie, the words triggering my fucking gag reflex.

"Until next family dinner, Dommy," Dana coos.

"And feel free to bring your new friend around whenever," Doyle agrees with another grin aimed at Ellie.

God, one day...

One day I'm going to murder everyone in this fucked-up family.

Until I do, I'll just have to be content with stabbing them repeatedly in my dreams.

The house is even more dilapidated up close. Fast food wrappers and empty beer cans litter the front yard and street surrounding it.

It's funny how my imagination changed some things to make it feel more...homey. I knew it was a piece of shit, but I'd forgotten just how bad it truly was until now, when I'm standing directly in front of it.

Have the front windows always been broken and covered with a bright-blue tarp? When did the rain gutters fall down to dangle precariously on both sides of the house? When did the roof lose the majority of its shingles?

God, I hate returning to this section of town, where the sky always seems darker, the weeds slightly longer, and the buildings more rundown. I know it's just my own perception of it, but I swear it's true.

The sky had been a brilliant shade of blue highlighted by a rich, yellow sun and fluffy white clouds. Now, it's a shade of gray so dark it almost appears black in certain areas.

The sun has been pushed behind dark clouds, promising that rain is imminent.

I suppose it's fitting—a dark thundercloud gliding over the town, just as it does our fates.

My mother stands on the rickety front porch, eyeing me as intently as I do her. Her face is gaunt and hollow, and purple crescent moons mar the skin under both of her eyes. Her dark hair resembles an oil spill that cascades around her shoulders in loose waves.

She lowers her gaze to my blue cast, and her cracked lips purse even farther.

"What do you want, Ryker?" Her raspy voice always makes me feel like a piece of shit.

Maybe because, at one point in time, she held more power over me than anyone else in my life. I was desperate to please her, to make her love me, to be the son she wanted. But through my friendships with the other guys and my relationship with Ellie, I've come to realize...she doesn't matter.

Nothing she says or does matters to me anymore.

An anvil pounds against my brain as I hurl daggers with my eyes at the sorry excuse for a woman who birthed me... and then abandoned me. I suppose her son came second to her love for drugs, alcohol, and shitty, abusive men.

It's funny how knowing you're going to die soon alters your entire worldview. Even a few days ago, I wouldn't have dared to travel back to this desolate home and come face-to-face with the conniving bitch who birthed me.

I notice that this time around, she doesn't pretend to be a doting, loving mother. How could she, when she had her dealer beat the shit out of me the last time I saw her?

She fiddles with the ties of her stained, blue bathrobe as I continue to stare at her, not answering her question.

She formulates an answer all on her own. "Are you here to get your revenge?" Her upper lip peels away from her yellowing teeth in disgust. "Hurt your own momma, boy?"

Again, I don't answer, and I can tell that unnerves her more than anything else. She begins to shuffle from foot to foot even more rapidly, her hands continually fiddling with the loose ties of her robe.

She tries a different tactic. "Ryker, baby..."

"Do you remember that one time when I was eight?" My voice is almost as raspy as hers, but while her ailment is a product of cigarette use and drugs, mine is of disuse and abuse. My throat aches painfully, but I continue on regardless, needing to get this off my chest, to allow these words to spring free. "When I snuck into the living room in the middle of the night and hid behind the couch to watch some television with you? You were watching a documentary. Do you remember?"

The glazed, confused expression on her face suggests that she has no fucking idea what I'm talking about. And that's okay. Some moments... Some moments stick with us. Those same memories may not have even registered to the others involved. I suppose it comes down to perception—what we perceive as life changing may not be significant to anyone else, thus making it forgettable to them.

"It was about a man on death row. Do you remember?" I take a single step towards her, and she flinches.

I find that I don't take any pleasure in the way her face twists in terror, in the way her hands ball into fists as if she hopes to fight me off, the way she shifts her weight.

"I don't know what—"

"I remember thinking... What would I do if I knew I was going to die? How would I want to spend my final days?"

For weeks after that documentary, those questions haunted me. I found myself staring at the scarce objects decorating my room and deciding which ones I wanted to play with one last time.

And then I thought of the people in my life... Who would I want to see before death inevitably claimed me? Whose faces flashed before my mind's eye? There were the obvious answers, but surprisingly, my mother was one of those names that reverberated around and around in my head.

Pain arrows through my heart, but I shove the instinctive reaction away. It seems to always make an appearance whenever I think about the inevitable conclusion of my story—death.

And...surprisingly...I find that I'm not scared.

Sure, the unknown is vast and terrifying, but the fear I thought I'd feel remains suspiciously absent. I know it's waiting just outside, raking its long claws down the window, banging incessantly and demanding to be let in. But as long as I keep the windows locked tightly and the doors closed...that fear won't come to me.

All I feel is a deep and agonizing pain that I'm leaving Ellie behind.

She doesn't need you, Ryker, I think bitterly—the same thought that has been ricocheting through my brain since I first made that deal with The Divine One. *She has the others. She doesn't want you. She doesn't love you.*

Doesn't love you.

Even still, I think of the note she wrote on my cast.

I heart you.

Did she mean it?

Does she mean it?

And if she does…as a friend or something more?

I always wondered why love was spoken in terms of "burning" and "fire." But just thinking of her has heat flowing through my veins. It's the only answer I need to that lifelong question.

I swallow, razor blades scratching at my throat, and focus on the reason I came here.

"You're my mother," I rasp out. "Blood."

She gives me a look of haughty dislike, one that has the hurricane in my stomach writhing madly.

"And you're a pathetic excuse for a son," she spits.

It seems as if my little story has helped her gain back some of her confidence. Perhaps she's secure in the knowledge that I won't kill her.

"You're a horrible mother, though," I continue on, acting as if I haven't heard her. "I know exactly what you get up to." This time, I don't hide my loathing for her on my face. I allow her to see all of the hatred I harbor for her, all of the disgust. "The way you sell your body to get your next fix. The way you'll rob and hurt your own fucking son to keep your dealer and pimp happy. The way—"

"Don't talk to your mother like that, boy!" she snaps, taking a single step down the steep staircase.

It creaks loudly beneath her feet, and I have to bite down a smile.

Even after all of these years, she still hasn't bothered to get that damn step fixed.

"So I'm giving you one last chance to redeem yourself. Live your life. Be fucking happy the way you truly don't deserve."

I can tell my words take her by surprise. Her mouth pops open, shock splaying across her haggard face.

"What—?"

I move towards the car I left idling on the street outside her house. It's one of Dominic's that he allowed me to use —fucking rich prick.

Feeling my mother's eyes on my back like branding irons, I pop open the trunk.

She descends the last few steps and gasps in horror.

Lying on a translucent tarp, his face covered in blood and his eyes unseeing, is Mom's dealer and pimp.

Fat, chubby cheeks.

Thin red hair that does very little to cover up his bald spot.

Huge potbelly.

Mom releases a gasping breath and then collapses onto the grass, her body heaving with sobs.

"W-what did you do?" she cries out, turning her tear-stained face up to me. I keep mine perfectly blank as I allow her to get one last fill of the disgusting man in the car before I close the trunk. "You're a monster!"

"You have one more chance to prove yourself, Mother." My voice is as cold as the frost permeating the air and no doubt decorating my onyx hair with snowflakes. "Make a life for yourself."

Mom can't speak through the great, rasping sobs that leave her.

"You can start over," I continue. "Get a motherfucking job. Make a life for yourself that doesn't involve whoring or drugs or—"

"I'll turn you in to the police!" Abruptly, my mother jumps to her feet and charges towards me, her finger extended. She jabs it into my chest as her mascara makes black tracks on her cheeks.

I blow out a heavy breath. It really is a shame when your parent disappoints you.

"I wouldn't do that if I were you," I say softly.

It's the barest breath of sound, almost lost in the howling wind pummeling the trees and houses surrounding us. A gray fog has descended, a gently blurring veil over the harsh lines of the neighborhood.

It seems as if the universe is agreeing with my dark, dour mood.

Mom trembles but remains standing in front of me. "What do you mean?"

"I'm very, very good at hiding bodies…but I'm also very good at making sure bodies are found." I allow a cold grin to tug up my lips, allow her to see the devil just underneath the surface of my skin. I'm the monster she created and cultivated with every verbal berating and slap to the face. Now, she's paying the consequences for her horrific actions. "Where do you think the evidence will lead if the police choose to investigate?"

Her lower lip wobbles, and her face drains of all color, becoming ashen. "You're lying."

"Am I?" I cock an eyebrow. "I wouldn't want to find out if I were you, now would I?"

"You murderous son of a bitch!" She aims a punch at my face, but I grab her wrist before her knuckles can connect.

I don't tighten my grip on her, though. Call it my fatal flaw, but despite everything she has done to me, I find that I can't truly hurt her. Not physically.

"You're a disgrace! A disgusting piece of shit! I always knew you were a monster! No wonder no one loves you!"

I release her as if her skin is toxic and take a step away, towards the car. I try not to let her words get to me, but they burrow under my skin and find a home there regardless.

"This is your last chance, Mom. Why don't you do something with your life?" I pull open the driver's side door and slide inside.

Still, I can hear her scream cutting through the air like a thousand knives. "I wish you were dead! I wish you were fucking dead, you disgusting asshole!"

My fingers whiten around the steering wheel.

In a broken whisper, I say, "In a few days, I'm going to be."

I don't look back as I put the car into drive and flee.

CHAPTER 21
Ellie

"I thought you said we were going to your moms' cabin?" I demand as Dominic pulls his car up the twining, gravel driveway.

He casts me a sideways look. "This *is* my moms' cabin."

"A cabin?" I snort and wave a hand in the air. "No, cabins are small and cute and cozy. This is…"

Honestly, I don't have words to describe the imposing building we drive up to.

The word "cabin" conjures up images of log houses with fires burning in the hearth. This monstrosity is what you'd get if a millionaire decided they wanted to try living in the "great outdoors." Which I suppose is actually kind of true.

There are three wooden garage doors that dominate the entire first floor of the house. Each one is separated by columns of what appear to be limestone stacked on top of each other. A huge, winding staircase ascends up a tiny hill towards the front door, which is nearly twice the height of me. The roof is shaped in an exaggerated V that slopes over a wraparound balcony. The top two levels of the house are constructed out of huge, burnished-brown logs.

"This is..."

"A sexy-as-fuck cabin that you can't wait to be alone in with me?" Dom asks with a teasing grin.

Or maybe it's flirtatious. I find that I can't tell for certain. My heart beats like a warm drum in my chest.

Laughing awkwardly—my face feeling as if it's on fire —I jump out of the parked car and move around the back to grab my luggage. Dom's already there, though, before I can even pop open the trunk. He throws his own duffel bag over his shoulder before doing the same to mine. When I move to grab my rolling suitcase, he casts me a frosty look, gently swats my hand away, and grabs it for me.

"You know I'm perfectly capable of carrying my own stuff," I protest, the heat in my cheeks turning into a blazing inferno.

Dom tosses a smile my way over his shoulder. "I know. But I like carrying things for you. Hell, I'd carry you as well if I didn't have my hands full."

Dear god. That did absolutely nothing to dampen the heat coursing through my body and sizzling in my veins.

Is he being serious?

Joking?

Why isn't there a manual for this type of stuff? I would call it—*What To Do When Your Five Best Friends Start Flirting With You.*

Dom waits for me to catch up with him before fishing in his jacket pocket for the mansion's—excuse me, I mean *cabin's*—keys.

"So...?" I ask as he fumbles with the door. "What happened with your father?"

Dominic had been uncharacteristically quiet the entire drive back home. I knew it wasn't intentional—he wasn't trying to keep me out or leave me in the dark. I could see the way his mind was working, the way he was constantly twisting all of the information he gathered around and around in his head.

I allowed him that time to process his thoughts, but now... Now, I want answers. I'm practically bursting at the seams in nervous anticipation.

"I think... I think he invited me to join the Paragons of Prosperity," Dom says numbly, pushing the door open.

Still, neither of us immediately enters the cabin.

"Is that what he said? He wanted you to join?" My heart rate accelerates at this revelation.

So it's true, then.

Harvey Rollins is a member of POP.

Why am I not even remotely surprised by this news?

"He never said the name POP specifically," Dominic admits. "But he did mention an exclusive club that the wealthy can join to gain more power and blah blah blah."

I offer him a soft, sympathetic smile. "What did he do when you told him no?"

I can't imagine Harvey would allow a slight like that to pass. He seems to be a proud man who rules his household and family with an iron fist. Dominic going against him would be seen as a personal affront.

Dominic blanches, the move nearly imperceptible. If I didn't know him as well as I do, I would never have noticed the way his face seems to drain of all color or the widening of his eyes.

Horror singes my blood as I gape at him. "You did say no...didn't you?"

"Ellie..." Dominic's entire chest seems to shake with the

force of his sigh. "You know it's not that easy. We need information, and if joining POP is a way to get it—"

"The Divine One knows you're not loyal to the cult," I whisper-hiss, suddenly feeling as if there are thousands and thousands of eyes on us. The tiny hairs on the back of my neck stand on end. "He'll kill you."

"If he even knows I'm a member." Dominic shrugs in a way that infuriates me. "There seems to be hundreds of members, and if I'm understanding my father correctly, this extends throughout the entire United States. I doubt The Divine One knows about each and every member, especially since they're all masked."

He slowly drops both duffel bags to the ground at his feet and takes a single step towards me. One of his long, golden fingers taps underneath my chin, forcing my eyes to his. I momentarily lose myself in those dazzling green orbs before I manage to regain my wits. Even still, I don't pull away.

"Dom..."

"I have your back, and you have mine, remember?" he says softly. "We're a team."

A tiny, tentative smile flutters across my face before I can contain it. "You're throwing my own words back at me."

"And is it working?"

"Dom...what you're doing with Harvey... It scares me, if I'm being completely honest." I grab his wrist and force his hand away from my face. Then, I interlock our fingers together so we're now holding hands, heat migrating from his palm to mine. "I don't want any of you guys to get hurt."

"We'll be more hurt if something happened to you," Dom whispers, and something in his tone—some sort of suppressed emotion—snaps my head up in surprise.

"Dom…"

He clears his throat and immediately lets go of me. When he takes a single step backwards, my body cries out for him, desperate to once again breach the distance between our bodies.

"But on a lighter note, I was able to steal my father's phone!" Dom says with forced cheer, grabbing a familiar-looking phone out of his pocket.

My brows furrow. "Isn't that your phone?"

"My case," he confesses, "but Harvey's phone. My phone had a…bit of an accident involving a garbage disposal." He makes a cross over his chest and then turns his stare towards the heavens. Above, a cloud passes in front of the moon, giving it a pearlescent luster. "Rest in peace, Phonie."

"Phonie the Phone?" I ask, bending down to grab my duffel bag before he can stop me. I throw it over my shoulder as he offers me a feigned glare of disappointment. "Real original."

"Would you rather I name her Bertha?" He tries to grab my bag from me, but I stealthily move out of the way so his fingers merely end up grazing the edges of it instead.

"Bertha the Phone?" I move inside the darkened cabin, willing my eyes to adjust.

It's almost…unnerving. All I can see is darkness and lumps of darkness and silhouettes of darkness and outlines of darkness.

So much darkness.

"What's wrong with Bertha?" Dom demands from behind me.

The door swishes shut—cutting off the dim glow of the moon—but before I can panic, the room flares with light.

"Bertha is…" I can't seem to articulate my thoughts as I

spin in a circle, unsure of where I want to look first. "A horrible name…"

If I thought the outside was grand, that's nothing compared to the interior.

A candelabra crafted out of antlers hangs directly overhead, casting soft, gold light over every available surface. While the floor is marble, there's a stylish red carpet directly in the center of the room, with a single table on top of it. And on top of *that* is a sculpture of what appears to be a…monkey. Maybe. Either way, it's crafted out of stone and glossy.

Two staircases, both constructed out of thick mahogany, branch outwards and upwards, joining together on a mezzanine overlooking the front entrance.

In the distance, there's a living room complete with darker floorboards, three red couches, a huge fireplace, and a flat-screen television. There's an immense window that spans the back wall overlooking the wilderness beyond.

I can't see anything on the floor above—only the internal balcony—but I imagine that's where the bedrooms and bathrooms are.

"Well, this is it." Dom rubs his hands down the front of his pants as he stares around the cabin with a curious expression.

I wonder what he's thinking, if he's trying to see it through my eyes. His features are unreadable.

"Upstairs, we have the bathrooms and bedrooms. Straight ahead is the living room. To the right of the living room is the kitchen and dining room. To the left are the game room and another bathroom." He places a hand on the small of my back. "There's a staircase that leads downstairs as well. Right now, it's still in construction, but my mothers hope to make it into more bedrooms and maybe add an indoor swimming pool. However, you can use the basement to access the garages and the outdoor hot tub."

"Holy shit, Dom." I stare at him, wide-eyed.

I've always been wealthy—both because of my parents' shipping business and Fischer's position as a state senator —but I've always considered that old money.

Dominic's parents, however, are self-made. They started from nothing and worked their way to the top. It makes me respect them even more.

A blush tints Dom's cheeks as he leads me up the staircase, his fingers gliding over the glossy railing.

"I know it's a little...much," he confesses sheepishly.

"It's gorgeous," I rush to say. "A lot of times homes like these look like...pictures you would see in a catalog. Beautiful, elegant, ostentatious, but not lived-in, you know? But I can see signs of your mothers' influences everywhere. And yours, too."

I smile at a painting taped to the wall—a tiny, stick-figure boy with golden hair holding hands with two women.

Dom laughs lightly. "I'm surprised my moms still kept that piece of crap. I made it when I was, like, six years old."

"Because they love you," I say simply as we head down a long hallway lined with doors.

Dom stops at one at the very end of the hall.

"This is the primary bedroom," he says. When I open my mouth, he rushes to add, "Don't worry. We have a maid service that stops by every week to clean and dust. It has been thoroughly cleaned since my parents last used it."

He reaches around my frozen body to push open the door and flick on the light.

"Dom... Are you sure? Don't you want the biggest

bedroom for yourself?" I ask as I hesitantly venture a step forward.

Like the rest of the mansion, the room is massive and elegant, encompassing a modern feel mixed with the rustic outdoors. A huge, king-sized bed rests in the center of the room covered in patterned quilts. It's flanked by two nightstands, each one holding a lamp and alarm clock. There are two dressers—one tall and one wide—and another flat-screen television, almost the same size as the one in the living room. A sliding glass door leads to a balcony that overlooks the forest.

"I'm taking the room next door," Dom explains. He points towards the door beside the wide dresser that I had initially dismissed as a closet. "That's the bathroom. It's between our two rooms. So...just lock it whenever you're in there, okay?"

"Yeah...yeah, okay," I murmur dazedly, still in awe over the sheer beauty of this place.

If I ever have a home...I want it to look like this.

A place made of warmth and love.

A place brimming with happy memories, evident in every framed picture, every arts-and-crafts project, every sculpture.

A place colorful and inviting and peaceful.

"I'll give you some time to shower and get ready for bed." He leans against the doorframe and crosses his arms over his chest. "It's getting late, and I imagine you're exhausted."

"Talking to those brothers of yours certainly took a lot out of me," I joke, but he doesn't laugh.

If anything, a frown touches the corners of his lips, twisting them down.

"They didn't...? They didn't try anything, did they?

While I was with Harvey in his office?" Real fear splays across his face. His hands are folded into fists where they still rest over his chest.

I rush to reassure him before his imagination can lead him down a nightmare-like path. "No. They just made a bunch of...crude comments." I make a face. "And a lot of sex jokes."

"I'll kill them," Dom says.

I can't tell if he's joking or not.

"No killing your brothers, Dom." I offer him a tiny smile. "I promise I've dealt with much worse."

He returns my smile with one of his own—the barest twitch of lips. After a long moment, he sighs and begins to move back down the hall, pausing when his back is to me.

In a voice like water trickling over rocks, he whispers, "Thank you for coming with me tonight."

The ache in my soul lessens, and my chest constricts. I'm suddenly crushed under the weight of my feelings for him, feelings I'm terrified to look at too closely, to put a name to. Either way, the intensity of it makes my stomach feel as if a large stone is sitting in it.

My heart leaps into my throat, causing my words to be choked and raspy. "Thank you for trusting me to have your back."

"Always," he says.

With that, he shuts my bedroom door gently. His footsteps sound in the hallway before he retires to his own bedroom.

Still, I don't immediately move from where my feet are rooted to the ground.

Oh god.

Am I...in love with Dominic?

Shit.

◆◆◆◆◆◆◆◆◆◆

I SHOWER QUICKLY and hurry to my bedroom in nothing but a towel. I put on a pair of clean panties before throwing on my pajamas—a thin tank top and a pair of shorts.

I use the towel to absorb most of the water in my tangled brown hair. I should probably blow-dry it, but I find that my body is too leaden, too heavy, to even consider that. All I want to do is collapse in my bed and sleep for hours.

Worry for Dominic is compounded with fear for the other guys. I haven't allowed myself to think too much about what they're getting up to, but I know they're doing it for me.

What have they found out about Senator Reece?

What is Ryker doing?

When are they going to return?

I only know they're okay from the occasional texts they sent me. Even Ryker—who is borrowing one of Landon's old phones—has sent a few assuring me he's fine and that he'll be at the cabin soon.

Still, knowing that they're all okay doesn't negate the worry swirling in my chest.

Dom...may be joining the Paragons of Prosperity.

Zane, Beckett, and Landon...are attempting to stalk a freaking United States Senator.

And who the heck knows what Ryker is up to?

With a huff of frustration, I toss the towel onto the chair in the corner of the room...and then immediately wish I hadn't when my wet hair sends goose bumps skittering across my arms.

I move to grab the towel and head back towards the

bathroom. I need to grab my clothes from today, anyway. I threw everything on the ground when I jumped into the shower—a huge, multifaceted monstrosity that could probably fit five people. The last thing I want Dom to think is I'm a major slob with no respect for his parents' house.

I inwardly cringe at just the thought.

Using my hip, I push open the bathroom door, already reaching towards the sink where I left my clothes.

Only to freeze when low, heated grunts reach my ears.

My heart is a speeding race car in my chest; I can't focus on anything but the repetitive thumping of it, the way it batters at my rib cage.

Dominic stands in the center of the room, naked, his hand around his erect cock. And wrapped around his hand is my pink, lacy underwear.

He hasn't seemed to have noticed me yet, too lost in what he's doing to have heard the door squeak open. I take a moment to study him unabashed, a burning sensation alighting in my lower stomach. I travel my gaze over the broad slope of his shoulders, his skin an enticing combination of gold and tan.

And then I look lower, towards the chiseled, hard curves of his ass cheeks and his straining member. My skin tingles with the intensity of it all.

But then I realize what, exactly, I'm doing—what *he's* doing—and panic daggers through me.

What the hell, Ellie?! Get out of there!

Dominic's eyelids droop, languorous and heavy, as he works his cock faster, my pink panties caressing his cock with every stroke.

My heart beats so loudly I can barely hear my own thoughts over the tumultuous pounding of it.

I know I should look away, should leave, should—

Dom's eyes snap open and home in on me. His mouth pops open in horror, his eyes turning to saucers, but he can't stop himself. Still maintaining eye contact, he comes all over my panties, a silent roar escaping him, the most beautiful kind of oblivion.

"Ellie…" His tone is rife with dread as he drops my underwear onto the ground. "It's not what it looks like."

"It looks like…" I swallow, my gaze instinctively dipping back towards his cock, long, thick, and golden. It seems to twitch at my attention, becoming hard once more. He immediately moves to cover himself. A blush turns his cheeks scarlet. "It looks like you were…masturbating into my underwear."

Oh my god.

What the hell am I supposed to do now?

Every inch of Dominic is smooth, masculine perfection. His chest and stomach seem to be carved by the gods themselves. And maybe that's what Dominic reminds me of—a Greek god from the time before, coming to smite unworthy humans and capture the hearts of women everywhere. He certainly looks like one with all of that golden skin and golden hair.

"Ellie." That blush doesn't leave his cheeks as he begins to back away, towards the door that will lead him to his own bedroom. "I'm so sorry. I thought you were done with the bathroom and were already in bed. I thought—"

"I should've knocked," I interrupt. Fire consumes my own face as I shuffle from foot to foot. "I should've…"

I can't stop thinking about what I walked in on.

The way his long lashes were like charcoal sticks against his cheekbones.

The way his lips were parted on a silent exhale.

The way his hand moved across his cock with a familiarity that suggested this wasn't the first time he had done this.

The way he exploded into my panties.

The heat in my face seems to migrate south, and I find myself shifting for an entirely different reason. Lust spears me, almost staggering in its intensity.

The thrashing organ in my chest seems to gain wings as I take a single step closer.

"Dominic," I whisper, and then swallow, "do you...*like* me?"

I don't just mean as a friend, and we both know it.

His face turns white—ashen, chalky, ghostly. He reminds me of a Victorian ghost haunting the halls of his house hundreds of years after his death.

"Ellie..." he begins helplessly.

I take another step closer, and this time, he doesn't counter it with a step backwards. Despite his hands still covering his cock from view, his eyes remain intent on my face. They focus on me with that unnerving gravity I've come to expect from all of the guys.

I don't know what comes over me then. It's like I'm no longer in control of my body—as if my time spent with The Divine One and the Paragons of Prosperity and even Raymond have reminded me how fragile and fleeting life truly is.

If I want something, I need to take it.

The crap I've been through over the months has been designed to make me bow.

But they're about to find out I'm a queen meant to rule.

With only a tiny bit of hesitation, I lift my hands and run them across the broad width of Dominic's shoulders, reveling at the softness of his skin. I move them lower until they graze his corded biceps and strong, muscular arms.

"Ellie, what are you doing?" he whispers.

"I don't know," I confess, my voice just as soft. It could almost be the wind that rattles the leaves on a tree branch.

I slowly push myself onto my tiptoes and press my lips to his.

When I kissed Beckett, I swore fireworks exploded all around me, butterflies erupted in my stomach, and my entire focus shifted until he was the only person I could see. It was the same with Zane and Ryker.

It's different for me and Dominic. Not better or worse... just different.

Fireworks don't detonate all around me, but I swear the world dims, becoming indistinct and hazy. Dominic is a blazing beacon in the blackness; a star shining through the darkest of nights. I'm keenly aware of him in a way I can't articulate. His hands are fire where they touch my skin, his lips an inferno.

And those butterflies? They don't come. Instead, my stomach seems to curl in on itself, flipping upside down and then twisting itself into a thousand knots.

All that exists, in that moment, is Dominic Black.

"Ellie..." Dominic moans against my lips, a hungry,

desperate sound that crashes over me like a tidal wave. "We should stop. We should—"

"I...I don't think I want to." I'm not sure he can understand my words, not when I'm still kissing him.

But he seems to freeze at my words regardless. His cock is rock-hard and straining against my stomach.

"What are you saying?" Dom pulls away from me and searches my eyes with a sort of desperation I've never seen from him before. Those green gemstones are physical caresses that send chills down my spine and lift the fine hairs on my arms.

"Would you believe me if I said I don't know?" I whisper as I lower my hand to his cock and stroke him the same way I did with Beckett.

Dominic's hips jerk forward instinctively, a low, pained grunt escaping him.

"We should..." He can't get the words out. His eyes have already begun to roll into the back of his head as his golden chest heaves.

"Don't you want me?" I tilt my head to the side as I study him.

His body... His body definitely desires me. I know that without a single doubt. But what about his mind? His heart?

The bravery I felt just moments before begins to dissipate, burning away quickly like paper in a fire.

Oh god. Did I read this all wrong?

Does he not want me?

Heat burns my cheeks as I slowly pull away from his cock.

Dominic grabs my wrist, keeping me in place

"Of course I fucking want you, Ellie. God, I've wanted you for so damn long, I've forgotten what it was like to not want you. To not be consumed by you. But you... You deserve better than me. Than any of us, really. We're bad, bad men, and you're so...pure."

"I'm not," I whisper shakily. "Not anymore."

Not after what I've witnessed.

What The Divine One made me do.

What I willingly did in my quest to end him.

What I'll continue to do.

"You are," Dominic insists softly. The hand not wrapped around my wrist lifts to cup my cheek. His thumb brushes against my lips, and another round of full-body goose bumps explodes across my skin. "But god help me, even if I destroy you, corrupt you, eliminate everything good inside of you, ruin you...I'll still want you. You're my greatest fucking sin, Ellie, but one I'd willingly get down on my knees in penitence for."

"Dom," I breathe, gunfire ripping through my chest.

How could he say that about himself? Doesn't he know that he and the rest of the guys are the best men I know? The most loyal and caring and loving?

"You asked me if I wanted you...and that's never been the question. I don't just want you, Ellie. I fucking love you."

His words rush over me like a gust of wind that just blew all of the blossoms from a cherry tree, and now they're dancing in front of me—impossibly magical and painfully beautiful.

"Dom..." My heart's beating too fast. Is that normal? Is a heart supposed to sound like a train speeding down the track and heading straight towards a brick wall?

"And I shouldn't. I know I shouldn't, but I do." His eyes are open and earnest, allowing me to see everything. "I hate myself for saying this to you—we agreed not to—but you're here...and staring at me...and I can't..." His lashes flutter shut. "Fuck, Ellie. I'm sorry."

"Dom..." I can't seem to say more than just his name.

"I know... I know it's not just me." He still doesn't open his eyes, but his hand also doesn't leave my face. His thumb continuously moves across my lip, the back-and-forth motion almost soothing. "I know you kissed Zane and did stuff with Ryker and Beckett."

My mouth opens, but what can I say to that? It's the truth, and I don't regret a single second of any of it.

I don't know what the heck I'm doing with these men, but every interaction, every touch, every kiss, feels inherently right, like my soul is being stitched back together after being separated for too long.

"And you still love me, even knowing all of that?" I ask in a choked voice.

"I don't care about that, Ellie," he whispers. "They need you just as much as I do. They lo—*care* for you too. I don't need to be your one and only. Just... Just give me a piece, and I promise to cherish it until the day I die."

Holy crap.

I have no idea how to respond to that confession, what to say. A part of me wants to jump into his arms and scream that I love him too. Because I do. God help me, I do.

And yet...

He's right.

It's not just him I love.

Would it be fair to say those three words to him when I still don't know what the heck is happening between me and the others? When I'm feeling split down the middle, my soul ripped into five perfectly proportionate pieces?

But there is something I can give him—me.

I want him.

That ache in my belly...

The heat in my core...

The fluttering of my heart...

They're all leading towards this one moment.

I've never given much thought to my virginity. It wasn't as if I wanted to be a virgin until I turned eighteen, but I never found a guy I liked enough to give it to. And perhaps a part of me was secretly waiting for a certain man.

Or five men.

But here and now, staring into Dominic's wide green eyes, I know that this is the right time. There's no doubt or hesitation in my mind. I want him just as fiercely as I want Landon. As I want Zane. As I want Beckett. As I want Ryker. They all may hate me because of it, but everything I've done has felt innately right.

My heart seems to crawl up my throat, becoming lodged there, as I twist my head to kiss his wrist. He shivers at the contact, his lashes fluttering once more.

"I want you, Dom," I say. Clearly. Succinctly. Without a hint of hesitation.

Shock splays across his face. "What?"

"Don't make me say it out loud," I say with a tiny, slightly hysterical giggle. And then my laughter tapers off. "I've never... I've never done it before," I confess. "But this feels right. Don't you agree?"

"God, Ellie..." He pulls me closer to him, until my body is practically merged with his. "Are you sure?"

I can feel how desperately his heart beats, the way his hands shake where they're resting on my hips, just above my waistband.

"Have you...ever done this before?" Like with Beckett, a part of me doesn't want to hear the answer, but at the same time, I can't expect all of the guys to be inexperienced.

They're the most popular and richest guys in school; they practically exude sex. Wouldn't it make sense that they'd have a plethora of girls over the years when I was nothing but their friend?

"No." Dom actually sounds appalled by the prospect. "I'm a virgin too. But are you sure you want to? With me?"

"Why do you sound so stunned?" I ask lightly, grazing my fingers down his smooth-shaven jawline.

I've never seen Dominic with anything remotely resembling a beard. I'm not sure he even knows how to grow one —not that I'm complaining. There's something appealing about Landon's stubble and Beckett's five-o'clock shadow, but I love seeing the sharp angles of Dom's face.

Heat spreads through the pit of my stomach.

"I just thought...out of all of us..." He shakily brings a hand up to run it through his hair.

I interlock my fingers with his and guide him back towards the room I've claimed as my own. He watches me with rapt fascination, almost as if he can't believe this is real, as if a part of him thinks this is nothing but a dream.

I wait until he sits on the bed before pulling my tank top over my head. I didn't wear a bra when I dressed in my pajamas, so my breasts immediately spring free, my nipples already beaded.

A lump in Dom's throat bobs as he swallows. "God, Ellie, you're so beautiful."

"You can touch me...if you want," I say shyly.

Dominic hesitates, but only for a moment. With a growl that almost sounds primal, he grabs me by the waist and hauls me forward until I'm directly between his naked legs. He splays his hands across the small of my back before moving them outwards, tracing the curve of my spine and the dip in my stomach. When he reaches my breasts, he pauses there to give my nipples some attention, flicking the buds back and forth with his thumbs.

I lean down to kiss him, and he moans against my lips, his fingers twisting and plucking at my sensitive nipples. I've never really thought too much about my breasts before. But the way Dominic plays with them sends a direct signal straight to my sensitive clit.

I rake my fingernails through his mussy blond hair, and another one of those strange growls escapes him. I freaking love that sound, so I do it again, tugging just enough to arch his neck.

"Fuck, Ellie…"

"Do you like that?" I whisper hesitantly.

Instead of answering with words, he nods.

For a few moments, we simply hold each other and kiss. Dominic doesn't stop his relentless torment on my breasts, but he also doesn't take it any further than that. I can feel how hard he is for me, though, how desperate.

"Do you have a condom?" I whisper.

I may be inexperienced, but I know I'm not ready to become a mother. At least we don't have to worry about any sexually transmitted diseases.

Dom freezes, his eyes popping open and spearing me with a "deer in headlights" look.

"Fuck." He quickly moves me away and hurries towards the bathroom.

All I can focus on is his golden ass as he searches the drawers and cupboards.

While he does that, I hastily remove the rest of my clothes until I'm naked and lying on the bed. It takes considerable effort to force away the pesky sting of self-consciousness that threatens to overwhelm me. Only a few people have seen me like this, and every time, I can't help but fear they'll find me...lacking.

Dom suddenly straightens triumphantly, a wrapper held in his hand.

"Ha!" He smirks at the condom. "I'm honestly surprised we even had any, though I suppose, knowing my moms, they were trying to—"

He cuts off abruptly when he finally notices me on the bed.

He swallows.

And stares.

Just...stares.

He doesn't say a single word as his gaze burns across my body, creating pathways of flames that blister and scorch in the most delicious way possible. I actually begin to feel light-headed from the force of it.

"Dom..." I sit up and extend a hand. "Come here."

He licks his lower lip but does as instructed, stopping when he's standing directly over the bed. For a long minute, he simply stares at me, his gaze unwavering, intense, penetrating.

Surprisingly, the self-consciousness from before has vanished. Maybe because he's staring at me with so much love, so much adoration, that I feel like the most beautiful girl in the world. My hair is still wet and wildly disheveled, and my body is covered in scars...but he doesn't seem to care about any of that.

He sees me. All of me—the good and the bad, the pieces of me I wish to hide away, and the ones I show the world. The light in my soul but also the darkness that creeps around the edges.

His gaze dips to the self-inflicted scars lining my wrist. So far, only Beckett has been made aware of what I did to myself in the days following Blair's death and the sacrifice I witnessed by the members of POP.

I can see the emotional turmoil raging in Dom's eyes as he swallows heavily.

"Ellie..." he whispers brokenly.

"Not now, Dom." I reach for him and drag him onto the bed with me. I'm not strong—there's no way I could've moved him if he didn't want me to—but he comes willingly, his hard, strong body hovering just above mine. "I don't want to talk about it now."

"But Ellie..." He pauses when I plant a kiss to the underside of his jaw. His breath hitches. "How long?"

"What?"

"How long have you been doing this to yourself?" He sounds anguished, broken, shattered.

When he stares down at me, I can barely understand the plethora of emotions flicking across his eyes.

"Not long." I gently cup his cheeks and run the tips of my fingers over his sharp cheekbones. "It was...a moment of weakness, I promise."

"Depression isn't just a moment of weakness, Ellie," Dom says. "Hell, I don't consider it a weakness at all. It takes a considerable amount of strength to fight the demons in your head day after day. But you don't have to do it alone, Ellie. I'm here for you. All of us are. If you have the urge to hurt yourself again...please...let us help you. I hate to see you hurt. I hate that you feel you have no other option."

He twists his head to kiss one of my scars, the softest press of lips against mutilated skin.

"Do you think they're ugly?" I don't know why I bother to ask that. Maybe it's that pesky self-consciousness once again banging on the door, demanding to be let in, persistently screaming at me to listen to her.

But I need to know.

"Nothing about you is ugly, Ellie," Dom declares passionately. "Absolutely nothing."

He leans down to kiss me again, and I lose myself in every press of his lips, every sweep of his tongue against my own. He places his hands on either side of my head to hold himself up, so I use the opportunity to run my fingers down his toned body, his spine, his ass.

Dom's lips leave mine, but only so he can move them to the hollow of my throat. I arch my neck to grant him better access, and he leaves a pathway of heated kisses down my neck and stops when he reaches the swell of my breast.

His eyes remain locked on mine as he licks around my aching nipple, never actually touching me where I want him to. I grip at his blond hair, but he simply smiles and continues his teasing torment, peppering kisses across my breast.

Finally, when I think I'm going to go insane, he sucks my nipple into his mouth and runs his tongue over the peaked nub.

My back arches instinctively at the contact, and it also serves to drive my breast deeper into his mouth. He bites down just hard enough that my nipple grazes between his teeth before he releases me and does the same to my neglected breast—teasing kisses followed by languid swirls of his tongue and the slightest pressure of teeth.

After he's certain my tits have received ample attention, he continues his descent down my body. My stomach. My belly button. My hip bone. And finally, my pussy.

The first swipe of his tongue against my most sensitive area has an explosion of lights detonating behind my eyes. I writhe on the bed, my fingers digging into the comforter as if it's a lifeline, as a surprised gasp escapes me.

"Does that feel good?" Dom's voice is husky—pure, carnal sex.

I wonder if anyone has ever heard him use this particular voice before or if I'm the one and only. I find that I like that prospect...maybe a little too much.

"So good," I moan.

He returns his face to my core and continues his slow, almost indolent laps against my slit. Everything about it is lazy and controlled. It's not the feverish frenzy that Ryker displayed when he ate me out on the piano.

"You taste delicious," Dom murmurs as his fingers grip my thighs, forcing them up. This new position has my ass lifting from the bed and my pussy arching closer to his face. I can feel his nose against my pubic bone as he licks and sucks at my most sensitive areas. A single finger joins the ministrations of his tongue, thrusting in and out of me, and I cry out.

"Dom..." I whimper, squirming.

"You want to come, baby?" A second finger joins his first, and he finally brings his lips to the bundle of nerves that has been neglected this entire time.

For someone who's inexperienced, he certainly knows exactly how to please a woman. I wonder if he's watched porn or read smutty romance novels or looked this up on the internet. The thought makes me flush from head to toe, lust rippling through me.

That, combined with Dominic's teeth grazing my clit, has me exploding, my fingers fisting in the blankets, my back arching, my mind blanking. It's the type of agony that's so pleasurable, you forgot it hurt in the first place— the sweetest, most exquisite type of torture. Bliss crashes through me as I come down from my high, feeling sweaty and sated...and still hungry for more.

"Dom, come here," I plead, tugging at his hair so he's forced to crawl up my body.

His hard chest presses against my nipples, creating a delicious friction, as I kiss him long and hard, allowing him to hear everything I'm too darn cowardly to say through the movement of my lips.

My heart rate accelerates when he pulls away to slip the condom on. He fumbles a little bit, his hands shaking, but he eventually gets the latex over his twitching dick.

When he notices me watching him, he offers me a slightly embarrassed smile. "This is nothing like the cucumber Mr. Morrison made us practice on."

A bark of laughter escapes me, and his eyes fixate on the way my breasts bounce with the movement. "I thought they only did that in movies."

"Nope." Dom grins as he holds himself above me, his golden arms straining. "Unfortunately, we had to correctly put a condom on a cucumber five times before we were able to pass the class. And Dane? He had a baby carrot."

I slap at his chest as another round of laughter escapes me. "You're full of crap."

"It's true! Mr. Morrison wanted to accommodate Dane's...smaller size." His smile is full of mischief as he looks down at me. "Of course, I got the biggest cucumber he had—"

I shut up his ramblings by pulling his head down to kiss him once more. As our tongues tangle, he lines himself up with my entrance, still dripping with the evidence of my arousal.

He hesitates, the tip rubbing against my folds, and whispers, "Are you sure?"

"I've never been more sure of anything," I promise.

He doesn't need me to say any more than that.

With a single thrust of his hips, he sheaths himself inside of me.

The pain… It's intense. I don't think I expected it to hurt as badly as it does. He's incredibly big, and the way he stretches my walls is almost harrowingly uncomfortable.

"Shit, Ellie? Are you okay?" Dom asks desperately, his fingers tentatively caressing my face.

"I'm…good," I promise, wincing at the sensation. "But I need you to move."

Dom hesitates, his eyes intent on my face as if gauging my sincerity, before he nods and does as instructed.

A gasp of pleasure escapes me at the friction of his cock pistoning in and out of me. It's unlike anything I've ever felt before—and certainly different from my own small fingers or even Ryker's and Beckett's. Pleasure ricochets through me as I hold on to him for dear life and allow him to fuck me into the headboard.

His touch renders me useless; I'm nothing but putty in his surprisingly skilled hands as he drives me to ruin.

"Dom!" I cry out.

"Not yet," he growls. In a move that surprises me, he pulls out of me and then spins me around so I'm on my stomach. "Hands and knees, baby girl. I want to watch your ass while I fuck you."

Oh my god.

I hastily follow his commands, unsure if my trembling arms will even be able to hold my weight. I just want to collapse downwards.

Dom lines himself up with my pussy once more, and I feel his hands on my waist, his fingers digging into my skin.

In one swift thrust, he enters me from behind, filling me up and stretching me completely.

I cry out, but he doesn't stop, doesn't slow down, pounding into me as his fingers tighten on my skin, branding me as his.

My breasts sway against the blanket, and the softness rubs against my nipples in a way that feels amazing.

"God, Dom!"

"You have such a perfect ass, Ellie," he rasps out. "I love watching it bounce as I fuck you."

Abruptly, he grabs my hair and hoists me upright—this new position has me on my knees with my back to him. The hard planes of his chest rub against my spine as he holds me up.

And still, he never stops fucking me.

"I've dreamed about this more times than I care to admit," he confesses huskily. "I touched myself to thoughts of your sweet pussy every night since I first knew what lust was. What sex was. Every time I touched my cock…every time I came…it was with your name on my lips, baby girl. Your." Thrust. "Fucking." Thrust. "Name."

He grips my breasts and resumes playing with my nipples.

"I wondered what color your nipples were. I thought time and time again what they would taste like. Every time you wore a fucking bikini… God, Ellie, all I could think about was ripping it away and sucking on those perfect tits." One of his hands drops lower and stops at my swollen clit. "And your pussy… Your sweet, perfect pussy. So pink and pretty for me. So wet. I always knew you would taste like heaven, and I was right." He begins to strum my clit as I gasp and cry out and scream his name. "But I never, not in a million years, thought you would allow me to touch you like this. I thought it would only ever be a fantasy of mine—an illicit daydream that I shouldn't fucking have but indulged myself in anyway. Who would've thought that this demon would eventually get the angel he loved for so many years?"

"Dom… Fuck, Dom…" His words rip apart a piece of my soul—a piece that belongs solely to him—and molds it into something new, something terrifying. My love for him is branded in my genetic makeup, etched onto my skin, tattooed into every fiber of my being.

"I love it when you swear, baby girl. I love it when you say 'fuck.'" His fingers move even faster over my clit. "Do you want to come?"

"Yes!" I all but cry.

"Then come for me, baby girl. Milk my cock."

I heard from more than a few girls that guys aren't always able to make the woman orgasm during their first time. I can happily say that isn't the case with Dominic.

My climax rampages through me, leaving tremors in its wake. All I can do is scream Dominic's name and pray that my body won't completely malfunction as wave after wave of pleasure ripples through me.

Dom's grip tightens on my waist a second before he comes as well with a possessive snarl. I can't help but wonder what it would be like for him to spill his seed inside of me…

If there wasn't a condom prohibiting us from being skin to skin…

Holy hell.

"Fucking hell, baby girl," Dominic murmurs, kissing my neck. He's obviously on the same wavelength as I am—the wavelength of unable to do or say anything but gasp and curse.

I collapse onto the bed facedown. A part of me cries out as Dominic removes himself from my throbbing pussy, but I'm not sure I can take any more today.

I hear him move to the bathroom—no doubt to take care of his full condom—and he returns with a wet washcloth. Gently, with the attentiveness I've come to expect and love from Dominic, he wipes at my core. I notice that the washcloth comes away red with blood. When I glance down, I see that the blankets are stained as well.

Embarrassment creeps over me, and I can feel my cheeks heat.

"I'm sorry about the..." I gesture towards the mess.

Dom's amused chuckle tinkers through the room.

"Now I have an excuse to bring you to my bed and cuddle the shit out of you," he says with a teasing grin.

He tosses the washcloth aside, stands, and then scoops me into his arms bridal style. I rest my head against his shoulder as he moves through the connected bathroom and into his bedroom. He sets me at the very foot of the bed, but only to pull back the covers. I crawl forward until I'm able to snuggle beneath the blankets.

Dom moves to lie next to me, and his arm comes up to spoon me from behind, pulling me flush against his body. He presses a kiss to the nape of my neck.

"I love you, Ellie," he whispers.

And in my sleepy state, I don't even realize I say, "I love you too."

But I mean it.

I really, truly mean it.

That's what scares me the most.

CHAPTER 23
Ellie

Something feather-soft brushes against my cheek, rousing me from my slumber. I've been having the most amazing dream, one that involved me, Dominic, a fluffy bed—

Not a dream.

Every muscle in my stomach tightens in delight at the feel of Dominic's muscular arms wrapped around my body, pulling me flush against his chest. I can feel the hard ridge of his cock pressed against my bare ass cheeks under the covers.

Is this what heaven feels like?

Dominic asked me if I'd ever envisioned hell, and I can honestly say that I hadn't. But my heaven... My heaven involves the five men who make my heart beat anew, who pump lust directly into my bloodstream, who make my skin tingle with emotions I still can't entirely fathom nor do I dare articulate.

Last night was...amazing. No, more than amazing.

Incredible. Is there a word that's even better than incredible? It was unlike anything I've ever experienced before. I feel tired and sated and so incredibly happy that my lips curl into a smile even before my eyes flutter open.

There's a little bit of pain between my legs, but even that is overshadowed by the pure adrenaline and contentment cascading through my veins.

Pure, unbridled *ecstasy*.

Heaven.

Definitely heaven.

That same touch from before traces the contour of my cheek before drifting to my jawline, soft, teasing strokes that have me squirming in Dom's arms.

But if he's holding me...

Then who's touching my face?

I snap my eyes open to see a familiar man staring down at me, so many emotions flickering in his gaze that it's impossible to tell what he's thinking.

Panic beats through me like a snare drum as I sit upright in bed and pull the blankets to my chest, suddenly keenly aware that I'm naked.

Holy crap.

Ho-ly. Crap.

The hallway light reflects on Landon's silvery eyes like a sunset on water. The tight set of his shoulders relaxes just a bit when he sees me looking back at him.

Oh god. What does he think of me?

Does he hate me?

Does he...feel nothing?

I don't know which one is worse.

Fear thrums headily through my veins as I hold his molten stare, willing myself to understand all of the thoughts percolating in his head. Why are his eyes always so unreadable, a blank slate wiped free of chalk?

He holds a single finger to his lips and nods his chin towards Dominic, who still sleeps obliviously beside me. For a moment, I can't help but soften staring at Dom's angelic face. He almost looks like an entirely different person in sleep.

The lines deepening the corners of his mouth are nowhere to be seen, and that perpetual frown—one that makes him look as if he's always attempting to decipher a difficult math equation—has smoothed out as well. He looks...peaceful, almost happy. It makes my heart skip a beat and my skin tingle.

But then I think about the man still standing by the side of the bed—the man who no doubt knows exactly what I was up to last night and who I was up to it with—and that familiar panic thrums through me. It brings about a sense of impending doom and despair, as if I have just messed everything up, ruined all of my relationships irreparably.

What did you do, Ellie?

What the heck did you do?

Tears prick the backs of my eyes before I can contain them, and a look of panic momentarily distorts Landon's strong, handsome features. He gestures towards the hallway before hurrying out of the room.

Quietly, so as not to disturb Dominic, I crawl out of bed and make a beeline towards his unpacked duffel bag on the floor by his bed. I unzip it and grab out the first sweatshirt I find and a pair of clean boxers. I know I need to change into my own clothes, but I'm almost desperate to hear what Landon has to say, overcome by a feverish need to face my punishment.

Will he be angry?

Will he tell the others?

Out of all the guys, I'm most confused about Landon's feelings towards me. The four others have made their intentions known, but not Landon. Everything he does is purposeful and meticulous. Does he even look at me that way? With lust and desire? Does he see me as a little sister? Is that why he didn't appear jealous at finding me naked in Dominic's bed?

But more than any of that, I'm terrified that I'm going to lose him. Lose them all.

What if they make me choose between them? I couldn't do that any more than I could choose a limb to sever. They're all an essential part of me, as vital to me as breathing. I can't live without my heart, just as I can't survive without a brain.

I would rather remain just their friend than lose any of them.

I can be their friend, can't I? I can forget about these stupid...crushes I have on the five of them, right? I can eradicate the memories of Zane's lips on mine, of Ryker's mouth claiming my pussy, of Beckett's cock in my mouth, of Dom pushing himself inside of me and stretching me to the limit.

I can, can't I?

It feels as if I'm walking to my execution, coming face-to-face with a firing squad, awaiting a noose to be wrapped around my neck and the floor to cave in under my feet. The finality of something ending hangs heavily in the air.

Landon's waiting for me in the hallway when I step out of the bedroom, shutting the door softly behind me.

I want to ask him how it went with Reece, if Beckett and Zane are with him, if Ryker returned from whatever mysterious errand he had to do, but I can't. The words get caught in my throat like a snowball rolling down a hill and coming to an abrupt halt when it finds resistance against a protruding rock.

Landon takes one look at my face and then pushes himself off the wall, coming to pull me into his arms. I can't help but breathe him in, though I'm not sure I should. I'm not sure I'm *allowed* to, especially after...

"Do you hate me?" Those four words escape unbidden, the softest of caresses, a gust of spring wind ruffling the tree branches.

"What?" Landon sounds stunned...and maybe even a little hurt. He pulls me away just enough to study my eyes. Those silver, metallic orbs lock in on my face, consuming the entirety of my attention. "Don't be ridiculous."

"I...and Dom..." I don't know how to articulate what I'm trying to say.

My heart beats just a little too fast to be healthy. That repetitive thumping sound is all I can hear, all I'm aware of.

"I know," Landon tells me gently. "And I know that you kissed Zane. And that you and Beckett shared a moment at the rest area. And you and Ryker...well...I won't go into details." A tiny smile curls up the corners of his lips before he turns serious. "Don't ever think any of us could hate you for something like that."

"Do you not...?" Once again, words fail me. "Like me? Like that?"

Does Landon not have feelings for me the way I do him? It seems ridiculous to believe that all five of my friends would have the same crush on me that I've been harboring for them. Perhaps I misread the entire situation. Perhaps Dom's dick has scrambled my brain. Perhaps—

"What did I say about being ridiculous?" Landon asks softly, his heated words fluttering against my lips. Another one of those soft, reserved smiles flutters across his face. "If you don't know the way I feel about you, Ellie, then either I'm an idiot or you are."

"How would you be an idiot?" My gaze can't help but flick to his lips before I force myself to meet his eyes.

God, what is wrong with me? I just slept with Dom, and I'm already thinking about kissing his best friend.

That can't be normal behavior.

"Because I thought I made it abundantly clear that I literally worship the ground you walk on, kitten. But if you're telling me I failed...then I'm an idiot," he answers simply.

"But...with Dom...and..."

The answer, surprisingly, doesn't come from Landon.

A pair of warm hands clasp down on my waist from behind, and soft lips brush against the underside of my ear.

"I told you, Ellie." Dom's voice is languorous, dripping with sleep and sex. It heats my skin more effectively than any furnace or fire could. "I don't need all of you...only a piece. That's good enough for me."

My heart feels like a battering bull in the middle of an arena. "I don't want to just give you guys a piece," I whisper. "I want to give you all of me."

"And you are." Landon brushes at a strand of my snarled brown hair. "I don't think you understand your capacity to love, Ellie. What you may only consider a piece... It's more love than any of us deserve."

"But Beckett...Zane...Ryker..."

"We'll talk to them," Dom assures me, his hands creeping underneath his baggy sweatshirt to brush across the smooth skin of my tummy.

Goose bumps pebble on my skin at the contact, the most delicious type of torment.

"And then we'll talk to you," Landon says. "No more

secrets, okay?" He presses his forehead against my own. This close, I can feel his stubble grazing against my cheeks, his lips feathering against mine in a mockery of a kiss. "Every single one of us got to have a first with you, Ellie... except for me." His voice is so low I'm not even sure Dominic can hear him, despite being directly behind me. "Zane had your first kiss. Ryker got to taste you first. Beckett got your perfect mouth around his cock. Dom got to make love to you. But me...?"

The smirk decorating his face now is positively devious—definitely unlike anything I've ever seen on Landon before. It's primitive and carnal and full of so much lust that I actually begin to feel dizzy.

Any thoughts that Landon may not feel the same for me as I do for him dissipate. There's no way he could be looking at me like that if he didn't desire me, want me, and—dare I say?—love me.

God, just the thought that he may is heady and intoxicating, more potent than any drug on the market.

"But you?" I ask softly, when it becomes apparent he isn't going to immediately finish the sentence.

"I get your ass," he whispers.

Sweet baby Jesus.

My heart rate spikes as a distant storm builds in my ears. Everything burns, a match striking against my flesh, but it's the sweetest agony imaginable. Desire beats through my blood as I hold his silver gaze edged with violet. They stand out starkly in the illumination of the room, promising me the world.

Promising me *everything*.

The two of us are as inevitable as a wave crashing against the beach and then returning back to sea.

"Landon..." I begin, my voice husky.

Our conversation is interrupted—and I'm not sure if I should be grateful or annoyed. But then both of those emotions are eclipsed by the pure joy I feel at seeing the face of our new arrival.

"Oh, *princesa!*" Zane all but throws himself at me, pulling my body flush against his muscular frame as he squeezes the life out of me.

"Can't. Breathe." I gasp exaggeratedly as he murmurs my name over and over and spins me around.

I laugh loudly, giddily, feeling buoyant and free. I don't know if it's because of Landon's words, my night with Dom, or the fact that Zane is here. And if Zane's here, that means Beckett is here as well.

And as soon as Ryker arrives?

We'll all be together again.

Maybe we were always meant to be like this—six broken souls who have somehow found each other in a world full of chaos and dissonance.

Maybe that's why I crave them all equally.

All too soon, Zane puts me back on my feet and then sheepishly runs a hand through his dark hair.

"I hate to...you know...interrupt all of the reunions, but..." He stares at Landon pointedly, and I swear a dark thundercloud rolls across our leader's face.

He folds his arms over his chest and glares at Zane. "Care to explain to Ellie and Dom what you're rambling about?"

Landon's tone reminds me of a disapproving parent who already knows what terrible thing their child did and wants them to admit it.

"Well, this is kind of awkward..." He rocks back on his heels. "But we sort of have a kidnapped victim in the back seat of the car." Zane holds his hands up innocently, as if to say, 'This isn't my fault. I'm innocent.'

"You *kidnapped* Senator Reece Whipers?" Dom explodes, incredulous.

"I wouldn't *technically* call it a kidnapping. More of a... grabbing someone off the street without their permission and bringing them to an undisclosed location in the middle of the woods to potentially torture and murder them." Zane scratches at the stubble lining his chin. "You see, we were doing normal surveillance, and I got really, really bored. All the good senator did was drink coffee, do paperwork, and talk on the phone to people. Super boring. Super-duper boring." He beseeches me with his eyes to understand, but I'm too stunned to do more than gape. "So I decided to do... you know...just do a tiny little kidnapping. Make things more exciting."

Landon pinches the bridge of his nose. "*A tiny little kidnapping.*"

"I nabbed him when he was stepping out of his favorite coffee shop," Zane continues proudly. "Shoved him in the back of the car. Drove away."

"Oh my god, Zane!" I place a hand over my mouth in horror. "Are we going to have Secret Service agents breaking down our front door?!"

"Don't be ridiculous." Zane waves a hand in the air dismissively. "Secret Service is only reserved for the president and vice president and their families. I think. At least, I'm eighty percent sure." His frown deepens before he forces an exuberant smile. "Anyway, no one will notice Reece is gone. Pinkie promise. He has a meeting in a small town in the middle of ass-crack nowhere. I had Beckett cancel the meeting...so yeah. His DC friends will believe he's at the meeting, and his small-town homies will believe he's still in DC. See? No one will notice a thing." His smile is forced, this baring of white teeth that eerily reminds me of a rabid animal. "Hopefully. Probably."

"I'm going to kill him," Dom mutters to no one in particular, gritting his teeth.

"How about instead of killing little ole me, we go talk to our mysterious senator, yeah?" Zane bounces from foot to foot eagerly. "And then afterwards...we can consider doing some light killing. But still not me. I like doing the killing, not being killed."

✦✦✦✦✦✦✦✦✦✦

SENATOR REECE WHIPERS looks surprisingly young.

I know all United States Senators have to be at least thirty years old, but Reece doesn't look a day over twenty-five. His face still has a young, guileless quality that gives him a youthful innocence—even when he's screaming obscenities at a frowning Beckett and a pissed-off Dominic.

He's not tied up, but then again, I don't think the guys need to do anything to restrain him.

Despite still being teenagers, all five of my guys are the same size or larger than Reece. Even without Ryker present, there's no doubt who would win if a fight were to break out between the five of them.

I take a moment to study Reece unabashedly from where I stand in the kitchen beside Landon and Zane.

He's a handsome man—even I can admit that—with light-brown hair, similarly colored eyes, and full, straight lips. Wearing a pressed dress shirt and khakis, he looks as if he's on his way to a business meeting.

Everything about the senator is utterly ordinary.

So what the heck does The Divine One want with him?

252

What does *POP* want with him?

Questions tumble around in my brain as I watch him scream at Dom and Beckett, demanding that they let him go.

"I'm going to have you all arrested!" he bellows, red splotches erupting on his cheeks, just above his cheekbones.

I zone out his incessant yelling and turn towards Landon and Zane. "Did you discover anything?"

"He seems like...a normal, law-abiding guy," Landon confesses, a prominent crease manifesting between his brows. "Beckett couldn't uncover any dirt on his computers, and he doesn't seem to be in contact with any known players of the Paragons of Prosperity."

"So why does POP want him?" I twist my head to stare at the man once more, noting the way his broad shoulders seem to strain against the fabric of his checkered dress shirt. He paces back and forth over the red rug in the center of the foyer, forking his fingers repeatedly through his mussy brown hair. "Do you think it was just a test? To see if I would be willing to do it?"

"No." Landon presses his lips together stubbornly and stares straight ahead, drilling holes into Reece's head with his eyes. "The Divine One could've made you take anyone... and he knew you would, mainly because he knew *we* would. He would use the opportunity for some sort of nefarious purpose. We just need to figure out what that is."

"Beckett's been trying to go through all of the stuff Reece has been most recently working on," Zane interjects, sucking on a chocolate Popsicle in a way that really, really shouldn't be sensual.

I blame Dominic. And Landon. And Beckett. And Ryker. And Zane himself.

Ugh.

"But Beckett's also been trying to go through Seth's and Harvey's phones as well," Landon confesses. "It's been taking time. He still hasn't been able to crack the code of that damn app."

"But if anyone can, it's Beckett," Zane declares with absolute certainty, not an ounce of doubt in his voice. "He's the second smartest man I know. Second...to me, of course. He's unable to sing and dance to Britney Spears while stabbing someone in the eye. Only smart people can do that. I call it interpr-*eye*-tive dance. It usually only works if you keep the victim alive—"

"Zane," Landon hisses, his gaze flicking to me.

No doubt, my face has drained of all color, my cheeks turning white as parchment.

Zane immediately glances at me and begins to laugh, the noise slightly hysterical. "I'm totally, completely, one hundred percent kidding. Obviously." And then, in a lower voice, he adds, "You need to listen to Miley Cyrus for eyeball stabbing. Britney is good for some limb severing, though."

Um...he's joking, right?

Is it wrong that a part of me doesn't care?

That a part of me welcomes his darkness, because I know it's an innate piece of him?

Maybe, maybe not, but I choose not to focus too hard on my own turbulent thoughts and the emotions they evoke within me.

Clearing my throat in an attempt to change the subject, I jerk my chin once more towards Reece. "What about his wife? Wouldn't she notice he's missing?"

"Ha." Zane claps his knee as if that's the most hilarious thing he's ever heard. "Yeah...that marriage? A total sham. It's the most loveless, twisted, fucked-up thing I've ever seen before. In just the few hours we've stalked them, I saw her hook up with five other people—Reece's driver, his head of security, his aide, his assistant, and even his female secretary." Zane winces in feigned sympathy. "That shit ought to hurt, man."

"And Reece?"

"Not oblivious to it," Landon confesses, "but he doesn't seem to care either way. I think he knows that his relationship with his wife isn't normal. It seems to be one of political convenience more than anything else. I doubt she'll even notice he's missing."

"It's rare that they even sleep in the same bed," adds Zane, wrapping his hand around his mouth to speak in an uncomfortably loud whisper only an inch away from my ear.

Loud enough that Reece's head snaps up and swivels in our direction. His eyes automatically home in on me.

And then immediately widen in terror.

CHAPTER 24

Zane

It's tiring work being a serial killer.

Honestly, I don't think people consider that when they sign up for the job. The lack of benefits, for one, puts a huge damper on what may have been an enjoyable career path. No health insurance for accidental stabbings? No dental for when you get your teeth knocked in by a wayward punch? No freaking life insurance? I don't even get a 401k.

It's bullshit, I tell you.

Bull. Shit.

And now, I have Landon pissed at me for what he calls, "going rogue," a senator who immediately clammed up after gaping at my girl like he just saw a ghost, and a knife that doesn't have any blood on it. Not a single droplet.

I mean, seriously, what's a guy got to do around here to get a warm body to stab?

Maybe the bloodlust in me would be abated if Ellie were to come over and cuddle with me, but *nooo*. She's currently in the kitchen with Landon, Beckett, and Dominic as they try to decide what to do next. Our friendly, neighborhood senator has been locked in a room upstairs.

We hadn't bothered with chains, ropes, and gags—much to my disappointment. Instead, Dominic simply placed the senator in a room...and then locked the door.

That's it.

Locked the freaking door.

It's entirely anticlimactic, if I'm being completely honest.

Not that it looks as if Reece is going to escape. He immediately sat on the bed and stared blankly at his pale hands, as if each finger held a different answer to the universe.

I've seen your hands, buddy. The only answer you may find is how to keep them incredibly soft-looking—because you sure know how to moisturize.

Beckett's typing away at his computer at the kitchen table, while Landon studies Harvey Rollins's phone, a furrow between his brows.

Me? I'm kicking my legs from side to side where I sit on the banister, wishing I were either balls deep in Ellie or blade deep in The Divine One.

Thoughts of Ellie have that familiar flash flood of fire coursing through my veins.

I saw the way she looked sandwiched between Dom and Landon in the hallway, her brown hair mussed, her lips parted, her eyes glazed with hooded desire and lust. My girl had just been thoroughly fucked, and I never felt more aroused in my life. More desperate for her.

If anyone else were to put their hands on her, I'd cut off said hands, shove them down their throats, and then skin them alive just for fun.

But if one of my friends touches her?

Fuck...can't they let me watch next time?

I'll be super-duper quiet. Honestly. The only thing they'd hear would be my hand around my cock as I jerked myself off and my low, heated grunts. That's it. Just some nice jerking and grunting.

Finally, when it feels as if I can't take it anymore, when I'm worried my body will burst with this strange, turbulent energy coursing just beneath my skin, I jump to the ground and head towards the door.

"Zane?" Ellie calls softly.

Trust my *princesa* to notice me leave. A warm, fluttering feeling explodes in my chest at the prospect.

Fuck, I love that woman.

"Yes, *princesa*?" I shove my coat on and slip on a pair of boots.

"Where are you going?" Her voice is rife with concern.

When I glance in her direction, I find that she has taken a tentative step closer. A frown tugs at the corner of her lips as her shadowed, blue-gray eyes penetrate all of my defenses as easily as a missile hitting concrete.

"Getting some fresh air." I flash her a cheeky smile and wink.

Getting some fresh air...so I stop thinking about fucking you against the table while Beckett, Dominic, and Landon watch.

But I can't really say all of that out loud, now can I?

She may think I'm insane or something.

She nibbles on her lower lip anxiously. All I can imagine is replacing her teeth with my own.

"Are you sure that's safe?" she asks softly.

Dom glances up then and offers her a look that curdles my blood with jealousy and avarice. I want to look at her like that, dammit—like I just fucked her into next week and know every inch of her body intimately.

Ugh.

One day.

One...day...

To...day...

Today...

Nope, dammit, Zane! Stop it!

"It's perfectly safe, Ellie," Dom reassures her. "No one knows this cabin even exists."

"And..." I pull open my winter coat so she can see the plethora of knives I've duct-taped into the interior. "I'm prepared. I have here my stabby knife, my super stabby knife, my super-duper stabby knife, my...well...this isn't really a stabby knife. It's actually a butter knife, but eh. Never really know when you're gonna need to butter some toast, huh?"

I pull my coat closed and zip it up as Ellie offers me an expression I can't quite read.

It's...soft.

Awed, even.

Warm.

Whatever it is has my stomach doing a running nose-dive straight off the highest cliff.

"Be careful," she says softly.

"Always am." I wink once more, turn on my heel, and step outside.

The frigid air immediately wafts over me, the chill finally cooling the heat in my veins and lowering my raging hard-on.

God, Ellie...

Princesa...

Just the thought of her pumps helium directly into my bloodstream. I feel light as air—floaty, even, as if I could soar hundreds and hundreds of miles above civilization and not worry about crashing back to the cruel world below.

For years, I wondered what true, genuine love would feel like. My parents never exhibited anything remotely resembling that—and if they did, they certainly didn't show it around me. I always considered love to be a beautiful painting slashed to ribbons with a knife. Something that exquisite couldn't last for long without being inevitably destroyed.

But then Ellie came into my life, warm and real and vibrant, and I realized that a man like me was actually capable of falling in love. Of putting someone above himself. Love can cut you like the edge of a blade, but it's worth it if the person you're bleeding for deserves your sacrifice.

In a span of days, she became my entire world.

The fact that some sick, sadistic fucker is trying to *destroy* my world now...

I growl low in my throat—the sound more animal than man—as I lean against the outside railing. The morning sun softens the ragged edges of the clouds, painting them in shades of red and orange. It's shaping up to be a beautiful day, even with the snow on the ground and trees.

A twig snaps to the right of me.

I unzip my coat and reach for one of the knives at the same time I spin towards the noise.

Who the fuck is there?

The Divine One?

A member of POP?

Ryker?

A frown dances across my lips when I realize that, out of all my blades, I accidentally grabbed my butter knife. Dammit.

Not impossible to kill with, but definitely harder.

I take a step down the steep staircase, staring into the shadowy forest...

When a monster plucked straight from hell emerges.

The scream I make could rival the high whistle of a train. If I were to shove a cattle prod up my ass and then circle it around, I imagine I'd make the same type of sound.

I jump onto the ledge of the balcony and then grab onto the nearest tree branch, hauling myself up. More and more high-pitched screams escape me as I eye the monster with horror.

The goddamn Chihuahua barks, a high-pitched squeaking noise that makes my ears bleed, as it hurries across the snow towards me.

"NO!!!!" I scream in terror as I attempt to climb even farther up the tree.

My hands and feet scramble for purchase as I cling to the branch directly above me, forcing myself up.

It's nearly impossible to breathe past the tightness in my throat. Fear jangles my nerves as the creature moves closer, its brown paws slamming against the stairs, its ears perked...

A car rolls into the driveway directly behind Landon's, and the dog stops below me, its head canted to the side.

I hold my butter knife in front of me with one hand as my other curls around the tree trunk.

"Be gone, demon," I hiss. "Go back to hell!"

The dog releases a pathetic whine, but if it thinks I'll fall for that shit, then it's even stupider than it looks.

It may appear sweet and innocent, but there's something repellent and malignant about this particular creature that makes me want to turn away and retch.

"I will make you a freaking toast sandwich, you motherfucking—"

"Are you...yelling at a ten-pound Chihuahua?" Ryker's voice is incredulous as he moves up the stone staircase leading to the front porch and my hiding space in the tree, his hands pushed into his back pockets and his customary scowl firmly in place.

The dog turns towards the newcomer, and panic spears through me as its tail begins to wag.

Oh god. It's going to eat Ryker, and then I'll have to explain to Ellie how one of her potential lovers got turned into dog chow. She'll blame me for not saving him, and then she'll come to resent me and hate me and—

The dog races at Ryker with a bark, and I scream in horror. If I jump down, I could throw myself between the two of them, maybe even tackle Ryker out of the way. I will only have a few seconds to get us both to safety, but it's definitely possible.

Ryker slowly lowers himself to a crouch...just as the dog runs at him with an excited yelp, its disgusting, slobbering, pink tongue coming up to lick his face.

"It looks like a stray," Ryker muses as he tentatively runs his hand across the creature's matted fur.

The monster continues to wiggle its tail as it rolls onto its back, presenting its belly for Ryker's inspection. Despite my protests, Ryker begins to scratch at the beast's tummy with slow, hesitant strokes.

"He's cute," Ryker says.

"So we're giving monsters genders now?" I ask haughtily.

Ryker gives me a look dripping with disdain. "Grow the fuck up, Zane...and get the fuck out of that tree."

"Nope." I cling to the tree even tighter. "No can do, my friend. I know what will happen if I were to come down."

One of Ryker's black brows arches. "And what would that be?"

"The demon creature will jump up and rip my dick straight from my body with his sharp, monstrous teeth. Then, he'll toss it back and forth like a damn chew toy. I'll, of course, be screaming in agony as Big Zane gets swallowed whole, but will that stop the mutt? Nope. He'll prance right over to me and then pee in the gaping hole that once housed my anaconda. So...no, I will not be coming down from the tree until that thing is gone. You got it?"

Ryker stares at me for a long, long moment, not saying a single word. Like always, his face is entirely impassive, not a hint of emotion flickering in his icy-blue eyes.

Then, a slow smile cracks across his face, and he says, "You named your dick Big Zane?"

"Perriwrinkle Teertime Toot Toot was already taken," I deadpan.

"Well, I need you to come down," Ryker rasps, still kneeling beside that wretched creature as he pets it—him, whatever—behind its ears. "I require...your assistance."

He makes a face at those words as if they cost him physical pain to speak out loud. It's immensely rare that Ryker will ever ask for help. He's usually so standoffish and independent, even with us, that the fact he's asking now pierces my heart like a javelin being thrown.

But...

"Not until the dog's gone," I huff.

The look Ryker casts me could turn lava to ice. "I have come to realize that I care more about this dog already than I do about any human aside from Ellie. If you hurt him, I will rip your insides out and then use them as a noose around your neck. You won't have to worry about the dog eating your dick off—I'll cut it off instead. Only when you're screaming in absolute agony, praying for death, will I drop you off a twenty-foot building and allow you to hang yourself with your own internal organs."

Ryker says all of this without pulling his eyes away from me. The dog, at some point, has practically crawled into Ryker's arms, his head nuzzling my friend's chest.

I blink.

"Did you just monologue about my death to me while holding my mortal nemesis in your arms?" I ask, incredulous.

Ryker doesn't respond.

"You know...if I wasn't entirely obsessed with Ellie, I might've gotten a little boner right then and there," I confess, much to Ryker's disgust. "You can't tell me that you don't like getting threatened with bodily harm. Like, if Ellie were to say she wanted to skin you alive, you wouldn't be a little, itty-bitty, tiny bit hard?"

I give him a conspiratorial wink, but he simply growls and stomps towards the front door, the dog still firmly in his arms like a smug motherfucker.

"Wait!" I bellow. "Where the fuck are you going with that thing? I haven't had time to apply holy water to the property!"

"I told you," Ryker growls. "I need your help. So I'm going to have Beckett look after the dog for a second. And I'm going to make sure to tell him—and Ellie—how much of a fucking coward you are."

Oh god.

I can already hear their voices in my head now.

Beckett will say something along the lines of, "Oh, I love

me some tea on this bloody fine afternoon. Oh! Crumpets! Tea. More crumpets! Monarchy! Bloody hell. Tea, tea, tea."

And Ellie will say, "Oh, Zane! You poor thing! I can't imagine the pain you've been through. Let me kiss every inch of your body to make you feel better. I love you so, so much. You're the best man in the entire world...and the best lover too."

Yeah. Totally nailed it.

I hold my breath as Ryker disappears into the house. He appears only a few minutes later with that familiar scowl firmly etched onto his face and the dog, thankfully, gone. Without paying me a second glance, he stomps down the staircase and heads towards the car he borrowed.

I remain where I'm crouched, my gaze intent on the door. What if that creature kills Ellie? Oh god. Maybe I need to go in there and protect her. Maybe I need to—

"Are you fucking coming?" Ryker snipes as he pops open the trunk of his car.

With one last reluctant look at the front door, I hop down from the tree and hurry towards where Ryker stands, his arms folded over his chest and a frown touching his lips.

"What the hell is your deal and...oh." I blink repeatedly. "Is that a dead body?"

My day certainly just got more interesting.

CHAPTER 25
Ellie

I move briskly around the kitchen, trying futilely to get my thoughts in order. There's a sort of desperation in my movements as I pull down a huge glass bowl and then begin grabbing ingredients at random from the cupboards and fridge. Eggs. Milk. Cocoa powder. Sugar.

"What are you doing, Ellie?" Landon asks, finally glancing up from Harvey's phone.

"Baking," I answer simply.

When he continues to stare at me in disbelief, I pull out my own phone and then begin to look up recipes at random before eventually deciding on chocolate fudge brownies. It doesn't look...too difficult. I'm ninety-nine percent sure I won't burn the house down, at the very least.

Beckett glances up as well. The glow from his computer screen lends a rosy flush to his cheeks and accentuates his multicolored eyes—the green as bright and vivid as a cedar tree while the brown resembles the soil it grows in.

"You don't bake," he points out, frowning.

"Well, I'm baking today." I drop the flour onto the table with a little more force than necessary.

White powder shoots out from the top and sprays across my face and the counter. Without breaking eye contact with Beckett, I aggressively wipe the flour from my face and then pour the entire bag into the glass bowl.

Beckett's eyebrows reach his hairline.

"Where's your guitar, Ellie?" Dominic asks gently.

I'm not surprised he's the first one to pick up on the turbulent emotions roaring within me. He knows that I'm fighting back in vain against the questions that crowd my mind.

"At." I toss some chocolate into the bowl and frown when the brown powder remains stagnant at the top. Oh...I probably need...water or eggs or something liquidy to stir everything together. Duly noted. "School."

I had packed the darn thing...and then forgot it after, what I like to call, Hurricane Landon.

When the guys continue to stare at me in bewilderment, I blow a strand of light-brown hair out of my face and plead, "Let me do this. Please? I just need... I just need to do something with my hands, or I'm going to go insane."

The warmth from my moment with Dominic seems to be fading from me like the sea drawing back from the land. Question after question piles up in my mind into a skyscraper of confusion, until I fear it's going to topple over and crush me under its immense weight. I feel as if we're no closer to solving this mystery than we were a few days ago.

"Has anyone been able to get the senator to talk?" I ask as I attempt to find a measuring cup amongst the plethora of drawers.

I swear Dominic's parents keep every cooking utensil known to man, most of which I've never heard of or seen before… Except for a measuring cup, which I can't seem to find anywhere. I sigh and pour half the bag of sugar into the bowl alongside the flour and chocolate.

"He won't talk to any of us," Landon confesses, scrubbing a hand through his brown hair.

Dark shadows rim both of his eyes, the only outward sign of his distress. I wonder how much sleep he has been getting. Maybe I could suggest we take a nap and regroup—

A high-pitched scream rips through the cabin, and all four of us pause. I swear I've never heard a sound quite like this before, more shrill and keening than even Dana's voice.

"Is that…?"

"Zane," Beckett agrees, already moving towards the window that looks out into the front yard.

Fear thrums through my veins as I venture a tentative step closer.

Oh god. What if something happened to him? What if The Divine One found him or POP or—?

Beckett pulls away the curtain…and then breaks into peals of raucous laughter. He actually clutches his stomach as he bends over, tears filling his eyes.

"Is Zane okay?" Landon asks briskly, the muscles in his shoulders tensing.

Beckett continues to laugh, ignoring his question.

Dominic, with a grunt of irritation, pushes the Brit out of the way and stares out the window as well. I watch his profile intently, searching for any signs of distress—his jaw unhinges, and shock seeps into his green eyes. For a moment, all he does is gape before he, too, falls apart in laughter.

Landon's taut posture relaxes marginally as he gives his friends an annoyed look.

"I'm assuming, by your responses, that Zane is fine?"

Landon asks dryly just as another terrified cry pierces the morning air.

"Oh yeah. He's perfectly fine," Beckett assures us, finally getting his chuckles under control.

He dabs at his eyes with his pointer finger and moves back towards the kitchen, Dominic a few steps behind him.

I eye the door warily, that same fear from before pumping into my veins. I know they assured me Zane was fine, but what if—

"Ellie." Dom places a hand on my shoulder, and warmth migrates from where he touches me, unfurling in my chest like a tulip in spring. "I promise you, Zane is one hundred percent fine. If something happens to him, it'll be his own stupidity that causes it."

My confusion mounts at his cryptic words, but Landon breaks into the conversation, steering it back in the direction of POP and Senator Reece.

"So what have you been able to find, Beckett, about our senator friend?" Landon's voice is cool and domineering— the type that warns us all what will happen if we don't get back on track.

I love the way he seamlessly takes control of the room without even so much as raising his voice.

I wonder if it would be the same in the bedroom...

The thought startles me enough that I almost drop the salt container I'm holding. Heat races through me, and I feel it settle in my cheeks.

Oh my god, Ellie, I mentally chastise myself as I begin to pour a little salt into the mixture. *Where did that thought come from?*

But I can't deny the delicate flutters that explode inside of me at just the thought of Landon using that tone of voice with me in the bedroom.

And what about Beckett? Would he be gentle and caring, the way he was in the rest area? Would he ravage my heart, body, and soul the way Ryker did in the music room? And what about Dominic? Now that we're both more... experienced, what will he do with me if he had the chance? While Ryker's kisses were all fire, Dom's were pure air, like being trapped underwater for minutes and finally breaching the surface. What would Zane be like? His unpredictability makes him exciting and passionate. His kiss proved as much.

What would it be like with all of them?

"Sweetheart." Dom gently wraps his hand around my wrist. "I'm pretty sure any chocolate recipe you may be creating wouldn't require two cups' worth of salt."

I blink repeatedly and instantly come crashing back down to Earth. Well, maybe not crashing—I quite literally dive headfirst through the air and go splat on the cool, unforgiving ground below.

Embarrassment creeps over me as I stare down at the pile of salt intermingled with the sugar.

"Oh."

"Yes, oh." Landon flashes me an amused smirk, and I wonder if he knows the direction my mind unwittingly went.

But that's impossible...right? He may be the smartest man I know, but he's not a mind reader. And I'm not so much of an open book that he'd be able to pick up every illicit, sexual thought rampaging through my brain.

Right?

Right?!

But the heat in Landon's silver eyes suggests otherwise.

I turn back towards my brownie mix just as Beckett clears his throat.

"As I said before, there's nothing overly exciting about the senator's activities." He pauses, and in the silence that follows, I can practically feel his unspoken words clawing at my skin like talons.

There's something he wants to say, something important, something he knows I may not like. It makes my skin prick with unease.

"What is it?" I try to keep my voice light and airy as I begin cracking eggs and tossing them into the bowl.

"One of Reece's most recent...bills," Beckett begins hesitantly, stumbling over that one word. "Or is it laws? Fuck, I can never keep up with American terminology and politics."

"Beck, focus," Landon instructs.

Beckett's lips purse, but he continues without complaint. "Reece has recently introduced a bill to the floor —though I have no idea why you call it the floor. I swear you Americans are so strange—"

"Beckett..." Landon warns in his low, rumbling voice.

"It's supposed to limit international imports," he admits. "I don't really understand everything, but from what I gathered, it's to help build more jobs on US soil."

A dark thundercloud crosses over Landon's face. I can practically hear the wheels grinding together in that analytical brain of his—dissecting all of the information, examining it beneath a microscope, and then coming to some sort of conclusion. "That would hurt a lot of shipping companies."

"Like Fischer's—" Dominic begins.

I grip the egg so hard that the shell cracks in my hand. Yolk and runny whites drip across my fingers and into the goo.

"Don't," I warn them all as I attempt to wipe the

eggshells off of my hand—not even caring when the majority of them land in the batter.

"Ellie—" Landon begins.

"I know what you're thinking, but I'm telling you, you're *wrong*," I insist earnestly. "Fischer isn't a member of POP. And he certainly isn't The Divine One." I know this truth in my very soul. It's embedded in my genetic makeup. There is no way that Fischer is a part of an organization that kills people. Not Fischer. And he would never, *ever* hurt me. Not ever.

Landon's saved from responding—and digging himself a deeper grave that I wouldn't offer him a shovel to climb out of—by the front door opening.

Ryker stands in the entryway, highlighted by the morning sun trickling in from behind him. It creates a hazy halo around his dark hair.

My heart beats frantically as I take in the strong lines of his face and the soft curve of his lips. I didn't even realize how badly I've missed him—how worried I've been—until he reappeared like a dark, avenging angel.

A beautiful, deadly, dark, avenging angel.

I quickly search his body for any injuries as he appears to do the same to me, his ice-blue eyes roaming over me in a way that, ironically, sends heat skirting up my spine. My pulse skitters as he takes a step closer to me.

For just a moment, before the door swishes shut behind him, I swear I see Zane clinging to a tree branch—

"What the hell is that?" Landon demands as both Dom and Beckett break into laughter once more.

My gaze finally homes in on the tiny creature in Ryker's arms.

"Oh my god," I breathe in awe as the dog yips and begins to wiggle its tail enthusiastically. I practically race across the room as I barrage Ryker with questions. "What's its name? Is it a boy or a girl? Where did you get this adorable baby?"

Ryker awkwardly attempts to hand me the dog, being mindful of the arm he still has in a cast.

"It's a boy," he grunts. "No name. Found him outside."

The Chihuahua is light brown and surprisingly fluffy, with a single white streak over his nose. His fur is matted, though, suggesting he hasn't been looked after in quite some time. He's also painfully thin when I wrap my arms around him.

"Well, I'm going to take very good care of you," I murmur in a baby voice. "Yes, I am. Yes, I am."

The dog stares up at me with wide brown eyes that cave my heart in on itself. Oh yeah. I'm a goner already.

Is this what love at first sight feels like?

"Dear god..." Landon breathes, a slight hitch in his voice.

Dom mutters something that sounds suspiciously like, "I always knew you had a breeding kink," but I ignore him.

I have no idea what he means by that, anyway.

Quickly, I move around the kitchen until I find a can of tuna and a bowl I can fill with water. I then place the little pup on the ground. He immediately runs to the water dish and begins to lap at it as my heart swells with happiness.

"Ellie and that dog are the two most important things to me," Ryker rasps, crouching in the entryway, his dark hands curled into fists. "If anything happens to them, I'll kill you all."

"You're choosing a dog over us—the friends you've had for years?" Beckett sounds more amused than upset by that prospect.

Ryker simply answers, "Yes."

He stands then and turns back towards the door.

"Wait!" I reluctantly peel my eyes away from the dog. "Where are you going?"

"Be five minutes," Ryker grunts, not bothering to turn around and face me.

Even still, I know I have his complete attention. It sends the butterflies in my stomach into overdrive.

Things have been different between us for a while now. I know I hurt his feelings when I claimed I wasn't his girl-friend...but how could I confess that I also had feelings for his four best friends? I can't even admit that to myself completely, let alone to him. All of this is so confusing, so discombobulating, that I feel as if I'm on a tiny sailboat in the middle of the ocean, attempting to survive the onslaught of waves. They toss me around until my only choice is to hold on for dear life or risk going overboard.

"Be safe," I whisper.

He tenses like I've struck him with a cattle prod before he finally glances over his shoulder. His eyes ensnare my own. I feel hot all over.

"*You* stay safe."

And with that, he hurries outside.

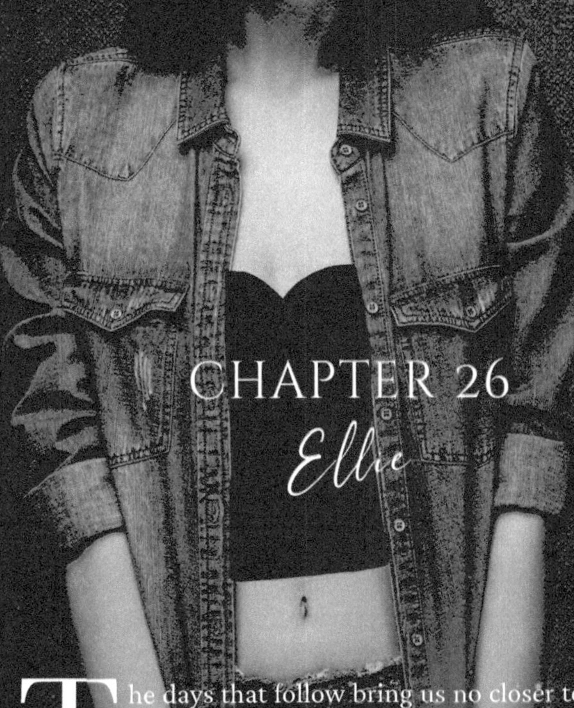

CHAPTER 26
Ellie

The days that follow bring us no closer to answers than we were when we started.

Senator Reece has refused to talk to any of the guys, and Landon is still convinced my brother is somehow involved, despite my adamant declaration that he isn't.

I feel as if I'm walking on eggshells around all of them as tensions crest—and no, I'm not talking about the eggshells in my failed creation that Zane called "Salt Chocolate Piss."

The only saving grace has been Frodo who has quickly become my new best friend, much to Zane's horror and the others' amusement.

But now....

"December sixteenth is tomorrow," I say where I sit on the couch with a freshly clean Frodo in my lap. I swear I had to give the pup five baths to eliminate all of the dirt encrusted in his fur.

Dominic sits on one side of me with Beckett on the

other. Ryker's crouched on the armchair opposite us, while Landon stands.

And Zane?

I tilt my head back to see him still lying on the rafters overhead, his arms crossed underneath his chin as he glares down at me. Or, more specifically, the dog in my lap.

"We have to hand Reece over to The Divine One." Landon scrubs a hand down his face.

His shadow has begun to grow into a full-on beard that only seems to emphasize the sharp angles of his face. His brown hair is in desperate need of a trim. But, more than any of that, is the exhaustion evident in his eyes—silver rimmed with violet. They're practically red from how little sleep he's gotten, made more evident by the purple crescent moons underneath each of them.

"We can't do that," I insist, noting the way Ryker tenses on the seat across from me. I ignore his strange reaction and turn back towards Landon. "Not until we know why The Divine One wants him. He could be completely innocent."

"No one's completely innocent," Dom murmurs darkly.

"Especially that demon pup in our girl's lap," Zane pipes in.

We all ignore him.

"Let me talk to him," I insist, the idea forming in my head like a tiny snowball being pushed down a hill. As it rolls, it collects more snow—just as my idea gains more merit every second I consider it. I'm practically shaking with barely suppressed energy. "You've seen the way he reacted to me. Perhaps I could get some answers out of him—"

"No." Landon shakes his head vehemently. "I don't want you near him."

Overprotective fools.

"One of you guys can be in the room with me," I contend, knowing that there's no way in heck they'll agree otherwise. "But please...just let me try. I'm the only one who hasn't talked to him yet."

"For good reason," Dom murmurs.

"Sweetheart," Beckett begins gently, "we don't know if he's dangerous—"

"Which is why one of you guys will be in the room with me." I fight the urge to roll my eyes, even as my heart swells with love for them. The way they protect me and look after me... God, I feel like a princess in a fairy tale surrounded by five sexy knights. It's like every one of my reverse harem novels coming to life. Just the idea of it makes me flush from my head to my toes. I push away my instinctive reaction and add, "Unless you guys don't think you can protect me."

It's a low blow—I know it—but if there's one thing I know about men, it's that you have to play on their egos if you hope to get anything done.

My five are no different.

They all immediately puff out their chests as indignation splays across their faces.

"Of course we can protect you," Landon growls instantly.

"I literally keep a knife tied to my penis just in case," adds Zane seriously.

Once again, we all ignore him.

I'm not surprised when it's Dominic who relents first, casting me a soft smile that has his green eyes glimmering.

"She's right. We agreed that we'll be a team, and as a team, we need to trust in Ellie's judgment. If she thinks she can get Reece to talk, then we have to let her try."

"Even though I hate the thought of Ellie near that asshole, I have to agree." Beckett makes a face. "Besides, while Ellie is interrogating Mr. Senator, I can continue working on the two phones. I'm so close to cracking that damn app."

Landon looks as if he would rather stick a hot poker in his eye than agree to allow me to meet with Senator Whipers. After a moment of silently staring down at his hands, he heaves out a breath and lifts his head.

"All right." He flicks his gaze to the silver watch on his wrist. "But we should go now. It's only a few hours until midnight. The Divine One may not know where we are, but I have a feeling that if we disobey him, he'll do everything in his power to track us down. We need to decide what to do with Reece, and soon."

Nervous anticipation thrums through my veins as I stand and wipe my sweaty palms down my pants.

I can do this, can't I? Talk to a simple senator?

I still remember the look of terror that flitted across Reece's face when he first set eyes upon me. My heart constricts at just the memory as something uneasy scuttles across my skin.

"Ellie."

Ryker's raspy voice turns my attention towards him, where he's still crouched on the armchair. The sight brings a timid smile to my lips. Trust Ryker to not actually sit in the chair but stand on it instead, as if he's worried he'll need to spring into action at a moment's notice. My heart expands and then meets resistance around the barbed wire surrounding it.

God, I want to fix things between us almost desperately, but with everything going on, we haven't had the chance to sit down and talk.

"Yes, Ry?" I take a step towards him.

A look of utter anguish paves its way across his face. The sight has my heart pounding erratically and cold terror streaming through my veins.

"Ryker?" I repeat.

"I—" His eyes shadow over; his lashes flutter against his cheekbones.

"Ellie," Landon calls from the staircase. "Are you coming?"

I twist my head to call up to him, "In a second!"

But when I glance back at Ryker...he's gone.

••••••••••

THE STENCH of sweat and body odor immediately assaults my senses as I step into the room we've chosen to lock Senator Reece Whipers in.

Despite being provided an en suite bathroom with a shower and toilet, it's apparent he hasn't bothered to use the former at all. His brown hair clings to his forehead in greasy waves, and his shirt is crumpled and smells vaguely of the beef stew Beckett brought up to him the night before.

He sits on the edge of the bed with his face in his hands, entirely still, almost like a statue.

Something I can't identify pinches my heart at seeing the obvious signs of his distress. When have I become so... flippant with other people's lives? It leaves an uncomfortable, nagging sensation in the center of my chest that's nearly impossible to ignore.

"Come to torture me?" Reece doesn't remove his hands from his face as he speaks, making his words muffled and indistinct.

Landon gently shuts the door behind us as I take a step

closer. He moves to stand in the corner of the room, though he never takes his eyes off of me. I can sense how tense he is, how unnerved he feels by having me so close to a man he considers a threat. He reminds me of a cobra coiled tightly, just waiting to spring and nip the ankle of the unsuspecting prey.

"I just want to talk," I whisper, my gaze flitting towards the locked window that looks down the side of the mountain.

According to Dominic, the window is constructed out of bulletproof glass, making it impossible for Reece to break. And even if he did, he would have to find a way to rappel down the side of the house and the mountain that looms below.

Overhead, the stars twinkle brightly, softening the trees in the distance and bathing them in a hazy, golden glow. There's no moon that I can see, and it somehow makes everything appear even darker and more ominous, despite the stars.

At the sound of my voice, Reece's head whips up, and that fear from before distorts his face.

"What do you want from me?" he rasps out in a broken, anguished voice.

My heart cracks down the center, and tears prick the backs of my eyes.

For the first time in my life...I feel like a monster.

My skin suddenly feels too tight, too itchy, too electrified, almost as if live wires have replaced my veins. I scratch absently at my arms as I hold Reece's despairing eyes and force myself to accept responsibility.

I... I did this to him. I broke him in ways that I'm not sure I can fix.

Guilt pierces my heart, but I force it away and take another step closer.

Landon tenses but doesn't argue with me as I stare down at the cowering, terrified senator.

"We just want to know about the Paragons of Prosperity," I say softly, trying to infuse my voice with warmth.

He blanches noticeably at the name. "I-I already told those guys." He turns towards Landon and then immediately away. "I have no idea what you're talking about."

"No?" I swallow and move to pull up the desk chair opposite the bed. Once I'm settled, I fold my hands on my lap and eye him gravely. "So you have no idea why The Divine One would demand I turn you in to him by tomorrow?"

His face whitens. "I...I..."

"We can help you, Reece," I continue gently, my heart pounding like a hummingbird in my chest. "But only if you tell us the truth."

His gaze flicks to Landon for a fraction of a second before he focuses once more on me. "Only you. I'll only talk to you."

"No way in hell," Landon barks, folding his arms over his chest and glowering. Possessiveness and protectiveness permeate his entire body.

"You know that's not possible," I tell Reece, maintaining that gentle, almost coaxing voice.

Reece's throat moves as he swallows. A bead of sweat trickles down his forehead, but he doesn't lift a hand to wipe it away.

"I'm not a bad guy," he whispers. "I've tried... I've tried so damn hard to make up for the sins of my past."

Nervous energy skitters just underneath my skin as I lean in even closer. "What do you mean?"

"I mean...that I tried to make amends for the things I've done...the things they made me do." He trembles, a despondent expression tainting his handsome features. "I've honestly tried."

"They... You mean the Paragons of Prosperity?" I whisper.

His words strike a chord of fear in me.

Reece nods once, terror dancing in his dark eyes. "I used to be a part of them...when I was younger. I was a stupid kid. A complete and utter idiot who wanted power and wealth and everything that was promised to me." He swallows again and moves his gaze so it's fixed on something just above my shoulder. It seems easier for him to speak to me that way. The words pour out of him like water surging down a waterfall. "But then...they started killing people, and they wanted me to do the same. I couldn't. I *couldn't*. Every life they forced me to take broke something inside of me."

His lower lip begins to tremble, and he finally reaches up to dab at the sweat on his face.

"So you left them?" Landon demands, pushing himself away from the wall and stalking closer.

Reece flinches at the suddenness of Landon's movements and curls in on himself.

Still, he answers, in a voice as cold as a gravestone in winter, "Can you ever really leave a cult?"

A frown touches Landon's lips. "Is that why The Divine One is after you? Because you tried to leave them?"

Dark laughter escapes Reece as he throws his head back. The noise scratches at my already frayed nerves like the long, twisted, gnarled fingers of a monster.

"I didn't just try to leave them," he hisses, the laughter

abruptly dissipating to be replaced by something significantly more malicious. "I tried to *destroy* them."

His words send a jolt through me.

I gasp. "What?"

Landon stares down at Reece with eyes the color of a stormy sky. "What do you mean?"

Reece scrubs a hand down his face. The anger from before seems to leach out of him as he slumps back on the bed.

"I worked with a division of the FBI, one that specializes in this sort of thing. I provided them with intel on the down-low. But..." He chews on the corner of his lips as his eyes flick to me and quickly back away again.

"But what?" I press soothingly.

"But the Paragons of Prosperity have eyes and ears everywhere. It may have started here, but it's much bigger than that. It's much bigger than anything you could ever imagine. They have judges, political officials, FBI agents, millionaires... You can't possibly begin to understand everything." Tears well in his eyes as he turns to me with a sort of desperation I've never seen before. "You guys are just kids. There's no reason to involve yourselves in this mess. Just keep your head to the ground, and you'll stay off their radar—"

"It's too late for that." My heart squeezes in my chest.

God, what I wouldn't do to just go back in time and do everything over again. Perhaps if I never begged Fischer to allow me to live in the dorms, this never would've happened. Perhaps I would've continued living my life in merciful oblivion, unaware of the horrors plaguing my small town right under my nose.

But...

That wouldn't change the fact that POP would still be

around, would still murder innocent women, would still haunt these streets like Grim Reapers with the capability of choosing who lives and who dies. And maybe that's what terrifies me most of all—The Divine One, the cult... They don't just consider themselves a religion or a group.

They like to play god with people's lives.

Smite down those who wrong them.

Build up the ones who worship them.

How long will it be before my guys are one of The Divine One's victims? Before I am?

An emotion I would almost describe as yearning crosses Reece's face as he maintains eye contact with me. In a breathy voice, he whispers, "You look so much like her."

"Huh?"

I don't get the chance to hear his answer.

The door to the room is thrown open, and Beckett stands in the doorway, looking wildly disheveled and flushed. His eyes are almost feverish as they land on first Landon and then me.

"Guys, you need to come downstairs. Quickly."

"What's going on?" Landon asks curtly.

"I was finally able to get into Harvey's phone," Beckett whispers. "You guys are going to want to see this."

Reece's confession rattles around in my head as I grab Ellie's hand and race out the door, stopping only to relock it behind us.

When we arrive downstairs, Dominic, Ryker, and Zane are already sitting around the television, their faces grave.

Fuck.

I push all thoughts of Reece aside to focus on this newest development. It's the way my brain has always worked—compartmentalize, choose what's most important to focus on, create patterns out of events that may appear insignificant to a normal person.

"Beckett, explain," I growl curtly as I throw myself onto the sofa.

As Ellie moves to go by me, I grab her waist and haul her onto my lap, her tiny body molding against mine instantly. I close my eyes and breathe in her scent, taking comfort in the fact that she's safe in my arms. If I were to lose Ellie...

I'm not sure what I'd do.

Beckett's face has tinged green as he moves towards the television. I see that Harvey's home page is pulled up on the screen—he must be mirroring it so we all can see.

"I was finally able to hack into the app. I just had to plug in a series of codes," Beckett whispers, and I hate how ashen he looks, how pasty.

It ramps up my unease almost instantly.

My arms tighten around Ellie, and I have to bite back a growl.

Patience has never been my forte, and I'm practically bursting at the seams.

"What did you find?" I demand.

Dominic scratches absently at his jaw.

"Fuck, man..." he rasps. "Just...fuck."

Beckett, after only a moment of hesitation, clicks on the dating app on Harvey's phone.

I expect to see the familiar lines of numbers and letters, but that doesn't show up. No. What I see is so, so much worse.

My heart batters like a charging ram as I take in the message boards and links.

"What the fuck am I looking at?" I squint to read a line better. "*I found a cute redhead with a great pair of tits. I strangled the bitch out while fucking her tight, little cunt. And then, when I was sure she was dead, I fucked that body for another two hours—*" I stop reading as disgust churns in my stomach and acid sears my throat. "Jesus Christ."

I'm suddenly desperate to get Ellie away from such depravity. I want to cover her eyes and shield her the best I can. Protectiveness permeates my body as I tighten my grip on her.

"It's… It's even more awful the deeper you go." Beckett's eyes are shadowed, the only indication that the things he's seen have scarred him irreparably. He flicks his gaze to Ellie once more, hesitates, and then reluctantly clicks on a link.

This one is a video. The person recording is hovering over a girl and shoving the camera in her tearstained face. Blood oozes from a wound on her forehead as she gasps and cries out in pain.

"You see this little bitch? Isn't she a pretty thing?" a male voice demands as he moves the camera down to her breast, mutilated with thick, zigzagging red scars. He pinches her nipples hard enough to get her to scream out.

"Please," she begs in terror as he continues to fondle her breasts.

I turn my gaze away in horror and disgust as the unrecognizable male continues his vulgar tirade.

"I wonder how pretty she'll look with her pussy wrapped around my knife?" he continues, and her scream echoes through the room, high-pitched and agonized.

It lasts for over five seconds before it cuts off abruptly.

Silence pervades the room. I'm not even sure I'm breathing anymore. My lungs seemed to have stopped working.

In the corner, I hear Dom dry-retching.

"Well, shit." The man laughs giddily. "I thought she would last a little longer than that. What a shame."

Beckett stops the video abruptly and squeezes his eyelids shut.

"What the hell is this?" Ellie breathes in horror. "Is this…murder porn?"

"There are all sorts of videos," Beckett whispers. "Some are similar to this, but some are…different."

"Games," Ryker rasps out. His ice-blue eyes are unreadable, but his jaw is clenched so tightly I can practically hear the bones grinding together. "There are videos of people playing games—but fucked-up versions."

"Tag with automatic assault rifles," Dom whispers.

"Dodgeball with bombs," adds Beckett.

Ellie squeezes my arms so tightly I can feel her nails digging into my flesh.

"Jesus Christ," she breathes, echoing my earlier words.

"This app allows you to..." Beckett pauses, swallows, and tries again. "It allows you to bet on who will survive these games."

"Like horses on a racetrack," Ryker growls.

"It also allows you to pay a ridiculous sum of money to watch these murder porn videos," Beckett confesses raggedly. "They even—god, this is so fucked up—allow you to buy these women and men for yourself to play with."

"Like human trafficking?" Ellie twists in my arms until her face is in the swell of my neck.

I hold her even closer, desperate to block out the rest of the world, the cruel, unforgiving fist of reality as it slams down on us.

Fuck. Fuck. Fuck!

"I don't know what the fuck this is." Beckett scrubs a hand through his hair, causing the meticulous strands to stick up in every direction.

"I do." Zane has been uncharacteristically quiet throughout this entire conversation. But just then, he glances up from where he's been studying the floorboards, his lips compressed in a perfectly straight line. Animosity saturates every pore in his body and has the flames from hell itself rippling in his dark eyes. It's a look that promises death—death on everyone who committed such unspeakable atrocities. "I imagine that this is how the Paragons of Prosperity have been making their money."

"The cult...their religion...Cassia... Has it all been a front so they can create *this*?" Ellie's voice is practically a screech against my skin. "A network for goddamn serial killers?"

I rub my hand back and forth across her skin, desperate to soothe her, to alleviate some of the tension I can sense running through her. I hate that she had to see that video, but I know what we promised each other—no more fucking secrets.

I just have to continually remind myself that Ellie is stronger than she looks.

"The rich being rich," Beckett responds dryly.

"And your father... He wants you to join this?" I swivel my head to stare at Dominic, who still appears as if he's going to vomit again.

Dark shadows line his eyes.

"What the fuck are we going to do, man?" he asks desperately.

"Maybe the senator is right." Ellie's voice is muffled from where she's still pressed against my skin. Her breath flutters against me in the softest of caresses. "Maybe we should just leave it alone."

"You don't truly believe that, do you, kitten?" I keep my voice low so the others won't hear, but I know Ellie.

She's not one to run from the injustices in the world. She may be meek and timid and soft-spoken, but she's made of steel. She's been forged in the fires of hell itself, and what emerged proved more durable than anything I could ever imagine. What she's been through... It would've broken most people. But not my Ellie. She's stronger than she's ever been, and I know she's only going to keep grow-ing, keep fighting, keep *surviving*.

"Wait!" Beckett's tense voice pulls my attention away from the girl in my arms and onto him. He's staring intently at Harvey's phone with a prominent furrow between his brows. "What the bloody hell is this?"

Instantly, I'm on alert, sitting upright on the couch with Ellie still in my arms.

"What's going on?"

The anger on Beckett's face... It's gone.

In its place is terror. Absolute fucking terror.

"FUCK!" Beckett declares, abruptly dropping the phone onto the ground.

Before I can even mount a protest, he brings his foot down and stomps on the thing until it's nothing but silver and black shambles at his feet.

"What the hell, Beck?" Dom demands.

Beckett glances up, his eyes as wild as his hair. "The app... It must've alerted someone... Or maybe Harvey got suspicious... Or..."

"Breathe, Beckett," Dom growls.

"I didn't notice it before. I swear I didn't. But they must've been tracking us for over a half hour, since I first was able to access the app—"

I cut off Beckett's ramblings with a sharp, "Tracking?!"

Beckett looks pale. "They were tracking the phone. They know where we are. I don't know how long until they're here—"

"It's too late." Ryker's voice is rife with a grief I can't even begin to understand.

He stands beside the window, only his fingers twitching to lift a corner of the curtains away to peer outside. I move to stand beside him, and my heart falls and shatters at what I see.

Standing on the driveway, in his blood-red robe and intricately engraved mask, is The Divine One.

And everywhere I look are more masked members of the Paragons of Prosperity. Each one carries a weapon—a knife, a saw, an ax, a gun, and even a fucking sword.

We're completely surrounded.

CHAPTER 28
Ellie

Terror seeps into my bloodstream like poison. It's the type of fear that makes you think you're choking on smoke—a thick, cloying substance that infiltrates your airways until you're gasping for breath.

Over Landon's broad shoulder, all I can see are members of the Paragons of Prosperity. They seem to be circling the house, huge, towering silhouettes bathed in a silvery light from the stars up above. Their black cloaks and faceless masks appear even more ominous in the darkness, as if they've been evanesced from the night itself.

"My god…" I breathe in horror.

My heart seems to be dragged up my throat as if barbed wire has been corralled around it and is now being tugged. Everywhere it touches, pain flares, white-hot and blister-ing. I bring my hands to my throat instinctively as if that could somehow quell the sudden and all-consuming pain.

Landon's face has drained of all color as he spins back

around to face me. Noting how close I am to the window, he grabs my shoulders and pushes me back a few steps.

Zane's there in seconds, wrapping his arms around me, seemingly—for the first time in his life—unconcerned about the dog I scooped up and now hold tightly. Frodo whimpers, obviously sensing the tension permeating the air, and leans up to lick my cheek.

"They must've tracked us using the app," Beckett whispers, the words seeming to be dragged up his throat, raspy and distorted. He looks as if he's going to be sick. "I'm so sorry, guys. I had no idea, no fucking idea—"

"It's not your fault," I rush to reassure him, recognizing the expression in his green and brown eyes for what it is —guilt.

It's the same emotion I saw every day in the mirror following Blair's death. The same emotion that twisted my insides into a dozen tight knots and ruined something in the depths of my soul, something I can't ever replace or even *name*. I don't want that for Beckett. The second he starts blaming himself for something he has no control over is the same moment he'll spiral. And if that descent into madness is anything like mine, he won't find himself in Wonderland at the end of it.

Beckett looks as if he wants to argue, but Landon is already hurrying away, taking control of the room once more. His silver eyes glint like two nickels in the dim glow of the room.

"They're after the senator," he growls out, already stomping towards the staircase to the right of the entrance. "They're here to make sure we hand him over at midnight."

Pain slices my heart to ribbons.

"You can't seriously consider handing him over," I

argue in disbelief. "He's actively trying to stop POP. He might be our only chance—"

"If we can believe a word he says," Landon points out, always the practical one.

"You saw his face when he told us his story," I tell him, resolute in my convictions. "He looked terrified of POP and The Divine One."

"It still doesn't change the fact that it's either you or him," Landon says fiercely. His teeth grind together as he holds my stare. "You know that we'll always, *always* choose you. Don't think for one second we won't."

Ryker, who has moved to crouch on the bottom step leading upstairs, winces almost imperceptibly. His face has been ashen since The Divine One and POP first arrived, as pale as a stick of chalk.

His aquamarine eyes meet mine and stay there. "Always," he whispers, and a dozen horrors I can't even begin to understand flicker in his gaze before he shields his expression.

"We could be handing over an innocent man to be killed!" I shout, my hands balling into fists.

There are some people who deserve death. Even I know that. There are depraved and twisted souls roaming this world—The Divine One included. But can I really say Reece Whipers deserves to die...or face whatever The Divine One has planned for him? He may not be a saint, but he's certainly no devil, and I have the distinct feeling POP plans to drag him down to hell.

My guys shouldn't be allowed to play judge, jury, and executioner. Who are they to decide who lives and who dies? I trust their judgment implicitly, but sometimes... Sometimes, I'm worried their morality is just a little too skewed, a little too biased.

An innocent man shouldn't die just to protect me.

I refuse to allow that.

"I'm not innocent." The rough, battle-worn voice sounds from directly behind me.

I turn, startled, to see Reece standing at the top of the staircase, Dominic's hand wrapped around his bicep. I hadn't even heard Dom leave the room to grab him.

The two of them make their way down the staircase, Dom's face drawn in taut determination while Reece just appears terrified. His entire body shakes like a leaf in the wind as he stops directly in front of me. Sweat plasters his brown hair to his forehead, and he appears thinner than he did even an hour ago—as if fear has sucked the life out of him, has vacuumed up a piece of him I can't articulate in words.

His throat bobs as he stares intently down at me.

"I'm not innocent," he repeats on a broken rasp. "The things I've done... They'd terrify you if you ever heard about them. They terrify *me*."

His gaze momentarily flits to the window, where the blinds have been drawn back just enough to reveal The Divine One standing in the center of the driveway, his cloak garnet-red in the twinkling starlight.

"Reece," I begin desperately. "There has to be another way—"

"I may be a lot of things, but I'm not a coward. And I refuse to allow a bunch of kids to pay the price for my sins." Reece's lower lip begins to tremble as pure terror flashes across his face—it's there and gone in less than a second, but it's enough time for me to see it.

For me to see it...and feel sick to my stomach.

I wonder if this is how lawyers feel when an innocent man they defended gets convicted of an unspeakable crime. My gut feels like it's full of boulders, and there's a dull rattling between my ears reminiscent of loose change.

"They could kill you," I whisper.

Reece offers me a sad, timid smile, one that doesn't reach his eyes. They remain as fathomless as a starless sky.

Tension thickens in the room as the inevitability of what he's about to do registers.

Isn't that what sets saints apart from monsters?

Sacrifice?

The ability to put someone else—even a complete stranger—above yourself?

I'm not sure if that's an adequate description for Reece Whipers, but just then, I'm grateful for him. Humans are arbitrary creatures who are capable of wicked, malicious deeds...but also beautiful, selfless acts.

"Maybe death is what I deserve," he responds, licking his chapped lips. With what seems like great reluctance, he pulls his gaze away from mine and turns to face the others. "I have some files hidden at this address. No one, not even The Divine One, should know about it." He moves towards a side table, grabs a piece of paper and pen, and quickly scribbles something onto it. "It's everything I've ever given to the FBI."

He turns to hand the paper to Landon; I note that his hand shakes so violently that it takes Landon two times to grab it from him.

"You said that you were betrayed...or at least, that you believe you were. Was it someone in the FBI? Is there anyone we can trust?" Landon demands, as matter-of-factly as possible. There's not a hint of inflection in his voice, not a hint of guilt that we're sending what could quite possibly be an innocent man to his death.

But then again...he was a member of POP once upon a time.

Can people truly change?

Or do the dark smudges on their souls remain no matter what they choose to do, like the grubby handprints of a child playing with charcoal?

Has Reece Whipers murdered someone before? Did he ever use the app that was on Harvey's and Seth's phones?

There are so many questions I want to ask the man, but none more so than one of his last comments to me—*You look so much like her.*

Did he mean my mom?

Zane's arms suddenly feel like iron around my waist as he pulls me flush against his chest. At one point, I would've found his embrace the most comforting place to be, but now, I only feel a sense of impending dread and horror as Reece surveys our group one last time. There's fear in his eyes, yes, but also a grave determination that once again reminds me of how handsome he truly is, even covered in sweat and days' old grime.

His hands curl into fists by his sides as he focuses on me —only me.

"I'm sorry, Ellie," he whispers.

And then, without another word, he pulls open the front door just enough to slip through and races outside.

My heart feels like a ticking time bomb in my chest as I watch through the window as he pauses on the front step, his hands raised in the air. Tears prick the backs of my eyes, and I imagine I may have fallen over if Zane's arms weren't around me. Ryker lunges forward and takes Frodo from my arms before I can drop the terrified, whimpering puppy.

God, what have I done?

What have *we* done?

Reece takes a single step closer, and the Paragons of Prosperity converge, five of them hurrying forward and forcing the senator to his knees. The Divine One remains where he stands in the center of the driveway, his golden mask canted to the side as he studies the scene before him.

I don't know what I expect—for one of the members to slice Reece's throat, for The Divine One to shoot the senator in the forehead the way he did to Blair, for Reece's blood to stain the snow bright red.

But none of that happens.

The members simply wrap some rope around Reece's wrists and force him to his feet. He stumbles, nearly falling over, but one jerk of his arm keeps him upright. With two members on either side of him and one behind, they march him away, disappearing around the corner of the mansion.

"Where are they taking him?" I whisper, my fingers grappling with Zane's arms, clinging on for dear life.

I know that I'm probably causing him pain—I can see the indents of my fingernails, like ten crescent-shaped moons on his tan skin—but he doesn't complain. He simply pulls me tighter against him.

"And why are they still here?" Landon demands, a note of indignation in his voice.

It's true. Despite the senator no longer being in view, The Divine One and the Paragons of Prosperity still remain, surrounding the mansion, their weapons held at the ready.

"Did they go back on their goddamn deal?" Zane hisses.

His breath stirs the fine hairs at the base of my neck and causes me to shiver.

"No," Ryker rasps.

We all turn towards where he crouches at the bottom of the stairs, the dog held in his arms. His pupils seem dilated, the black swallowing the blue I've grown so accustomed to, and his cheeks have taken on a rosy tint, almost as if he has a fever. Concern for him momentarily eclipses my fear for Reece and my worry over POP.

"What do you mean? Ryker?" My voice trembles.

And then, Ryker does something I never would've expected.

Not for the second time within a span of a couple weeks.

Not in front of Landon, Dominic, Beckett, and Zane.

He begins to cry.

He collapses onto the ground clutching the dog desperately to his chest as sobs wrack his body. He trembles from head to toe as he rocks back and forth.

"Ryker!" I fall to my knees before him, unsure of how to comfort him, unsure of what's wrong. I try to wrap my arms around his rigid body, being mindful of his cast and the dog still smushed between us. "Ryker, baby, please. What's wrong? Tell me what's wrong."

"I fucked up, Ellie," he whispers raggedly.

His husky voice—a voice that my mother may have called a smoker's voice due to its throaty quality—curls around me like smoke. I can feel his pain almost like a physical wound, a deep gorge directly over my heart that refuses to scab over.

"Ryker, what the fuck is going on?" Landon demands, but I detect something in his voice I've never heard before —fear.

And if Landon's afraid...

"I thought he had you," Ryker says desperately. He places the dog on the ground by his side and then pulls me completely into his lap, nuzzling the side of my face with his nose. "I thought The Divine One had you. When you were with Raymond. I thought..."

"He didn't have me," I murmur, running my fingers through his pitch-black hair. "He never had me."

"I...I made a deal with him." His eyes shine brilliantly under the fluorescent lighting as he stares down at me. They look like two tranquil puddles. "I thought I was doing it to protect you, and maybe...maybe I still am. But fuck, Ellie. FUCK!"

Cold spreads through me, stealing what little warmth remains.

"What deal, Ryker?" I whisper. When he doesn't immediately respond, I repeat, louder, "What deal, Ryker?!"

"Your life...for mine."

Those words seem to puncture something vital inside of me. A lung, my heart, another one of my internal organs... I suppose it doesn't matter. All I know is that a piece of me dies right then and there. It crumbles into dust particles so fine, no one will be able to reassemble it. Snakes slither in my stomach as I take a moment—just a moment—to digest Ryker's words, to turn them over and over in my head, to try to make sense of them in a way I can understand.

No. No. I refuse to believe it.

He couldn't have possibly...

No.

No!

My stomach lurches as terror like I've never felt before pierces me. It feels as if I put my soul up for sale and watched as it was won by the devil himself. That's what this agony feels like—hell.

Because losing him, losing any of them, would break me.

"No." I shake my head adamantly as I grip him tighter, wanting to meld our bodies together until you wouldn't be able to differentiate one from the other. "No."

"Ryker…" Dom's voice is rife with horror.

"No!" I say again as I grip both of his cheeks, forcing his eyes down to mine. "Ryker, tell me you didn't. Tell me—"

"I would do anything to protect you, baby girl." He desperately grabs at my waist. His hands curl in the fabric of my shirt as he tugs me even closer. "I love you, Ellie. I love you so damn much. I love you—"

"Stop it!" I scream, hating him for doing this, hating him for keeping it a secret, hating The Divine One, and, more than any of that, loving him so darn much that my heart physically aches. "Stop acting like this is goodbye."

"If it's my life or yours—"

"Jesus, man!" Beckett explodes. "You can't be serious!"

He kicks at the nearest table, not even bothering to watch it topple to the ground with a resounding smack.

"You should've goddamn told us!" Landon rages, beginning to pace. Desperation lines his face. His eyes are anguished, the silver appearing almost molten.

"If it's me or Ryker, maybe I could—" I begin, but all five of the guys immediately turn to stare at me.

"No!" they snarl simultaneously. Even Frodo gives a bark at that.

I turn my attention back to Ryker and run my fingers down the sharp lines of his face, wanting to memorize every square inch of him. God, he's so beautiful. Have I ever told him that? He needs to know that he's utter perfection —including his heart that he believes is jaded and tainted black.

Ryker and I have always been two flints rubbing against one another, creating flames where there was once nothing. We *burn* when we're together.

Doesn't he know that I need him more than air?

"You should've told me, you stupid idiot!" I cry as huge, ugly tears cascade down my cheeks.

"I'm so sorry." He places his forehead against my own, and for a brief moment, our tears mingle. "I'm so, so sorry. I love you, Ellie. I love you—"

"I love you too," I whisper roughly.

I've always been terrified of saying those words to anyone, but just then, they came out as naturally as breathing. I want him to know the depths of my feelings for him. Every scorching look he aims my way, every gentle touch of his hands, every brush of his lips against my own... It only solidifies how deeply I've fallen for him. He owns me.

They all do.

Shock splays across Ryker's face at my words, as if he didn't expect me to actually say them back.

"Don't—" he begs, cutting himself off abruptly. He squeezes his eyelids shut, and when he peels them back open, his eyes are glassy with unshed tears. "Don't say those words to me because you pity me."

I feel like an addict standing in front of a lit cigarette, just waiting for the plumes to blow in my face. All I can focus on is the contrast of his scars against my unmarked flesh. The warmth of his touch sends heat skittering through my body.

"I don't pity you, Ryker." Truer words have never been spoken. My breath hitches as I continue, putting every ounce of love, adoration, and reverence I feel for him into those three magical words. "I love you. I love you. I love you. I love—"

He slants his lips over mine, inhaling my final word. He tastes of salt and citrus—salt from his tears and citrus from the orange I saw him eating earlier today. Everywhere we touch, we dissolve into each other like raindrops sprinkling down onto the turbulent ocean, joining its swirling, fathomless depths.

I don't care that Beckett, Landon, Zane, and Dominic are watching.

I don't care that The Divine One and POP are waiting just outside the house.

I don't care that Reece Whipers may be dead.

None of that matters.

Only Ryker does.

And I refuse, absolutely refuse, to give him up.

It feels as if I'm cleaving my soul in two, but I'm finally able to tear my lips away from his. Before I can give in to the pleading in his blue eyes—which beg me to continue kissing him until the rest of the world fades away—I turn towards the others with a newfound sense of determination.

"There must be something we can do," I growl desperately, clinging to Ryker's shoulders as if I'm afraid he's going to run away if I release him.

"Ellie..." Ryker begins helplessly.

"We could fight," Zane suggests, his tone grave. "But there may be too many."

"Run?" Beckett suggests.

"For how long?" Landon demands. "They'll kill us if they ever find us."

"You should just let me go—" Ryker begins.

Landon whirls on him, the fires of hell spewing from his eyes. "Shut the fuck up, Ryker," he hisses. "You should've told us about your deal with POP the second it happened. And if you think for one second we'll sacrifice you, then you don't know us at all."

Ryker's jaw ticks as he holds Landon's molten stare.

"You'll sacrifice me in a heartbeat if it means keeping Ellie safe."

Dom moves to stand between the two men, a frown tugging at his lips. "No one will sacrifice anyone. We'll all get out of this shitstorm. Together."

He addresses the last word at Ryker, who appears as if he wants to argue but manages to hold his tongue. Even still, his body is rigid against mine, and his arms seem to be constructed out of granite.

"How close is it to midnight?" Zane demands.

Beckett glances at his watch. His face drains of color almost instantly. "One minute ago."

Before anyone can respond to him, the window behind Landon shatters in a flurry of shards. Ryker immediately twists his body to cover mine as the glass rains down on us.

"What the fuck?" Dom yells.

"Holy fuck!" Landon bellows.

A second later, he's yanking Ryker off of me and hoisting me into his arms. It's only then that I see the bottle at the base of the window, flames licking at the carpeting near it and climbing towards the lace curtains. Those catch on fire almost instantly, blazing red, yellow, and orange.

More and more bottles are thrown through the various windows surrounding the house until I'm practically choking on the pungent stench of smoke and ash. Fire licks at the wooden walls like a demon crawling out of hell.

"The basement!" Dom rasps, covering his nose and mouth with his arm. He coughs wildly. "There's an exit in the basement!"

And, with Landon's arms like impenetrable claws around me, we break into a run through the burning house.

CHAPTER 29
Ryker

It isn't long until the smoke engulfs me, encircling me in a wispy, gray hug. The only thing that propels me forward, that gives me the strength to put one foot in front of the other, is the sight of Ellie in Landon's arms.

She coughs, twisting her face until it's in the small of his neck, as Dominic leads our group down a wooden staircase that creaks beneath our feet. Behind me, Frodo barks, and Beckett murmurs soothingly to the dog.

My fault.

Always my fault.

My fault.

This time, when my breathing becomes ragged, it's not because of the smoke infiltrating my lungs. It's something much more carnal than that, more primitive.

Guilt.

Because of me, Dominic's cabin has gone up in flames.

Because of me, one of my best friends could become hurt. They could *die.*

Because of me, Ellie is a target.

Apprehension is a lead weight in my chest as I debate turning right the fuck around, charging out the front door, and accepting my fate like a goddamn man. Would it be a quick and painless death? Would The Divine One make me suffer?

Prickles of heat run up and down my skin, causing my heart to beat erratically. Fear is funny like that. It causes the sensations one would feel when experiencing emotions such as...lust. And love.

Your palms turn damp, your hands begin to shake, your heart races, and your skin burns as if it's been consumed by flames. But there's one fundamental difference between love and fear.

When your palms finally dry up, when your hands remain still, when your heartbeat slows to a repetitive rhythm, when the fire eating your skin is doused... After all of that, you're left with an airy, buoyant sensation, as if your bones are made of helium.

Fear, on the other hand, is the snake slithering beneath the undergrowth, searching for something to devour. Once it does, it sinks its sharp fangs into you and refuses to let you go, forcing poison straight into your bloodstream.

Everything comes down to this—I don't want to die.

But I may not have a choice.

Fire belches black smoke that eats at the walls on either side of us, but fortunately, the majority of the basement seems to be unburdened by the raging inferno.

Dom turns to us at the bottom of the staircase, soot darkening his cheeks and casting black highlights in his platinum-blond hair.

"My mothers are having a basement constructed," Dom pants, coughing into his sleeve. "I doubt anyone knows this area even exists. There's a door that should lead outside, at the base of the mountain."

Dom once again hurries through the concrete jungle full of cement walls, wooden floorboards, and pipes lining the ceiling. Tools litter the ground, and rolled-up rugs lean against the far wall.

Landon and Ellie are only a step behind him.

This is it.

I can turn around right now.

Go back upstairs.

Come face-to-face with The Divine One—

"Get moving." Beckett gives my shoulders a push, obviously reading my intentions in the sudden stillness of my body. His voice is like ice when he speaks next. "Don't make me knock you out and carry you, you goddamn bloody idiot."

I growl at him but do as he instructs, following the hazy silhouette of Landon, Dom, and Ellie.

Upstairs, something shatters, the noise almost deafening. It's quickly drowned out by the hiss and crackle of fire as it eats away at the walls and ceiling.

Fuck. Fuck. Fuck.

I quicken my pace until I'm practically running.

When Dominic pushes open a wooden door devoid of a knob, I'm directly behind him. All of us spill outside, greedily inhaling lungfuls of clean air. It's still smoky, but it's not nearly as pungent, the cloying smell replaced with the scent of pine and maple trees.

"What the fuck?" a masculine voice exclaims.

My head snaps up, and I focus on the POP members standing directly in front of us. There doesn't seem to be a lot of people manning this section of the house—probably because Dominic was right, and The Divine One didn't know this door existed.

However, there are two members of POP, and they're both standing perfectly still, their weapons raised.

"Stay back—" the second person begins in a trembling, high-pitched voice.

I'm across the clearing in three long strides then tackling the first man to the ground. Distantly, I'm aware of Dominic doing the same to the second POP member, but I don't focus on him. I trust my brother to be able to take care of himself and our girl.

The POP member bucks wildly underneath me, and his gloved fingers loosen around the knife he's holding. I place my arm to his neck and apply pressure as he begins to scratch desperately at my skin, trying to escape.

But I'm wrath.

I'm vengeance.

I'm a beast contained in a man, a devil wearing a human face.

These men tried to hurt the people I care about most in the world.

I won't allow them to live.

Gradually, the man's jerky movements begin to slow, and his hands slide off my arm and fall to the ground at his sides. I wait just a few more seconds before releasing him and pulling off his mask.

An unfamiliar man stares back at me, his eyes sightless and glazed over in death. He has a bald head with gray sideburns, a wide nose, and a goatee.

"Judge Luther Swollen," Landon murmurs from directly over my shoulder.

I turn towards him in surprise, having not heard him

approach, but he's staring pointedly at the dead body instead of me.

"He's been on our radar for some time now, but we never had any proof he was involved. Mostly, he's been helping known POP members get out of minor, petty crimes, such as drinking and driving and shoplifting."

"Wouldn't want anyone looking too close into the club's members," I say in disgust, then I spit on the corpse.

Sick satisfaction rumbles through me at getting rid of another twisted fuck, another threat against my brothers and Ellie.

"This is Deputy Ali Earl," Dominic whispers harshly from a few feet away from me, where he stands over a brown-haired woman with hazel eyes. "Jesus Christ. How deep does POP go? Judges? Police officers? Fucking senators?"

"I talked to Ali a few times," Landon confesses, scrubbing a hand through his brown hair and disrupting the soot in the strands. "I thought she could be an ally. I never would've expected her to—"

"Guys!" Ellie's shrill voice has us all turning to her. She stands like a blazing silhouette in the fire-lit sky, the orange, red, and yellow flames creating a pearlescent sheen around her. It also highlights the stark terror in her blue-gray eyes. "Where's Zane?"

"What?" Beckett glances around in confusion, his grip tightening on Frodo, who whines and shakes.

"Where the fuck is Zane?" Ellie seems to be growing hysterical. Tears create lines down her smudged face. "Oh god!"

Beckett immediately pulls her into his arms, squishing the dog between them, as we all stare at one another in horror.

Zane...is still in the house.

Fuck. Fuck. Fuck!

Wasn't he behind me and Beckett? I could've sworn I heard him singing, *"It's burning men! Hallelujah! It's burning men!"*

Unless there's some other crazy fucker I don't know about...

"Beckett, Dom, Ryker, stay with Ellie!" Landon instructs, already pulling his sweatshirt off to create a makeshift scarf around his head. "I'm going after Zane. If I'm not back in five minutes, get her the fuck out of here."

"No!" Ellie calls fiercely, but Beckett's arms simply tighten around her, keeping her pressed against his chest.

Landon takes a step towards the flaming house...just as someone skips—literally fucking skips—out of it, a body slung haphazardly over his shoulders.

"I'm burning, and I know it," Zane sings cheerfully, seemingly unconcerned or just utterly oblivious to the fire eating away at his shirtsleeve. Directly below it, I can see the evidence of charred, black flesh.

"Fucking hell!" Landon's voice is a mixture of relief, irritation, anger, and love. "Where the fuck were you?"

"Zane!" Ellie pushes away from Beckett and runs towards the psychotic, beautiful bastard. Fuck, I'm glad he's okay. "You're on fire!"

"Is this your way of telling me I'm hot, *princesa*?" Zane says with a cheeky grin. "Because, I have to tell you, I'm definitely into it—"

"No, you idiot! You're actually on fire!" Desperation bleeds into Ellie's voice as she points at his flaming arm, slightly raised to provide support to the dead body over his shoulders.

Zane's brows pinch together as he slowly twists his

head to look where she pointed. "Oh," he says at last. "Would you look at that?"

Landon uses his sweatshirt to put out the flames, and I have to give Zane credit. He only winces once before he plasters on his perpetual, slightly manic smirk that makes his eyes look like two gaping black holes—endless vortexes you can fall into and get lost in.

Ellie launches herself at him with a cry of relief, winding her arms around his waist.

Does she not care that he's holding a motherfucking dead body?

Or is she just oblivious?

"Did you really think I would leave you, silly goose?" Zane asks lightly, but when he glances down at Ellie, his face is so full of love and yearning that my heart pinches.

"What the fuck were you thinking, Zane?" Dom demands.

"And why do you have a corpse?" Beckett points out.

Trust Beckett to point out the fucking dead elephant in the room.

"Guys, we don't have a lot of time..." Landon warns, casting a quick glance in each direction.

Right now, The Divine One believes us to still be trapped within the burning building, but it won't be long now until he has his minions searching the perimeter for us. Fortunately, there are no windows on this side of the house—only a door that The Divine One didn't know existed. I'm hopeful this will be the last fucking place The Divine One will look.

"We need to kill Ryker first," Zane exclaims cheerfully, flashing me a wink that looks even more eerie with the firelight reflecting off his pupils.

I imagine Zane is what a demon would look like—his

pretty face does very little to hide the monster lurking just beneath his skin, demanding to be set loose on the unsuspecting world.

A cold chill races down my spine as I gape at him, even though I shouldn't be surprised. We always agreed to put Ellie first. I can't blame them for wanting to get rid of me in order to protect her.

"What?" Ellie pulls away from him with a look of alarm and horror.

"Ellie…" I whisper, resigned to my fate, to the certainty that this will be my last few minutes on Earth, to the fact that I'm going to be forced to leave her.

At least if I go now, her face will be the last thing I see.

"Ellie, meet Dead Ryker. Dead Ryker, meet Ellie," Zane chirps as he throws the body to the ground by her feet.

Ellie staggers backwards instinctively, a look of horror and disgust distorting her pretty features. Her eyes are comically wide on her face.

"What the…?"

The charred, black corpse appears like nothing but a lump of meat—meat that has been left over the fire for way too damn long. Even the bones are beginning to blacken, though I'm not sure if that's from the fire or soot.

The backs of Zane's shoulders are red and mottled from carrying the burning body, but he doesn't seem to notice as he rubs his hands together gleefully.

"Who the hell is that?" Landon asks, aghast.

"My mom's dealer," I rasp. The smoke is making my voice even more unrecognizable—it's merely a breath of sound, like sandpaper rubbing against the interior of my throat.

The body doesn't even look like the man who I

murdered. He's an unrecognizable bag of pulp and black-ened meat.

Zane helped me hide the body in the garage of Dom's cabin, and we began the painstaking process of removing all of the man's fingertips and any other identifying features, just to be safe. We then planned to take him back to Zane's farm to dissolve the bones in acid.

"The Divine One would know if one of his own members went missing," Zane continues brightly. "So...I decided we needed a body that The Divine One wouldn't expect. After all, he had no idea that we already had a dead body in the garage, did he?"

He sounds so damn smug that my own lips twitch upwards reflexively.

"A...dead body? In the garage?" Ellie breathes. Her face is whiter than the half-melted snow at our feet.

Beckett holds Frodo tighter in his arms and turns towards Landon. "Do you think... Do you think it would work?" he whispers. Hope and fear both vie for dominance in his multicolored eyes.

Landon bites down on his lower lip hard enough to draw blood before turning abruptly towards Ellie. "If we're going to pretend this body is Ryker's, you'll have to give the goddamn performance of a lifetime. You used to do theater, right?"

Ellie's face turns ashen. "In freaking middle school!"

"Ellie." Dom places his hand on her shoulder and bends so he's at eye level with her. He traces the seam of her lips with his thumb, a soft, wistful expression overtaking his face.

The sight of it makes my heart clench.

Fuck, he loves her.

He loves her so goddamn much.

The realization sits like a boulder in my gut.

"You can do this, baby girl," he whispers. "You *need* to do this. You don't have a choice. The Divine One needs to think Ryker is dead."

Tears stream down Ellie's face, but she manages a tiny nod.

Then, sliding her eyes towards me, she whispers, "For Ryker."

There's a promise in her gaze, and a reminder. Her words from before play on repeat in my mind as warmth surges through me, almost startling in its intensity.

And I swear I fall even more in love with her.

••••••••••

I CROUCH behind a tree in the forest, wind whipping at my face and carrying with it the pungent stench of smoke and burnt wood.

And then Ellie's horrified sobs pierce the night air like a shotgun being fired. I feel each cry like a javelin to my chest. I'm gripping the branch of the tree so tightly, my knuckles begin to ache.

Ellie screams and screams and screams, nearly inconsolable, as Beckett attempts to hold her back.

The Divine One materializes out of the darkness itself, a shocking vision of red that almost blends in with the flames at his back. Only his golden mask sticks out like a white dot on a black piece of paper. He glides forward as if gravity doesn't exist to him—or maybe it *does* exist, and he's just too damn powerful to abide by it. Four of his minions flank him, two on either side. All four of them bow their heads submissively when The Divine One stops directly beside Ellie and the charred body.

The Divine One stares down at my "corpse," and I suddenly wish he didn't have that stupid mask on. I'm desperate to see his eyes, to see the emotions etched across his face, to know the reason for his sudden and startling silence. All I can hear is the angry hissing of fire, the sound resembling thousands and thousands of snakes all coiled around each other. It has goose bumps pebbling on my arms.

Or maybe that's just my natural reaction to this all-encompassing fear.

Fear for the guys.

Fear for Ellie.

And...fear for myself.

"YOU MONSTER!" Ellie screams, and I know she claimed that she hadn't acted since middle school...but goddamn.

My heart cleaves down the center at her heart-wrenching scream. I never, ever want to hear her cry like that again. Tears prick the backs of my eyes irrationally. I know I'm not truly dead—I'm standing right the fuck here with a goddamn dog in my hands—but still.

Is this how Ellie would truly behave if I were to die?

Would she miss me this much?

Or is this all a show for The Divine One?

My heart patters like the wings on a hummingbird as I strain my ears to hear The Divine One's reply.

His mechanical voice sounds like cogs turning together. It scratches at my skin like the claws of a lion.

"Ryker knew what he was agreeing to," he says simply.

Ellie glares mutinously at him, tears continuing to cascade down her cheeks. And then...she explodes, a can of soda that has been shaken repeatedly and then abruptly opened. All of the rage and hatred and anger she has ever harbored for the man pools out of her in gasping torrents. The force of it makes me wince, even where I stand over a dozen feet away.

"YOU TRICKED HIM! YOU BASTARD! I'M GOING TO KILL YOU! I'M GOING TO—"

Beckett grabs Ellie abruptly and drags her back a few steps as she struggles and screams and cries. Through it all, The Divine One watches.

Just watches.

Then, he inclines his head towards the four goons and says, "Leave us. The job is done. The trash is dead."

Trash?

The four goons go to do as instructed as Ellie wails at him not to talk about me like that, threatens to skin him alive, cries my name in utter agony. Every word she says is another knife to the chest, a dagger to the gut, an arrow to the back. I'm bleeding profusely from multiple wounds, but I find that I don't care.

Maybe it's worth it to bleed for Ellie.

The Divine One, though, doesn't immediately move to follow his four followers. He stays behind for a long moment, his masked face trained in Ellie's direction.

"I did what I had to do," The Divine One says at last. "You're better off without the trash in your life."

For a moment, Ellie appears stunned. Even from this distance, I can see the tears drying on her blotchy face and her mouth popping open.

"W-what?"

Trash.

Trash.

Trash.

You're trash, Ryker. Trash.

The Divine One doesn't humor her with a response. He

simply turns on his heel, his red robe swishing around his legs like silk, and stomps back up the hill towards the front of the house. And through it all, Ellie screams and screams and screams and screams—

The sound breaks something fundamental inside of me.

I desperately want to move from my hiding space and comfort her, but I don't. I *can't*. I'm nothing but a ghost haunting the people I love, a translucent entity unable to truly interact with the real world.

Ryker's dead.

And I have no idea who—or what—is rising from his grave.

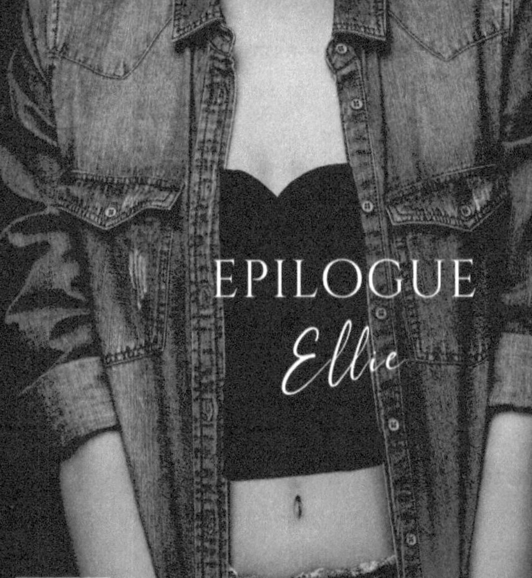

EPILOGUE

Ellie

The smell of burnt flesh is nearly overpowering.

I watch as the flames eat away at the sides of the house. The fire does very little to thaw the ice permeating my system.

Zane moves to stand beside me, covered in soot and blood. I can't discern what blood is his...and what blood is the dead man's.

Belatedly, I wonder if this is what it feels like to fall down an elevator shaft. My stomach flip-flops wildly, and the world blurs around me in a kaleidoscope of color, none more prominent than the lemon-yellow citrine shade of the fire.

Fuck. Fuck. Fuck.

Did The Divine One believe me? Was I convincing enough? My grief sure as heck felt real—like my soul was being tugged out of my body and my heart was being simultaneously stomped on beneath a metal cleat.

"I can't believe we did this." Beckett moves to join our makeshift group. He shakily runs a hand through his brown hair as he peers at the burnt corpse. "Bloody hell, I can't believe we did this."

I don't know what he's referring to—tricking The Divine One or using a dead body to do it. I suppose it's the former. I can't imagine my guys are squeamish about a lot of things, least of all corpses.

Who was this man at my feet?

I know from Ryker's description of him that he was a piece of shit, but did he have a family? A wife? Children? He certainly was someone's son. Would they grieve him?

Guilt squeezes my heart, and I force my eyelids shut for a brief moment to block out the images threatening to bombard me from every direction.

You can't think like that, Ellie. You can't.

Ryker's alive.

That's all that matters.

Even still, my heart constricts and then caves in on itself, becoming nothing but mush.

"It's done." Landon folds his arms over his chest as his lips straighten.

I wish I could read the emotions running rampant through his brain, but he's more closed off than ever before. I feel as if I'm turning the pages of a foreign book with no guide on how to translate it.

"Zane, Beckett..." Dominic twists his head to encompass the two men on either side of me. "The three of us need to make sure they're all gone. If they're not, kill them. Don't hesitate."

Kill them.

Don't hesitate.

Kill them.

Don't hesitate.

Kill them.

The three of them disband—two in one direction and one in the other—to ensure the Paragons of Prosperity have truly left.

Almost instantly, Landon turns towards me. His silver eyes are unreadable in the illumination of the fire, almost metallic in appearance, tinted with violet.

"Ryker's dead," he says simply.

A reminder that Ryker...to the rest of the world...is dead.

Oh god.

Grief for the man I love carves me open.

How can we hide this from The Divine One and POP? Will Ryker be forced to go on the run? Will he have to leave us?

"We need to get rid of the body. Then, hopefully," Landon continues, his voice like a frosted-over sword slicing cleanly through bone and muscle, "this will all be over."

"Hopefully," I murmur, scanning the trees.

Is Ryker there now?

Watching us?

I want to run into his arms, but I know I can't. I'm not sure I'll ever be able to do that again.

We may have saved Ryker's life, but at what cost? Is it worth staying alive if you have to give up everything you know and love?

Where would Ryker even go?

An idea begins to form—a ridiculous, absurd idea that gains traction with every passing second.

Landon kneels beside the corpse and closes his eyelids, his long lashes fluttering against his cheekbones and smearing the soot smudged there. I take his momentary lapse of concentration to move a few steps to the side—still in his line of sight but hopefully far enough away that he won't hear my conversation.

I know what we all promised each other—no secrets— and I meant it. There will be no more secrets.

But what had I told Dominic earlier?

It's better to ask forgiveness than permission?

Yeah...that.

And what better time to apply it than now?

I know what I need to do, and I also know the guys aren't going to like it. They'll fight me tooth and nail, claiming that my safety is on the line and blah blah blah. But this isn't about my safety—this is about Ryker's life, or lack thereof. We're not equipped to deal with something of this magnitude.

With shaking hands, I fumble my phone out of my back pocket and pull up my contact list. I hesitate for only a moment, ice skating down my spine, before clicking on a number I added only a couple of days earlier.

The phone rings two times before a gruff voice says, "Ellie?"

"Raymond," I whisper, the words carried away by the wind and the crackling of fire.

"Are you okay? What the hell is that noise?" Raymond's voice is rife with alarm.

"I need your help." I keep my voice low so as to not alert the others.

Raymond is silent for a long moment before he asks, "Do your fellas know that you're calling me?"

"Not yet," I confess. "But they will."

I won't keep this a secret from them.

Raymond blows out a heavy breath, the noise tinged with something akin to irritation. "Dammit, girl. They're going to rip my ball sack off, aren't they?" He mutters something I can't hear before asking, "What do you need? Don't act like you're calling for any other reason. You need something, don't you? So you need to tell me—"

"Not on the phone. In person," I say curtly.

He hesitates, but only for a moment, before relenting. "All right. I can give you an address—"

"No." I shake my head, despite knowing he can't see it. "We'll give you an address and time. Meet us there."

"So I can get my ball sack ripped off?" he jokes, but when I don't laugh, he blows out another breath. "All right. All right. Let me know when and where, and I'll be there. I meant what I said, Ellie. All I've ever wanted to do was protect you."

"Then tell me this." My hand shakes around the phone. Despite the inferno at my back, my body feels unpleasantly cold, as if I'm in the middle of Antarctica with the wind whipping at my cheeks and tangled hair. "Why do you hate POP so much? Why are you trying to take them down? Why do you hate The Divine One? And don't give me that bullshit excuse about wanting to make the world a better place. This seems...personal."

For a moment, I think Raymond isn't going to answer. Silence stretches between us, as taut and frayed as a one hundred-year-old rope.

And then, in a voice like thunder, Raymond says, "Do you want to know why I hate that fucking organization so much? Why I want to kill every last one of them? Why I dream about ripping The Divine One's head off with my bare hands?"

"Yes," I whisper.

What he says next chases what little warmth remains

from my body. I find myself swaying precariously to the side as black dots explode across my vision.

"Because, my dear Ellie, The Divine One killed your parents."

Make sure to grab book four, Delirium, here!

AFTERWORD

Okay, on a scale of one to ten, how badly did you want to murder me after you read that prologue?

But did you really think I'd be evil enough to kill off Ryker? I mean, I may like to torture my characters, but I prefer to keep them alive for that. MWHAHAHA.

Am I evil? Just a little bit. I think Zane would be proud.

Make sure to pre-order book four, Delirium, here!

ACKNOWLEDGMENTS

Thank you to my incredible team of alphas for picking this book apart and making it the best its can be! Ash, Kelly, Ellen... I don't know what I would do without you guys. I seriously have the best team in the world. I love you all so much!

I would also like to thank my family for pushing me to write, even when I thought my brain would explode. Your support and encouragement mean the world to me.

And finally, I would like to thank all of you incredible readers for sticking with me! Some of you hate Ellie, some of you love her, but she's a character I can relate to more than any other. So to everyone who put their trust in me... thank you. I hope you enjoy reading about her journey as much as I enjoy writing it.

ABOUT THE AUTHOR

Katie May is a reverse harem author, a KDP All-Star winner, and an *USA Today* Bestselling Author. She lives in West Michigan with her family, cat, and adorable puppy. When not writing, she can be found reading a good book, listening to broadway musicals, or playing games. Join Katie's Gang to stay updated on all her releases! And did you know she has a TikTok? Yeah, me neither. Follow her here! But be warned...she's an awkward noodle.

ALSO BY KATIE MAY

1. Torn to Bits

2. Ripped to Shreds

Tory's School for the Trouble (Bully Horror Academy Reverse Harem, COMPLETED)

1. Between

2. Beyond

3. Beneath

The Damning (Fantasy Paranormal Reverse Harem)

1. Greed

2. Envy

3. Gluttony

4. Sloth

5. Pride

Prodigium Academy (Horror Comedy Academy Reverse Harem)

1. Monsters

2. Roaring

3. Venom

4. Fangs

Kings of Grove Academy (Contemporary Academy Reverse Harem)

1. Mania

2. Psychotic

3. Pandemonium

4. Delirium

<u>The Death Whisper (Fantasy Reverse Harem)</u>

1. Of Rain and Wrath

<u>Supernaturalette (Interactive Reverse Harem)</u>

1. Introductions

2. First Dates

3. Group Outing

4. Game Night

5. Exes

6. Truth or Dare

7. Scavenger Hunt

8. Reveals

CO-WRITES

<u>Afterworld Academy with Loxley Savage (Academy Fantasy Reverse Harem, COMPLETED)</u>

1. Dearly Departed

2. Darkness Deceives

3. Defying Destiny

<u>Darkest Flames with Ann Denton (Paranormal Reverse Harem, COMPLETED)</u>

1. Demon Kissed

1.5. Demon Stalked

2. Demon Loved

3. Demon Sworn

<u>Darkest Queen with Ann Denton (Paranormal Reverse Harem)</u>

1. For Whom the Bell Tolls

<u>Dark Temptations with Ann Denton (Monster Reverse Harem)</u>

1. Ravaged by Monsters

2. Devoured by Monsters

3. Worshipped by Monsters

<u>Fae Revealed with Quinn Arthurs (Paranormal Reverse Harem)</u>

1. Courting Darkness

2. Seducing Shadows

<u>STAND-ALONES</u>

Toxicity (Contemporary Reverse Harem)

Not All Heroes Wear Capes (Just Dresses) (Short Comedic Reverse Harem)

Charming Devils (Bully/Revenge Reverse Harem)

Goddess of Pain (Fantasy Reverse Harem)

Demon's Joy (Holiday Reverse Harem)

Broken Howl (Wolf Shifter Reverse Harem)

Dark Paradise (Paranormal Motorcycle Club Reverse Harm)

Ruthless as a Cheetah (Paranormal Romantic Comedy Reverse Harem)

<u>BOXSETS</u>

Together We Fall